By Calia Read

Unravel
Unhinge

UNHINGE

UNHINGE

A Novel

Calia Read

BALLANTINE BOOKS

NEW YORK

A Ballantine Books Trade Paperback Original

Copyright © 2016 by Calia Read

Published in the United States by Ballantine Books, an imprint of Random House, a division of Penguin Random House LLC, New York.

BALLANTINE and the HOUSE colophon are registered trademarks of Penguin Random House LLC.

ISBN 978-0-553-39478-8
ebook ISBN 978-0-553-39479-5

Printed in the United States of America on acid-free paper

randomhousebooks.com

2 4 6 8 9 7 5 3

Book design by Dana Leigh Blanchette

UNHINGE

Prologue

WESLEY

October 2014

Love holds so many secrets.

How it will hit.

When it will attack.

Where it will happen.

We are its playthings, walking around this world unaware that at any moment it will strike.

Don't try to plan for it. Whether you fight or go willingly, love will wrap itself around you and when it does, you'll never be free again.

I stared up at the fan slowly swirling above me. It was time to get ready for work. I knew that. But my mind wanted to take a trip down memory lane. I refuse to get sucked into the past and turn my head, but that's a fool's mistake because even though my bed was empty, I saw the image of my wife.

She was quietly sleeping. The sheets were drawn around her shoulders. The tips of her lashes brushed against her upper cheeks. One hand was draped across her forehead, the other hanging off the side of the bed.

The moment I met Victoria I should've known I was doomed. I should've paid attention. Felt the wind against my neck and the goosebumps that prickled my flesh. But I didn't.

So I fell.

And I fell hard.

You could say our love was unreal.

Everything about Victoria was mysterious yet beguiling. Her smiles spoke of dreams, her lips the promise of something good to come. She held her secrets in one palm and her dreams in the next. And with her eyes dared me to choose one.

Ignoring them both, I went for her heart.

Then she became my wife.

Ripping the covers off, I got out of bed and walked over to the window. I jerked open the blinds. Clouds shielded the sun. A heavy fog swooped in and covered everything in a white blanket. I crossed my arms, musing that the fog was a lot like my wife. She covered herself around me, obscuring everything so I couldn't see a thing. I would reach for her, but she was this tangible thing that I couldn't quite reach.

There were no sounds of birds. No front doors closing or cars starting up. The world was silent, taking one big collective breath, waiting to see how Victoria and I would end.

Reluctantly, I stepped away from the window and went through my normal routine. I showered. I shaved. I dressed.

If Victoria were here she'd be asleep the whole time.

I glanced down at my watch. I had so many things I wanted to tell her. But our time was up.

Today's date flashed on my phone. A bitter taste filled my mouth. My hands flew across the keyboard as I wrote her a quick email. I never wanted it to come to this. But Victoria left me no choice.

Before I could think twice, I pressed SEND, knowing that I could never reverse this decision no matter how hard I tried.

As I walked toward the door, I grabbed my bag. I hesitated when I saw the empty bed. I keep obsessing over it because it just seemed wrong, almost criminal for Victoria not to be there.

If she were, I would bend down and kiss her on the forehead. I would tell her that I loved her and that I had to go. She wouldn't say anything, but her shoulders would tense and I'd know she heard me.

And then I would walk out of the room. At the doorway, I would look over my shoulder and stare at her body one last time, knowing that I would never understand my wife and how her mind worked.

1

November 2015

"Twenty-three, twenty-four, twenty-five."

Abruptly, I turn around and walk toward the other side of the room, continuing to count my steps. My feet are starting to ache; I don't exactly wear heels here. If ever. But for him, I'll wear them.

He'll be here soon. He comes almost every night, but what makes tonight different is I'm determined to get him to help me.

Thirty minutes ago, I started getting ready. I put on my favorite dress. A simple black wrap dress. It's his favorite too. I brushed my hair until the brown strands fell around my shoulders perfectly and I put a coat of lipstick on. Sprayed perfume on both pulse points.

I straightened up my room, smoothing the edges of my plain white comforter. Folding one of Evelyn's blankets and draping it over the back of the rocking chair in the corner.

I stopped my pacing, long enough to peek into the bassinet. Evelyn's wide blue eyes meet mine. She happily coos and kicks her legs rapidly. The smile she brings to my face is genuine—natural and pure. Everything in my life seems to be cloaked in fog, impossible to make out, but not Evelyn.

Very gently, I caress her cheek and brush the gossamer strands of her light brown hair away from her forehead. "I'm going to get us out of here. All right?"

She smiles widely as though she understands what I'm saying. I cover her small body with a blanket and kiss her on the forehead. Give her a few minutes and she'll be out like a light.

Loudly, someone knocks on the door. The door creaks open and Kate, the night shift nurse, walks in. She's in her midthirties. Her hair is always pulled back in a ponytail. Face stripped of makeup. She's a mom of three. Every time I see her, she looks distracted and bored. As if Fairfax is the last place she wants to be.

But Kate's not so bad. There are nurses much more terrible in this place than Kate.

"Lights out," she says loudly.

Evelyn eyes open and close. I shoot Kate a withering look.

"Why are you dressed up?" she asks.

"No reason."

Kate narrows her eyes. "Fine. Whatever. I don't feel good and I have a kid that's sick at home. Go have a night on the town for all I care."

"If you're ill why come to work? You could get my daughter sick," I point out.

She sighs. "We wouldn't want that, now would we?" Kate holds out a plastic cup with a colorful array of medication. "Here."

Without a word, I take the cup and toss the pills back. Then I open my mouth dutifully and stick out my tongue. She barely looks. She takes the cup from me and throws it away in the bathroom.

"You should be in bed," she calls out over her shoulder as she leaves, none too quietly.

I take this as my moment of opportunity and spit out the pills. I stopped taking them a month ago. In the three years I've been here, I'd always taken these pills. Never once did I question them. They did their job. They made me blissfully unaware of the world around me. They blotted out all the questions that danced around the corners of my mind. They made the days blur together.

But recently the questions had been getting louder. Loud enough that not even the medicine could block them out. Very swiftly, my body became sluggish, my actions robotic. And the whole time there was an all-out war in my mind.

So I stopped taking them, thinking the questions would just fade away.

But that only made things worse. Now the questions are accompanied by small flashes of memory. I realize there's so much of my life that I don't remember.

Sure, I remember *some* moments, but they're mostly from my childhood. Family. Teenage years. College. Graduating. Getting my first job as a nurse.

But when I became Victoria Donovan—it all goes blank. There's an enclosure around that part of my life that I don't know how to get around.

And I think . . . no, I *know* that the only person in the world who can help me is him.

"Did you hear me?" Kate appears at my door again. "You need to get ready for bed."

"I can't. I have a—"

"I know. You have a date," Kate cuts in. "Blah, blah, blah. I'll check up on you in an hour."

The chances of her following through are low, but I nod along and smile just to get her out of the room.

But, as she leaves, I quickly speak up. "Kate?" She turns. "Next time, can you not be so loud when you walk in? I'm trying to get my daughter to sleep."

Kate rolls her eyes. "Yes, Victoria."

The second the door shuts behind her, I push my bed away from the wall and stuff the pills in a little hole in the wall. It's no bigger than the tip of an eraser. I found the hole by accident one day when I dropped a piece of paper behind my bed. Many times I've wondered how it got there. I like to think that some other patient made that hole and did the exact same thing.

I sit at the very edge of the bed, my heels tapping against the linoleum floor. The clock on the wall ticks slowly, almost taunting me with all the time that I'm losing.

He'll be here any second. Of course he will.

Over and over I remind myself that I have to stand my ground and not give in to his words. If I follow these two rules then he can't seduce me.

Even though I turn into a live wire that only comes alive when he's nearby.

Skin tingles.

Heart races.

But not all of his visits are pretty. Sometimes he reveals the darker side of his heart and torments me with his knowing grin and cryptic words.

To put it simply, he's a bad habit that I just can't break. A habit that everyone around me thinks doesn't exist.

"Your husband's dead. . . ." My doctor's words run across my mind.

I hug my stomach and hunch over, reminding myself to breathe.

They're all wrong.

He's not dead. It's a lie.

He's as real as it gets. My reaction is proof. But no one here believes me. It doesn't matter how many times I tell them.

Abruptly, I stand up and start to pace the room. My heels clicking against the floor. I count my steps all the way to twenty-five before I start over and count again.

My eyes start to get heavy.

He'll be here soon and then I'll have my proof. One of the nurses will catch him and they'll let me go.

Because then they'll see I'm not crazy.

Right?

I settle on my bed and obsessively stare at the clock. Time ticks away.

10:45

10:46

10:47

My eyelids start to droop. I fade in and out before finally giving up and letting exhaustion take over.

The door opens quietly.

I lift my head and watch him as he steps into my room. I smile slowly. I don't know how much time has gone by. Maybe a few hours.

Maybe a few minutes.

All that matters now is that he's here. He's always owned any room he walks into. The half smirk he wears so well shows he knows the effect he has on people.

I stand up and follow him with my eyes. My hands toy with the hem of my dress.

He hasn't changed and I'm convinced he never will. His blond hair is cut short, his face freshly shaven. Those austere hazel eyes.

Even though the lights are off, my blinds are open, letting in stripes of silver light. They run across his face, making him look like an apparition.

If it weren't for the lines around his eyes I'd think he was immune to time. His clothes never change: a white undershirt, jeans, and a tan coat. It doesn't matter what the temperature is. His outfit never changes.

"Have you missed me, Victoria?"

My memories might go in and out, but his voice and presence are impossible to forget. Bright scenes play behind my eyes. The fog fades slightly. I think I'm going to see the truth, but then the scene turns into an old filmstrip. It flickers. My mind strains, trying to hold on to the memory. Black dots appear, getting larger and larger until there's nothing but darkness.

He asks his question again. This time, impatience is laced throughout his words.

I hesitate. I think no matter what the reaction he elicits from me, my heart and mind will always be at war with each other. One second I want to hold on to him and beg him not to leave, and the next I'm fighting the urge to get away from him as fast as I can.

"Yes," I finally answer.

I blink and he's directly in front of me. I stay perfectly still. This close and I get a whiff of his cologne. I stop myself from burying my face in his neck.

"I've missed you too," he says.

His fingers skim down my arms and circle around my wrists. With one tug he pulls me to him. His hand curls around the back of my neck and pulls me toward him. The air around us shifts. He guides my head closer. Our lips are inches apart and I know it's now or never. There's no pre-amble good enough for what I'm about to say.

"I'm leaving Fairfax." The words rush out.

The grip on my nape tightens imperceptibly.

An announcement like that should bring enthusiasm and happiness. Wes reacts with neither. He just smiles that confident smile, as if he knows something that I don't. "Why do you want to leave? This place is your home."

"Not anymore." With both palms on his chest, I gently pull back. "They need to see you. They need to know that you're not dead. You have to help me."

I glance down at my hands, seeing that they are curled into fists, tightly holding on to his shirt.

Wes extracts my hands and moves them away. "I can't help you."

"Yes, you can." My heart pounds like a drum; I have made it past the first hurdle. I can't give up now. "I know you can. Evelyn and I don't belong here anymore."

Wes doesn't spare Evelyn a glance. His mouth tightens as he rubs the back of his neck. "Do you really believe that if the doctors see me they'll let you go?"

"It'll show I'm not lying."

"Victoria, you put yourself here."

"No—" I stop abruptly. I want to deny his words, but when I rifle through my memories I can't find the days leading up to Fairfax. There's nothing but darkness. As always.

"Have you told anyone else this?" Wes asks sharply.

I stare at him thoughtfully. "No."

"Good. They can't help you." His voice is firm, leaving no room for argument.

"Then who can?" I whisper.

He gives me a sad smile. "No one."

Wes holds the answers to why I'm here. I can see them dancing in his eyes. If I can get him to open up, just a little, I know I'll capture a small piece of my truth.

His arms wrap around my waist. "Just stay here," he whispers into my hair.

He's going to touch you and you'll forget it all, my mind whispers. *Keep strong.*

At first I am strong. But one kiss turns into two. Then

three. And by the fourth I'm a goner. Any and all questions I wanted to ask him drift further and further away until I barely see them.

"You're going to get me out of here," I say with my lips.

He holds me so close I can barely breathe. I fall back on the bed and he quickly follows. His weight presses me farther into the mattress as he kisses me with purpose. I try to slow everything down, but it's useless. He bites down on my bottom lip hard enough that it starts to bleed. I feel the sting for a second. He pulls back an inch, his thumb gently rubbing the blood away.

My throat dries up when the face above me begins to change.

It's a slow metamorphosis.

Starting at the roots, his short golden hair turns black. The strands grow longer until they curl around my fingers.

Smooth skin is replaced with black stubble that rubs against my palms. Very slowly Wes lifts his head. Hazel eyes fade away like the sun and turn amber.

Shoulders expand.

His grip loosens and his hands trace the curves of my body, stopping at my waist. His touch for some reason feels reassuring, almost protective. He smiles, looking like he'd give me the world if I asked. I feel myself relax.

No, no, no. This is all wrong. I blink rapidly, hoping that Wes will come back into focus. But the face doesn't change. The man holding me looks dark and dangerous, like a fallen angel.

"What's wrong?" he asks. The voice is deep. It makes

goosebumps break across my skin. I stare at the stranger's face in a complete daze.

I squeeze my eyes shut, telling myself it was just a hallucination. When I open my eyes, it's Wes's face I'm staring at again.

My relief lasts only for an instant, though. I have no idea what just happened.

He frowns. "You're shaking. What's wrong?"

I take a deep breath. "Nothing."

Wes rolls off me. But our bodies are only apart for a few seconds before he wraps an arm around me. "You need to sleep."

Amber eyes are all I can see.

"No, I don't."

"Just try."

He laces his fingers through mine. Silence settles in my room yet I can't calm down. Despair settles in my gut. Tomorrow I'll wake up and still be here. And the day after that. Until I do something about it, this process will continue.

But I'm on borrowed time. In the distance I can hear the faint echoes of a clock ticking the time away. And yet I have no idea how to break this pattern.

"Help me get out of here." I swallow loudly. "Please."

He pushes my hair back and says softly, "I love you. You know that. But I can't help you."

"But I can't help you. . . ." It feels like my heart has been cut in half. If you love someone shouldn't their pain be yours and vice versa? Shouldn't you do everything in your power to help them?

His arm drops away from my waist and I take a deep breath. The voices start out as faint whispers—I brace myself for what's about to come. They morph into screams so loud I can barely understand what they're saying.

All I can hear is, *"I can't help you."*

My ears start to ring.

I cover my ears and close my eyes.

The mattress dips slightly as he sits up. Cold air touches my back.

"Stay," I whisper against my pillow.

He doesn't reply. It's useless for me to turn around; I know he's already gone.

The voices become so loud that my ears are humming now. They're so loud, almost as if they're trying to claw their way out of my mind.

I close my eyes and groan. I'm starting to realize that there's something about this place that renders people useless. It steals your soul and your identity.

I want to tell him just that, but when I turn around he's gone.

But he'll be back. He never leaves my side for too long.

There's a good chance I'm going crazy. But there's an even better chance that if I don't get the voices to stop, they'll grow bigger and devour me whole.

At the very thought, panic sets in, curling around my body. My eyes close and the voices in my head become amplified. But there's one that's louder, until it's practically screaming at me. It cuts through the barrier. Words wrap around my heart. They do their job right and very quickly I feel my fear dissipate.

My lips part and whisper the words softly against my pillow: *Hold your breath and count to ten. Soon it will be over before it ever began . . . hold your breath and count to ten. Soon it will be over before it ever began hold your breath and count to ten. Soon it will be over before it ever began . . .*

2

"Victoria . . ."

Somebody shakes my shoulder none too gently. My eyes flash open and I stare into a pair of cold green eyes.

Alice, the day nurse, removes her hand from me as though I'm dirty. "Time to wake up."

Of all the nurses at Fairfax, Alice is by far the worst. From day one she's been out for me. She's uncaring—devoid of emotions. How she's remained here for so long is beyond me.

"You missed breakfast," she says, her tone almost gleeful.

Instantly, I sit up and rub the sleep out of my eyes. I never oversleep. Ever. I like to be up and dressed before the nurses make their morning rounds. "You didn't knock on my door."

Alice looks at me with barely disguised disgust. "Yes, I did. You never responded."

My eyes narrow.

Liar.

Alice has one tone—patronizing—and an arsenal of three different facial expressions: anger, disgust, and contempt. She treats most patients with hostility, but I swear she takes a particular interest in trying to tear me down. I'm probably the most harmless person here, but you'd never know from the looks she shoots my way.

"I don't trust you," her dull green eyes whisper. *"Stay far away from me."*

"Besides," she continues, "you've been here long enough to know when breakfast is."

Another cup is thrust at me. This time there's only one pill to swallow, but Alice is much more thorough than Kate. She peers carefully in my mouth, turning my jaw left and right as if I'm a doll.

I'm seconds away from choking on the pill when she finally steps back. Her eyes flick briefly to Evelyn's crib. "Get dressed. I'll be back in a few minutes."

As she walks away I hear her mutter underneath her breath: "This is no place for a baby."

The minute the door slams, I jump out of bed and store the pill in my hiding spot. Turning, I glance around my room for remnants of Wes's visit last night.

I dressed up just for him. I glance down at my pajamas and realize that I don't remember changing. I run to the small closet in the corner. My dress hangs on the hanger. Right below it are my heels.

As I change, I think of last night. It felt too real to be a dream. Of that I'm sure. But I have no solid proof to back me up.

I go to the bathroom and wash my face. When I lift my head, I stare at my reflection. Now would be a good time to cover up the shadows underneath my eyes with concealer and swipe some blush across my cheeks for some color.

But I can't seem to do it. The whole process feels fraudulent, as though I'm trying to wear someone else's skin. No matter how hard I try to make it mine, it just doesn't fit right.

I don't know what makes me *me* anymore.

Evelyn cries out. I hurry out of the bathroom, and peer into her bassinet.

She's swaddled tight, but her hands are in tiny little fists as she stretches. It's fascinating that something so small can have such a powerful impact on me. With one smile she can obliterate my anger and sadness.

I can't get enough of her smile.

I make quick work of changing her diaper and dress her in a washed sleeper. When I'm finished, I swaddle her, grab one of the bottles on the desk, and sit down in the rocking chair. As I watch her feed, I softly hum a nursery rhyme. She always stares up at me with these incredibly bright blue eyes. I have her attention and trust, and that's the most important thing in the entire world. I love these moments. When her small body presses against mine, I can hear her little heart thumping away. It always calms me down. When she's done, I hold her against my shoulder and give her back a few gentle taps.

Alice arrives moments later. "Ready?"

No, not at all. Evelyn hasn't burped. A baby needs to burp or she'll be gassy. But instead of saying this, I bite my tongue and reluctantly stand up. "Yes."

Alice watches me coldly. She looks at me as if I'm vile.

"Since you overslept, you're going to have to skip your rec room time."

"Why?"

"Because you have to see your doctor."

My life here has an order. And that order has never been broken: Breakfast. Dayroom. Lunch. Therapy. Dinner. Back to my room for some free time and all too soon the nurses are walking down the halls, handing out medications and announcing lights-out.

It should get old. Real fast. But it's these moments that break up the monotony of this place. It keeps us sane.

"I want to go to the dayroom."

Everyone else here calls it the rec room. Besides meals and group therapy, it's the only time that male and female patients are blended together.

"Well, not today. You missed your allotted rec time because you were getting your beauty sleep."

"I wasn't aware I had a schedule."

"Just come on."

Stubbornly, I stand my ground. "No."

"You don't have an option. You're going to see your doctor."

The look in Alice's eyes suggests that she has no problem dragging me down the hall. No problem at all.

Never before have I crossed Alice; I've never had a reason to. But today she's ruining my routine. My mouth opens but I'm interrupted before I can speak.

"Look! It's the Memory Woman!" Reagan, who's walking circles around the new nurse, skips over to me.

"Reagan, what are you doing?" Alice says in that no-nonsense tone.

That's all most patients would need to hear to pull themselves together. But not Reagan. She is Fairfax's resident bad girl. She arrived two months ago and already holds the record for the most escape attempts. She's up to six.

She looks so innocuous with her green doe eyes and auburn hair that hangs down to her waist in a tangled mess. But there's a wild look in her eyes, like she's lost and has no idea where she is. Sometimes she wears hospital gowns with stains on the front, but after a few days the nurses make her change into sweats. To finish off her look, she has to wear a blue wristband with ELOPEMENT RISK written in bold, black letters.

Today she's wearing a hospital gown.

She pulls out a packet of cigarettes and taps the bottom of the package against her palm. She pulls a cigarette out. I stare at her with blatant shock. So does Alice.

Reagan just smirks as she reveals a lighter. She's starting to look less like a patient and more like a magician. How the hell did she get a lighter past the nurses?

Right before she lights up, she smiles and takes the cigarette out of her mouth. "Forgive me. I'm so rude." She extends the same cigarette to me. "Do you guys want a smoke?"

No one says a word.

"Alice? Mommy Dearest? Nobody?" Reagan glances at Evelyn. "What about you, little baby?"

Finally, Alice comes to her senses. "Give me those." She snatches the cigarette pack and lighter away from Reagan and stuffs them into her pocket. "You know you can't smoke inside."

"Says who?"

Alice gestures toward the nurses' station. Taped on the glass shield: SMOKING IS PROHIBITED INSIDE.

Everyone knows that smoking is only allowed after lunch and dinner. And it's always done outside, in a small section, monitored by the nurses. Inside, it's considered contraband. Reagan knows that.

"Hm. This is the first time I'm seeing this." She turns to Alice. "Are you sure that wasn't *just* posted?"

"Yes, I'm sure," she snaps.

"Whoa." Reagan lifts her hands in surrender. "Easy, Cujo. There's no reason to yell."

"You need to follow the rules like everyone else, Reagan," says the blond nurse. She seems nervous, constantly looking at Reagan as if she's a wild animal about to attack.

Reagan pouts. "I'm tired of all these rules."

"Bring it up with your doctor," Alice shoots back.

"You always say that." Gone is the snark and dark smirk. Now she's angry. This girl can turn on a dime. "The doctors do nothing!"

"You can always leave."

"I can't leave because, to quote my doctor, I'm 'a danger to myself and everyone else.'" Reagan looks directly at me, a malicious smile on her face. "Hey, you have some experience with that, don't you?"

I take a step back and then another. I need to get away from this girl. Reagan steps forward, her hands outstretched. "Let me hold the baby, Mommy Dearest."

I back away. She steps forward.

"Come on," she says, continuing her taunting. "Don't you trust me? I'm a good babysitter. I promise."

She looks me straight in the eye and then sighs. "Oh forget it. You're no fun."

Slowly, she backs away. It seems like she's done creating a scene. But then she snatches the cigarettes from Alice and skips down the hallway. Her laughter trails behind her. "Come catch me, you old bat!" she shouts.

Alice looks like she's going to kill her. She grabs the walkie-talkie hooked on her pocket and calls for assistance.

"Stay right there," she tells me and then she's chasing after Reagan.

I watch as she disappears around the corner.

When I glance around the hallway, I see that hardly anyone is giving the scene any attention. One lady peeks her head out of her room, looks around before she slams her door shut. This is the norm.

If Alice expects me to stay here and wait, she's delusional. Her telling me to stay put makes me want to defy her even more.

With Evelyn cradled in my arms, I hurry down the hall.

A social worker passes by. She's talking to one of the youngest patients in the women's ward. The girl can't be more than eighteen. She has a fight-or-flight expression.

She's way too young to be here. There's a part of me that wants to grab her by the shoulders and tell her to get out now. While she still has the chance.

I quicken my steps and look over my shoulder to make sure I'm in the clear. Still no Alice. Ahead of me, the doors to the women's ward are shut, as always. You need a passcode to get through them. Momentarily, I panic, but through the glass I see a nurse punching in the code. I slow down and glance out the windows to my right, pretending to be fascinated with the outdoors. She walks by me and I grab the door right before it's about to shut.

I walk confidently into my ward as though it's perfectly normal to be without a nurse. The nurse behind the front desk doesn't blink an eye and the one sitting to my left has her nose buried in a bodice-ripper romance. This place could catch on fire and she wouldn't notice.

The dayroom is the largest room in Fairfax, with tables scattered throughout, always full of patients. Because of that, you'd think they'd spruce this place up more but the walls are painted a dull white. There's a single painting of mountaintops during a sunset on the opposite side of the wall that looks like it's been here since the day this place opened its doors. Windows line the left wall. The blinds are open, letting bright light in, so it's not completely depressing in here.

Besides the dining hall, this is the only area that men and women share. We're constantly kept busy here with sessions, therapy, activities, and meals. The activities are all laid out in front of us and we're expected to reach out and take them. If you choose to go to your room for privacy, you can kiss the dream of leaving this place goodbye. Nurses will knock on your door every five minutes, to "check in on you."

The table that I normally sit at is unoccupied and I hurry toward it.

The television is on, but the volume is so low that captions scroll at the bottom of the screen. Most of us waste away watching talk shows where women sit around a table and "discuss" topics, but it's just a lot of yelling to me. We watch game shows. We watch soap operas. We watch the news. We watch anything and everything to avoid focusing on the problems haunting us.

Not so long ago, this used to be my favorite spot in Fairfax. I would make laps around the room, stopping a few times so Evelyn could look outside. When she was crying, angry and upset, I would hum a lullaby.

But now, no part of this place is my favorite; I see it for what it really is. A holding cell. It's dressed in frills and lace, giving the impression that there's freedom here, but there isn't.

In my arms, Evelyn starts to fuss. I gently pat her back and give her a quick kiss on the cheek.

The front doors slide open. People come and go all the time, and I usually don't pay attention. But today I lift my head and watch a man walk through. He brings in fresh air that drifts across the room and makes goosebumps break out across my skin. His hands are tucked into his front pockets. At first I think nothing of him. Then he turns and looks directly at me.

My heart becomes lodged in my throat.

This is the man Wes morphed into last night. I sit up

straight. He blinks rapidly. His brows form a tight V. He looks at me with confusion and I have no idea why.

The nurse behind the front desk greets him and he looks away.

Patients and staff—all eyes are on him. We share one thought: *Why is he here?*

A dazed smile graces the nurse sitting behind the front desk.

Picking up the visitor clipboard, he writes his name down. I wish I were next to him. I want to put a name to that gorgeous face.

Since I've been at Fairfax, I've perfected the art of people watching. You can't be obvious. In a place like this it's awkward to be caught. No, you have to take furtive glances spaced apart—that's enough for me to create a person's life story.

With this man, I picture power. Control.

With his elbows on the counter he leans in closer to the nurse. She's a newbie. Just last week she finished up her week of training. And the way she looks at him . . . I can already tell she'd give anything for him to continue talking to her.

He says something and she shakes her head. I try to read her mouth, but she's talking too fast.

Then he gives the nurse *the* smile.

The smile that makes smart women turn stupid.

The nurse sighs and her shoulders droop in defeat. She sneaks a peek behind her shoulder to make sure no one's watching before she leans over the counter and points straight at me.

The man looks my way. His eyes are intense. Strong. A force.

Pushing himself away from the front desk, he walks into the dayroom. He has a confident stride, as though every step he takes is fought for and earned. His chin is raised and eyes are forward, looking straight at me. My hands start to shake. I feel the blood rush from my fingertips, all the way down to my toes.

My heart starts to thunder.

Thump.

Thump.

Thump.

Each beat is louder than the last, until I am positive that everyone in the room can hear the pounding of my heart. I clutch Evelyn closer as the man stops directly at my table. I tilt my head back to make eye contact and I swear I feel a jolt straight to my heart.

"Can I sit down, Victoria?"

How does he know my name? I'm frantic, desperate to know what's going on. Is someone playing a trick on me? I glance around the room, waiting for one of the doctors to jump out from around the corner and tell me this is just a test.

When I don't reply, he lifts a brow and sits down across from me. He settles his hands on the table, lacing his fingers together. They're large, rough with calluses and blunt fingernails. My stomach flips because I remember those hands on me, last night. Not Wes's. His.

We sit in silence, but what exactly am I supposed to say? There's no easy way to start up a conversation with a virtual stranger.

He stares at Evelyn with those hard eyes. His gaze flicks

between my daughter and me. I shift Evelyn so her head is resting against my chest and gently pat her back. "I'm sorry, do we know each other?" My voice is firm, but kind.

He tilts his head to the side and looks at me beneath his lashes. The black slant of his brows brightens his eyes. "I'm Sinclair."

I stare at him, expressionless. I know he expects me to recognize him. I don't. I've never met him. Not counting last night.

"Sinclair Montgomery," he elaborates.

Still nothing. All I can do is shrug. His eyes close and his lips move into a flat line. I don't know him, but his pain is obvious. I wish I could help him. Yet how can I? I can barely help myself.

"You don't remember me," he says bluntly. No anger or hurt in his voice but there's a riot of emotions in his eyes. It's almost too much for me.

"Should I?"

His lips tilt up into the saddest smile. "You should."

It's crazy to have someone look straight at you, with thousands of memories playing in their eyes. Memories you can't retrieve but wish you could.

Crazy and terrifying.

"Your name doesn't sound familiar," I offer quietly. I feel like my tongue is too big for my mouth and that anything I say will sound pathetic.

Sinclair.

His name is Sinclair.

With his dark looks and intense eyes, the name fits him to

a T. He smiles at me, a slow smirk that spreads across his face, as if he knows what I'm thinking.

"I know you don't remember me. That's why I'm here," he says. "We have a lot to catch up on."

This seems all too . . . unbelievable. I hold Evelyn tighter. "Are you lying to me?" I whisper.

He leans in. "Since we've known each other I've never lied to you once," he says fiercely.

"And how long has that been?"

He swallows and I watch his Adam's apple bob. "Two and a half years."

My doubt shows in my eyes.

Sinclair sighs. "I know you don't believe me."

"You're right," I concede. "I don't. I've lived here for three years. There's no way we've met."

Sinclair frowns. His eyes flick across the room for a quick second and veer back to me. "Three years? You haven't been here for three years."

My mouth opens. I'm so close to insisting that I'm right. I should know better than anyone how long I've been here, but as I skim through my Fairfax memories and go back to the beginning I don't see much. And that was all in . . . 2011?

Frustration gets the best of me. What's the point in having a memory when it doesn't work? I close my eyes and rub my temple. When I finally look at Sinclair his expression softens as though he sees the brick wall my mind is running into. "You've only been in here for six months."

I want to challenge his word so badly. I want to have cold hard facts, but I don't. Three years. Three whole years I've been here and if we were such good friends why didn't he come sooner? I ask.

"Since you've been here, I've tried to visit you every day." His lips pull into a flat line. "I've been turned away every time."

"How do you expect me to believe that?"

"Ask any of the nurses. Go look at the visitor sign-in sheet from yesterday, the day before, and the day before that. You'll see my name on every page."

I swallow loudly.

No one told me about his visits. I feel anger blossom in my chest. Shouldn't it be my choice to decide who can and cannot see me?

"I promise you I'm not lying." And before I can say a word, he speaks again. "Do you remember anything that happened?"

I frown. "What are you talking about?"

"Your past," he says bluntly. "Do you remember?"

Patiently, he waits for my reply. My pulse skyrockets. "No."

"Well I do." His voice becomes gruff. "I can help you . . . if you let me."

His offer is dangerous and enchanting. I have no proof, but I believe he knows my past. He is part of it.

I glance down at the table. A fine coat of dust covers the surface. I write my name in clear block letters.

VICTORIA.

VICTORIA.

VICTORIA.

I see nothing. Just letters strung together. This man claims to know me and I can't help but wonder what he sees behind my name.

"How do you expect me to believe you?"

"You and my sister used to be best friends."

"Used to?"

He nods and hesitates. "Before everything happened."

When his words trail off, I have to stop myself from reaching across the table, grabbing him by the collar of his shirt, and demanding that he tell me everything.

But instead I just say: "Why doesn't she visit?"

"She did at the beginning, but like me, she's restricted."

Exactly how many people were barred from seeing me? Was there a list? Did Wes make that happen or my mother? Or maybe my doctors were behind it?

"Why would she not be allowed to visit me?"

He gives me a weary smile. "Because she was the one who brought you here."

The day I arrived at Fairfax, I remember slamming the car door and shielding the sunlight away with my hand as I stared at the building. I remember grabbing Evelyn from her car seat. I remember signing the admission paperwork and thinking to myself that while everyone else around me might be here to heal, I was here to rest.

Not once do I remember being accompanied by someone.

Sinclair looks like he wants to say something. His mouth opens and closes. In his eyes I see memories. Am I those memories?

"Victoria! What are you doing in here?"

Alice. The sound of her voice is like nails on a chalkboard. How long have I been sitting here? I jump out of my chair just as she walks over. She looks between the two of us and finally focuses on me.

"I told you to wait in your room." She doesn't wait for a reply and glares at Sinclair. "Mr. Montgomery, you're not allowed to be here. Who let you in?"

Sinclair stands up. He towers over Alice. The corner of my lips twitch, but I fight my smile. It's nice to finally see someone stand face-to-face with this woman and not be fazed by her harsh glare and scowl.

He gestures to the nurse behind the front desk, who looks ready to bolt. "She did."

"Well, you can't be here. You have to leave."

Not yet. No, not yet. For the first time in a while, I feel like someone's on my side. I'm not ready to let go of that feeling.

Evelyn starts to cry. I take a step toward Sinclair, but Alice blocks me. I'm a calm, patient person, but right now I want to shove Alice aside. I want to invoke that same level of fear in her that she vindictively shoots my way every day.

Sinclair reaches out. His large hand lands gently on my shoulder. It's only a second before it slips away, his fingers grazing my arm.

"I'll come back soon." Before he turns and walks away his gaze collides with mine and he says, so quietly, "If you never remember us, that's okay; I'll remember for the both of us."

And then he leaves.

Alice guides me toward the front desk. She speaks to the new nurse, no doubt reprimanding her for letting Sinclair through. I take this moment to peek at the sign-in sheet. His handwriting is unintelligible, but I clearly see the *S* and *M*. I go to yesterday's sign-in sheet and the one before that. I keep moving until I'm a month out. His name is on every single sheet.

Sinclair Montgomery is right.

3

Today, there's no outburst from Reagan. Or a visitor waiting for me in the dayroom.

All morning and afternoon I've held out hope that something would happen until the very last second. But as I stand in front of Dr. Calloway's door, I know I can't put it off another second. I have to get this session over with.

Taking a deep breath, I loudly knock on her door.

"Come in," she calls out.

I push it open and step inside her office.

I don't hate Dr. Calloway. In fact, she's not so bad. But I've never gone into depth with her about my foggy past. That's not a hit to her personally; I don't trust any of the doctors here. They crack open your feelings and you're expected to let the truth spill out.

Crazy or not, that's hard for anyone.

I can't remember how long I've been seeing her. Maybe a few months? In that time span Dr. Calloway has never pushed and prodded me to get information. Not like the other doctors who ask the same questions ad nauseam. *Your husband's dead. Tell us what you know.*

Some have different approaches though. Some have this astonishing ability to put me on—nodding their heads at everything I say, acting as though they understand me. Got me. Liked me. But inevitably, they always, *always* go in for the kill.

She doesn't give me the kid glove treatment like all the rest. At the beginning she asked the generic doctor questions, but after a while she stopped. Now when I see her, she'll ask how I'm doing. How Evelyn's doing. How I'm handling my medication. And then, when I offer up nothing else, she'll turn to lighter topics. I've actually had good conversations with her. Normal ones.

I know she's been married once. Divorced. She and her first husband drifted apart. She's been with a man named Tom for three years. Tying the knot is not in her future. No kids. She's not human until she's had a cup of coffee in the morning. She hates to cook and orders in a lot.

She's forty-one and loves her job.

Her openness is not common. Here at Fairfax she's the exception. At times we slip into a silence that is neither awkward nor comfortable. It's just . . . there.

This morning, I told myself that everything would be okay if I told Dr. Calloway that I wanted to leave this place. Now I'm incredibly nervous. Nervous to voice my thoughts. Nervous to get shot down.

"Good morning, Victoria." Dr. Calloway lifts her head slightly, gives me a smile, and goes back to reading the paper in front of her. Blindly, she gestures at the seats angled toward each other and facing her desk. "Please sit down."

I take a seat and almost instantly my legs start to bob up and down nervously. Evelyn shifts in her sleep and I stop moving my legs. I remind myself that I have to do this. I have to talk to someone. If not for me, then at least for Evelyn.

Dr. Calloway drops her pen and finally gives me her full attention. "How are you doing today?"

I start to break out in a sweat. I can't give her my routine reply of "I'm fine." It doesn't cut it.

"Great, great," I start out slowly. "Can I ask you something?"

"Of course."

"How long have I been here?"

Dr. Calloway cocks her head to the side. "How long?"

I nod anxiously. My nerves are getting the best of me. So I hold Evelyn a little bit tighter and grasp her hands in mine.

"Well, I'm not sure. That's something I'd need to look up." She glances at my mammoth file and back at me and then glances at her computer. She smiles at me. "It's much faster to look it up here."

Her fingers fly across the keyboard. It takes only a few seconds, but it feels like years. Finally, she turns the computer screen toward me. It's my admission sheet. She points at the very bottom of the screen. I see my signature and right next to that is the date: 5-19-2015.

Sinclair was right. Six months.

I sit back in my chair and my mind is running. Why did I think I've been here for three years? I feel Dr. Calloway's eyes on me and meet her gaze.

"Why do you ask?" she gently prods.

I answer honestly. "I thought I'd been here for three years."

"Three years?" Dr. Calloway's brows lift. "That's a long time. Why did you think three years?"

I shrug and go on to tell her I don't know, but just then I hear the sound of Wes's voice. It's very faint at first, but soon the sound turns up and it feels like his lips are against my right ear as he says, *We're coming up on three years of marriage . . .*"

I meet Dr. Calloway's eyes. "I have no idea," I say. Before she can prod any further, I change the subject. "I've been doing some thinking lately . . ."

Say it, my mind urges. *Just say it!*

Calloway says nothing, just waits patiently for me to continue. God, I wish I had her patience. Nervously, I lick my lips. "I want to leave Fairfax."

She doesn't look shocked, just nods agreeably. There's a look of interest in her eyes. "Why are you ready to leave Fairfax?"

Because I feel like I'm really starting to lose it. I need to take my life back. I need to feel normal again. No, I can't say that.

"Because I don't want to be here," I finally reply.

My words are met with silence. She laces her hands together and rests her chin on top of them.

"Why not?" Dr. Calloway finally asks.

Don't tell her about the voices, my mind whispers. *That will just fuck everything up.*

If I'm going to tell the truth, I have to go about it wisely. The last thing I need is for her to think I'm crazy.

"Has anything occurred that's made you come to this decision?"

My mouth opens and closes. I certainly can't tell her that I've stopped taking my medicine. So I give her a sliver of the truth. "No. I just know I don't belong here anymore."

Dr. Calloway stares at me carefully. I don't see judgment in her eyes. "In order for you to leave, you need to be evaluated by me and a board of doctors before we sign off on discharge papers. We need to see that you've made a vast improvement from when you were first checked in."

That's what I figured. And even though I prepared myself for how big a battle this will be, I'm still deflated.

I don't say a word.

Silence wraps around us. This is the worst kind of silence too. It eats at me. Dr. Calloway stares at me expectantly, waiting for me to say something.

"If you leave, I want to be confident. I'm not disagreeing with you that you might not belong here anymore, but . . ."

God. I hate that word. Has any sentence ever had a positive ending that began with *but*? No. I don't think so.

"But there's a lot of work to do before you can reach that goal. If you're willing to let me help you, I want to."

"You want me to open up and tell you how I'm feeling?" I ask skeptically. Just saying that out loud leaves a bitter taste in my mouth.

"No, not that."

"Then what?"

"It's nothing bad, Victoria. I know you're a private person." She glances at Evelyn, her smile slightly fading. "You love your daughter and want to protect her, but I need you to open up. I need you to trust me."

She stands up abruptly. With the sun shining in, her shadow dwarfs my own. Instinctively, I flinch. Dr. Calloway doesn't notice. She goes over to a filing cabinet and pulls out a file. My name is on the side. There are so many papers; it looks close to falling apart. "Is that my file?"

She nods and opens it up. Some papers are paper clipped together. Red tabs run the length of the edges. In the back, tucked into the pocket, is a thick stack of pictures. She only takes a few out and holds them in her hands.

"I want to show you some pictures."

I try to get a look at them, but Dr. Calloway hides them like we're playing a game of poker.

"Pictures of what?"

"Yourself. I'll start off slowly showing you each photo. Once you've got a good look at them I'll speed it up. If any of them are familiar tell me to stop and I will."

"Who gave those to you?"

Dr. Calloway lowers the pictures. "Your mother. When you checked into Fairfax she gave them to your doctor at the time in hopes that you would remember . . . something."

"Why am I just seeing these?"

"Because every time these pictures were brought out, you refused to look at them."

I refused? I can't remember, but I don't doubt her.

"Are you willing to try and look at these pictures?" she asks gently.

When someone wants to retrace their steps, where does one start?

The beginning.

The problem is, I don't know where my beginning is.

But here it is: my chance to taste life twice through a prism of pictures.

I'd be a fool to say no, but an even bigger fool not to be nervous. This is a quantum leap from my everyday routine and I have no idea where I will land.

Very slowly, I nod my head.

"Excellent," she says. "It's time to untangle your past."

First picture: Wes and me on what looks like our wedding day. We're walking down the aisle, our hands intertwined. Wes is smiling at me, and I'm beaming with joy. We look like the perfect happy couple. Deeply in love.

Second: my mother and me. We are sitting outside on my mother's back deck. It's the same house I grew up in. My mother holds a super-slim cigarette in one hand, a picture in the other. Stacks of photographs are in front of me and drinks are on the patio table. We're both smiling at the camera.

Third: I'm inside a hospital. I'm dressed in scrubs. An unknown blonde is standing next to me. I'm leaning against a counter, looking exhausted but extremely happy.

True to her words the process speeds up. One after the

other, the images appear until I feel like I'm looking at a flip-book. Soon the colors start to bleed together until I don't know when one picture ends and the next begins.

My head's starting to spin. I feel like I'm on a roller coaster, seconds away from making a hairpin curve. My stomach drops. I think I'm going to be sick.

"Stop," I say. The pictures move faster. "I said stop."

Dr. Calloway stops at the picture of Wes and me, but my mind doesn't. It's latched on to all those memories, clinging to them like starving animals. My heart is pounding a mile a minute. I can barely take a deep breath. I feel trapped, as the walls slowly close in on me.

I'm pulled into the memory, getting smaller each second, while the picture grows larger, slowly surrounding me. Dr. Calloway's office fades. She's still talking but her words are impossible to make out.

My ears start to ring and a bright, searing light surrounds the edge of my vision before it's all I can see. I feel myself detaching from the present and merging into the past. My clothes dissolve and are replaced by a cotton summer dress. My hair shines and my skin begins to glow. A breeze brushes against my skin. And in front of my very eyes, Evelyn starts to disappear. I cry out for her but it's too late. . . . I'm already gone.

4

I had no idea how my life would unfold the day I met Wesley Donovan.

I met him a year ago. We ran into each other on the street. Literally. I was in a rush, carrying a bouquet of flowers I had picked up from the florist. I hurried to my car and glanced down at my watch. I wanted to get back to my apartment and clean up some more before I had dinner with my mother. I wanted to put the flowers in a vase and display them on the table. It would be one less thing that my mother would tut about. I should've done this earlier. I know that. Five o'clock is the worst time to try to get things done, but I had a late shift at the hospital and got home around six this morning. I told myself I was going to get a few hours of sleep and ended up sleeping until three in the afternoon.

Cars waited in traffic. Horns honked. Radios were blasted so loud the ground seemed to shake beneath me. It was all annoying me, distracting me.

And then I walked straight into him. He was in a rush, talking on his cellphone. His BlackBerry fell out of his hand and onto the ground, skidding across the concrete before it stopped next to the storm drain. The flowers scattered everywhere.

"I'm sorry," he lamented and kneeled down to help me pick up all twenty of the long-stemmed roses.

One by one they were placed back inside the kraft paper. Here was this gorgeous man gently handling flowers. It left me in a daze. I watched him carefully. His blond hair was cut short on the sides and longer on the top. Not a single strand of hair was out of place. Light brown lashes touched his cheeks, concealing his hazel eyes. He was freshly shaved, making his cheekbones stand out. He glanced at me from beneath his lashes and my world shifted.

Just like that.

The look in his eyes showed me he wanted to own every single part of me. The crazy part was that I would let him.

Flustered, I grabbed his phone and handed it over to him the same time he gave me back the flowers.

"Is your phone broken?"

He slid it back into his pocket and shrugged and gave me a lazy smile. "Doesn't matter. I can replace it."

My voice was shaky as I said thank you and when I started

to walk away he gently grabbed my hand. It looked so small and delicate in his grasp. "I'm Wes Donovan," he said.

"Victoria Aldridge."

His hand drifted away from my wrist, fingers lingering on my skin, and shook my hand. My heart was in overdrive from one simple handshake. I knew then that I had to see Wes again.

Then he said to me, "You're bleeding."

I blinked away the fog that Wes had placed around me. "Huh?"

He extended my pointer finger and I saw bright red blood slowly traveling down its edge. "Must have been pricked by a thorn," he said.

"I guess so," I replied, my voice slightly breathless.

Without asking, he gently grasped my hand and wrapped it in a monogrammed handkerchief. He carried my flowers for me and walked me to my car. And when I was ready to get into the car he rested his shoulder against the side of it and dipped his head close to me. He told me he wanted to see me again.

I said yes. Of course I said yes. I thought that any woman who would say no to a man like Wes Donovan was a fool.

That was the prologue to our relationship.

Wes was ten years older than my twenty-three. At the time, the age difference didn't bother me. If anything, it was one more point in Wes's favor. Very quickly, I was pulled in by his unshakable self-assurance. I thought he was mature. Wise. He knew what he wanted and when he wanted it.

We had so many things in common: Books, even our childhoods matched up just right.

He was so perfect.

I wanted to be the woman who snagged the unattainable Wes. When I talked, he listened with rapt attention, soaking in every word. He handed out information about his life sporadically and when he did, it always made me feel special.

Wes grew up in McLean, Virginia. He told me he was an only child. His parents devoted all their time to him. He studied hard, graduating from Penn State. He came back to Falls Church to work at the law firm Hutchins & Kelly. His goal was to become partner.

It was through friends that I found out that before me, there had been a string of women. Did that bother me? No. If anything, it made me more proud that he chose me. *Me.*

Six months later, we were engaged. I loved being his fiancée. It was bliss. Knowing that I'd spend the rest of my life married to him felt surreal. I kept waiting for the other shoe to drop or for someone to tell me this was all a dream.

We set the date for May 18.

I would show off my engagement ring, displaying it to people with a sense of pride. I felt victorious. Maybe even a little smug—I had done what no other female had done before. I had Wes. And better yet, I had his love.

I always wanted to have my wedding outdoors in my mother's backyard at sunset. With white chairs and sheer material connecting the rows. At the end of the aisle would be an archway of flowers. The large oak trees that lined the property would have lights draped across their branches.

And I got just that.

With one hundred of our closest friends and family we said "I do" to each other behind two live oaks. Hand in hand, we walked down the aisle. The smile on my face wouldn't disappear. I don't know if I'd ever been happier in my entire life.

Married.

We were married. I couldn't believe it.

Extended family on my side smiled at us. Also in the crowds were friends of mine: some that I grew up with, others that I met in college. Of course my mother's society friends were there. Quite a few of Wes's friends showed up, but very few family members bothered to come.

I nodded and smiled at everyone. Inside, my heart was pounding. I was running on pure adrenaline and happiness.

I counted the steps I took as I walked down the aisle.

Twenty-four steps.

At the end of the aisle, Wes lifted our linked hands in the air. The photographer snapped picture after picture.

Wes gazed down at me. His blond hair appeared golden in the sunlight. A stray piece fell onto his forehead. His hazel eyes sparkled.

We were both so happy and neither one of us tried to hide it.

What the photographer didn't catch was the moment we walked up the pathway and turned toward the patio. Rosebushes and shrubbery hid us from plain sight. Secretly, I loved it. A single shared moment just between the two of us. My foot touched the first step when Wes grabbed my arm, holding me in place, and whispered into my ear, "I'll love you till the day I die."

5

June 2012

"So, how is the happy couple?"

I took a long drink of my lemonade and smiled softly. "We're good."

"Oh, Victoria, don't blush," my mother said as she rifled through the pictures. "You're married now."

Married.

Just a few days ago, Wes and I returned from our honeymoon. We spent two wonderful weeks in Paris. It was amazing to relax and spend every waking moment together without a care in the world. We left our worries behind the second we stepped into the plane. Even though we were home now, back to work and settling into a routine, there was still this electric charge around us. I watched the clock constantly while I was on shift, counting down the hours and minutes until I could see him again.

"Look at this one." My mother pushed a picture toward me. "I love this picture of you."

I picked it up and stared at myself. I looked so happy. "I love it too."

"Can you get it in an eighteen-by-twenty-four?"

"Mom, there's a whole other stack that you haven't gone through."

"Doesn't matter. That one's my favorite. I can already tell."

My mother was on cloud nine. She was the quintessential wife, born in the wrong era. When women were burning bras and fighting for equal rights, she was dreaming up the kind of family she'd have. And she got it: husband, son, and daughter. The perfect family. She loved living a hidebound life and she expected me to want the same thing. She looked at my years in college as some act of rebellion, as though it were some terrible black smear on my life record. She didn't understand why I wasn't willing to enjoy the imprimatur of married life. I didn't understand why she didn't recognize that I was already happy with what I had.

But marrying Wes put a fresh coat of white paint on that smear.

I continued to skim through the photos, smiling at every single shot. My mother was pickier. With her glasses perched on her nose, she would peer carefully at a photo, muttering underneath her breath: *"Who is that person? Why would I want a picture of a stranger?"*

"Oh! This one is gorgeous!" She held up the picture. I leaned forward to get a better look. It was a black-and-white close-up of Wes and me. He was kissing my cheek, while my eyes were closed, head slightly shifted to the left. "I want this one too."

I held up the previous photo. "You just said that you didn't need to see the rest because this one is your favorite."

She shrugged. "I changed my mind."

She continued to flip through each photograph but it was hard for me to focus. I looked out into my mother's immaculate backyard. A gardener trimmed the shrubs in the distance. The sprinklers went on. Beads of water were suspended in air before they fell to the ground. Directly off the deck was a pool with clear, blue water that sparkled in the sun.

I could count on one hand the number of times the pool and backyard have been used. My mother, she's a collector—gathering beautiful people and things around her, but never really using them. She was born into the echelons of the elite and never had to work for a thing. She's vivacious and outgoing. She goes from one event to the next and when there's no event, she creates one. As a child I used to watch her in awe; she was so different from me. I was okay sitting back and living in my imagination.

But for all her outgoing ways, she was never a hands-on parent. She watched from the sidelines: always there but a few steps away. I think it had to be that way. She was always on the lookout, always protecting me and my older brother, Mitchell. My father died when I was seven.

"Now that you two have settled in, when are you going to give me a grandchild?"

I choked on my lemonade. "Grandchild? We've barely been married for a month!"

The look on my mother's face said: *And your point is?*

"Babies are in the distant future," I elaborated. "Like, light-years away distant."

"Victoria, all I'm saying is that pretty soon you'll be dreaming of pink and blue onesies. It'll be all you can think about. Plus, babies make everything wonderful."

"So does alcohol but that doesn't mean I should run out and start drinking," I said smartly, a cheeky smile on my face.

My mother didn't look amused. "I'm being serious right now."

"I know, I know."

All kidding aside, I did want kids. I wanted two girls. I could see myself loving on them as babies, wiping runny noses, breaking up fights when they were young, and handing out curfews when they were teenagers. I had all these waiting memories on hold for my future kids. But that was the thing: Those memories were in waiting and I had no desire to reach for them now.

I reached across the table and held my mother's hand. "It's not happening right now."

She shook her head. "Well, that's disappointing."

"I'm not saying it's not in the cards. I want a family. But right now I want to enjoy my husband. I'm selfish and I want him all to myself." I smiled. "Can't I be selfish just for a moment?"

My mother smiled back. "Of course you can. Of course." We slipped back into a silence, scanning the photos, when my mother spoke up once again. "I forgot what it's like in the beginning."

I lifted my head. "Huh?"

She leaned forward and ground the butt of her cigarette into the ashtray. "Oh, you know . . . fresh love. Newlywed life." She sighed and tilted her head back so the sun shined down on her. "It's a beautiful time."

"It is," I agreed softly.

During our honeymoon, Wes and I made promises to each other. On how the future would be and how we would do things right. In a few years, we would break ground and build our dream house. If we had an argument we would work things out and we would never go to bed angry. We had plans and I was determined to keep every single one.

I glanced back at my mother and realized that she had been talking this entire time. ". . . And then you'll have a family and house like the one you grew up in." She gestured to the English, country-style monstrosity of a house beside us. Growing up in this house had been like growing up in a maze. I constantly found new places and dead ends. I think my active imagination was born from this place. There was such a wide age gap between my brother and me and on the days where my friends couldn't come over and play, I would create imaginary friends. They never complained. Or fussed. To them, all my games and ideas were brilliant.

If only imaginary friends stuck with you during adulthood. Maybe then things wouldn't be so rough.

I didn't know why she still lived here. I moved out after college and my brother had left three years before me. I suppose she stayed here for the memories. I know she wanted the same for me but I didn't have the heart to tell her that I had no desire to have a home so big that I could get lost inside it.

"What are you two talking about?"

At the sound of Wes's voice I turned around. He shut the patio door behind him and smiled at me. His black dress shirt was tucked into an equally dark pair of slacks. The sleeves were rolled up to his elbows. Sunlight reflected off the watch strapped around his left wrist. He came up behind me, his hands curving around my shoulders. My head rested against the hard muscles of his stomach.

"Oh, nothing," my mother answered breezily. "Just talking about how lucky you are to have my daughter."

Wes grabbed a chair and pulled it up next to me. He gave me that signature smirk of his. The one that pulled me under and never let go. "I'm lucky, all right."

6

December 2012

Her bruises were severe.

Her lip was busted.

The fluorescent lights didn't help her much; they high-lighted each mark. She cradled her right hand close to her chest, refusing to let me or Dr. Pelletier look at it. I was pretty sure it was sprained.

Dr. Pelletier was an older, gruff man. But if you looked past his demeanor, you saw he truly was a caring man. I'd worked with him on and off for the past year. Whenever he was on shift I knew the time would fly by.

For the sixth time he asked her how she had gotten hurt. Every time, though, he asked the question differently. Her answer was always the same: She fell down the stairs. She slipped on some water one of her kids had spilled. Just an accident, really.

I'd heard so many explanations for bruises and broken bones, I could write a book on it. From Dr. Pelletier's scowl I knew he felt the same. His eyes gave away nothing, but his shoulders drooped slightly.

Dr. Pelletier told her to get some rest and left the room. I stayed behind and waited for the door to close, before I gave her a comforting smile.

Her name was Alex.

She couldn't have been more than a few years older than me. But life hadn't been kind to her. Her skin was sallow, eyes blank, hair limp around her shoulders. If I could, I'd have locked her in that room until she finally agreed to leave him for good.

There was always a "him."

I should have been used to situations like hers, but I wasn't. It was just as painful to see as the first time. Mostly because I tried to help them, to fix the damage, but I knew that they'd go right back into the arms of violence. It was an awful feeling.

"You don't have to stay with him," I said quietly.

Alex didn't lift her head. It was almost as if she was used to this statement.

"There are shelters you can go to. Hotlines you can call. There's so much support waiting for you."

She sighed. "It's not that simple." Her voice was barely above a whisper. I had to lean in to hear her. "We have three kids. I can't just leave."

Lined up on the small counter was an array of pamphlets

ranging from how to quit smoking, to depression, pregnancy, domestic violence.

"Yes, you can," I said vehemently.

The woman snorted and slid down off the exam table. She put the pamphlet in her purse but I knew she wouldn't look through it. More than likely it would end up in the trash can by the exit.

She might come back.

She might not.

But if she did her story would be more airtight. Her guard would be up and her eyes would be deader than ever.

Unfortunately, she wouldn't be the last woman I'd see in such bad shape. The encounters never got easier. I wanted to block them from leaving. I wanted to try to convince them that they could really leave if they tried.

But I couldn't.

Finally, I left the room. The moment with the battered woman fell to the darker side of my job. I tried to think of the bright side: helping people. Comforting them.

It made me feel productive, like I was doing the one thing I was meant to do in this world.

I made my way down the hall, passing patients and nurses. At the kiosk, one of my close friends, Taylor, was checking in.

"I was hoping to see you," she said over her shoulder.

"Yeah?" I asked as I walked behind the nurses' station.

She nodded and rested her elbows on the counter. "I wanted to see if you were free for lunch on Saturday?"

"Do you mean to tell me that we have the same day off?"

"I do. Miracles do happen!"

I smiled. "That sounds good. What time?" I'd met Taylor

in college. She was flaky, scatterbrained, and if you gave her something she'd always lose it. But she was also kind and caring, the sort of friend who would stick by you through everything.

"I don't know yet. I'll call you with the time." She nudged me with her elbow and gestured down the hall.

Wes was walking toward us. He gave me a wink as if he knew exactly the thoughts running through my mind.

She sighed. "He's too good to be true."

I had to agree. Six months into marriage and everything couldn't have been more perfect.

"He doesn't happen to have a brother, does he?"

"If he did I would've already set you two up."

"Good girl."

Our conversation died as Wes stopped next to me. I went to hug him and he dangled the take-out bag in front of me. "Hungry?"

"Starved."

Surprisingly, Wes had the day off. He'd always been passionate about his job, but trying to make partner just added a whole other layer to his obsession. He was working his ass off on each case sent his way. A lot of times we saw each other in passing, with him going to work, me getting home from work. And as much as it sucked, it made those moments we were together that much greater.

He rubbed my shoulder gently. "When's your break?"

"Now."

Constantly moving from room to room left no time to be bored—or hungry. It was only when my stomach started to rumble that I realized I'd been on my feet for hours.

"Want to eat with me?"

"Why do you think I came here?" he teased.

Taylor pushed away from the counter. "All right," she sighed. "I can see that I'm not wanted here. I'll see you later, Wes."

As we walked toward the small break room at the end of the hall, I grabbed the take-out bag from him.

"Healthy lifestyle. I like," I said sarcastically.

Wes grinned. "Only the best for you."

The chaos circling around the nurses' station was nowhere near this area. In here there was always a hushed silence as doctors and nurses tried to get a few minutes of quiet.

Only one other nurse was in the break room right now. She sat clear at the other end of the table, her eyes glued to the magazine in front of her. A television was mounted on the wall, quietly playing a soap opera. There was a large corkboard on one wall, with a calendar tacked to it. Directly in front of it stood a magazine rack filled with outdated magazines. To the left was a mini kitchen where most of us usually warmed up our meals. Vending machines lined the wall behind me.

There was nothing much to this space, but most of the time, when we walked through the doors, we were so exhausted and hungry, we didn't care. We just wanted a moment to sit down.

Wes opened up the take-out bag and started pulling out the food. "When do you get off?"

I glanced at the clock as I dug through my purse for some change. "In about five hours. I told you this morning I had a twelve-hour shift."

"I know. I was hoping it might've changed."

"Nope." I walked over to the soda machine. "We're short-staffed today."

The smell of fries made my stomach grumble. I snatched the two waters and walked back over to the table, tossing one bottle to Wes. He caught it with one hand and sat down. For a few minutes there was nothing but silence as the two of us dug into our food.

The other nurse finally got up. She tossed her garbage away and left. The door slammed behind her. I wasted no time and leaned over to kiss Wes fiercely on the mouth. He seemed taken off guard, his lips unmoving beneath mine. It took him only a few seconds to react just the way I wanted him to.

When I pulled away, Wes had a slightly dazed look on his face.

"What was that for?"

I shrugged and took a drink. "I don't know how much time we'll have alone, so I might as well take the chance while I have it."

Wes leaned back in his chair and crossed his arms over his chest. He made an appealing picture, just sitting there with that serious expression of his. Right then, more than anything, I wished I could leave work and go home with him.

"When are the crazy shifts going to end?"

"The same time yours end," I teased.

He smiled and reached out, his fingers laced with mine. "I mean it."

I gently squeezed back. "I know you do. But this is how it always is. A few weeks of crazy shifts. A small lull and then more crazy shifts."

"Just don't overwork yourself."

I loved his concern. "I won't. I promise."

"Because the minute you do, you know you can stop working, right?"

I got up and threw my trash away. "Why would I do that?" I asked over my shoulder. "I love my job."

"And I love you. I want you all to myself. There's nothing in this world that I can't give you."

When I walked over to him, his hands curled around my waist, bringing me snug against his body. He squeezed my hip. I kissed the crown of his head.

"I love you, Victoria."

The look in his eyes showed he meant every word. Even if I was dressed in scrubs, he still made me feel beautiful.

There's nothing better than coming home after being on your feet for twelve hours.

Anxiously, I kicked my shoes off and walked right past them, not bothering to line them up against the rest of the shoes. The kitchen light was off, but light from the living room poured out into the hall. It was uncharacteristically quiet. Most times the TV was on, usually as background noise.

"Wes?" I called out.

My question was met with silence.

My legs felt like jelly as I walked down the hallway. All I wanted to do was slide beneath my sheets and go straight to sleep.

Entering the bedroom, I immediately collapsed onto the bed and pressed my cheek against the floral comforter. Since

Wes and I moved in together, we'd had to compromise on what items of ours stayed, what went into storage, and what had to go. His townhouse had been a complete bachelor pad, from the black leather furniture to the bland art on the wall. I liked splashes of color, flowers everywhere. The first time he saw the pale, yellow floral comforter, he reacted with horror. In the end he relented, and now the bachelor pad was gone. We met in the middle to create a cozy space that was all ours.

The bathroom door opened and out walked Wes, a towel wrapped around his waist. My exhaustion magically disappeared. Rivulets of water trailed down his ribs. His wet hair fell across his forehead, drops beading off it and sliding down his face like tears. He dried off his hair and leaned over to give me a quick, "Hey. Finally home."

"Finally. I've decided that it's probably a really bad idea for you to come have lunch with me."

He lifted a brow. "Why's that?"

"Because I was counting the hours until my shift ended. More so than usual."

I watched him closely. His body was lean, the cut of his abs prominent, his chest wide. The muscles in his back were pulled taut against his skin. He pulled out a pair of boxers and turned back to me.

Unabashedly, I continued to stare at him.

"Are you tired?" he asked.

"Yeah."

"Then stop looking at me like that, because now all I want to do is fuck you."

Wes had my attention the second he walked out of the

bathroom, but now I was transfixed. I slowly sat up, reached out, and hooked my finger around the hem of the towel and tugged him closer and gave him a wicked smile. "Suddenly, I'm not so tired anymore."

Seconds later I felt his warm body on top of mine, pinning me to the bed. With my eyes still closed, I smiled at the ceiling and wrapped my arms around his neck. I desperately wanted him to kiss me, but he had other ideas. He kissed my neck. The line of my jaw. My cheeks.

By the time his lips hovered over mine, my nails were digging into his skin, creating crescent-shaped marks. My breath was coming out in small little pants.

He waited another second and then he kissed me. There was nothing sweet and gentle. Like the one from earlier today. This one was fervent, as if he thought if he kissed me hard enough maybe he could tame this all-consuming desire between us. Propping myself up on my elbows, I kissed him back with the same intensity.

His hands slipped beneath my shirt, drifted up my stomach, and possessively cupped my breasts.

This was what I went crazy over. In public Wes was controlled and contained. Alone he was entirely different: wild, almost dangerous. He grabbed on to me, his fingers sinking into my skin. He issued commands and I followed every single one. It was a thrill to tap into this unknown side.

The hunger between us continued to grow.

I sat up long enough to take my top off. My pants were next to go. I reached out to touch him, and he captured my hands, holding them so tightly there was no way of breaking free and placing them above my head.

"Not yet," he panted.

The chase was a thrill, intoxicating. Seduction was a game to Wes and he played it well.

I smiled, feeling myself go half-mad. The towel dropped from his waist, revealing just how hard he was. His grip loosened and I reached out, my hand curling around the length of him. With heavy-lidded eyes, he watched. My grip tightened just the smallest bit. His mouth parted and he sucked in a sharp breath. I couldn't look away, even if I tried.

Wes always craved control in every aspect of his life, but in moments like these I called the shots and loved every second of it.

"Fuck," he hissed.

He pushed my legs apart. With his hands on either side of my head, Wes thrust into me. My eyes closed and I sucked in a sharp breath.

Wes slid in and out of me so agonizingly slowly that my hips bucked and my heels dug into the mattress. He watched every move I made with a possessive gleam in his eyes.

I could feel a buildup inside me: Blood rushed through my veins; my skin was hot to the touch.

Wes rolled his hips. Sweat beaded over his upper lip and hairline. His pace quickened and for one distinct second, we felt like one. So entwined in each other's lives that nothing could ever tear us apart.

I closed my eyes but behind my lids I saw only Wes.

7

November 2015

"Victoria?"

Gradually I come back to the present. The warmth of the sunshine on my skin recedes. The happiness of the memory fades. I'm back to wearing my black sweatpants, gray T-shirt, and a robe. The smell disappears and is replaced with that of Lysol.

This is a reality check if ever there was one.

"Victoria? Are you okay?" Dr. Calloway peers at me, concern etched on her features.

I hold up the wedding picture. "I remember this day."

"For the first time?"

I nod and, in detail, explain what I saw. She writes it all

down. Not once interrupting me. When I'm done talking she drops her pen and gives me a faint smile.

My hands are shaking at the memory and I can barely hold Evelyn. It was so vivid, so real that it's impossible that it happened years ago instead of right now.

"This is great," Dr. Calloway says with a big smile. "You remembered something."

I know Dr. Calloway is thinking about the bigger picture, but I'm impatient. I'm willing to do just about anything to get out of this place. I want instant results. Remember one memory, remember them all.

"How many pictures are there?"

Dr. Calloway flips through them. The action's all for show; I know she's counted the photos beforehand. "Around twenty."

"Can I take the ones from today?"

"Of course. They're yours."

I slip the photos into my pocket. I know that's me in the picture, but it's incredibly surreal to stare at a captured memory and not remember the moment. I stand up slowly, unsure of what to say or do. I think Evelyn picks up on my nervous energy. She looks up at me with those blue eyes, the expression on her face saying, "Well, did that help you at all?"

Like a coward, I look away.

"Are we going to go through all of those pictures?" I ask Dr. Calloway.

"If you want to we can. I think they are crucial to helping you remember things about your past."

This leads me to think again about getting the hell out of this place. That's the silver lining on all of this. I walk toward the door. My hand hovers over the handle and I glance at Dr. Calloway, hesitant about how to say my thoughts. "What happens if I remember something that isn't good?"

"We'll deal with that when we reach that point." Dr. Calloway smiles. "Everything will be fine."

I nod and say okay, but truthfully, I'm skeptical; there's three years' worth of memories mangled in a ball. And I have to untwist each and every one.

Alice is waiting outside the door. Without a word, I turn in the direction of the dayroom. She doesn't ask how my day is going. How Evelyn is. Or how the session went. But I know she'll never be that kind of nurse. Right now, I'm grateful for that. I have the opportunity to really think over each memory. Now that I have them back, I'm dumbfounded that I ever forgot them. And if I so easily lost good portions of my memories, what did I do with the bad ones?

I glance down at my hands. Now I remember all the times I used them to help people: holding the hands of scared patients, bandaging wounds. . . .

How ironic that the roles have been reversed.

Entering the dayroom, I sit down at my regular table and instead of playing a game of cards or watching television like everyone else, I people watch.

I've never questioned why people came to Fairfax.

New names were put on the outside of doors daily. Faces came and went. Not once have I made an effort to get to know them. Yet right now it's all I can think about. The girl rocking herself in the corner: Did she want to be here? Or the older woman—I think her name is Lottie—who's been here much longer than me and sings "God Bless America" on a nonstop loop: What compelled her to make Fairfax her home?

The TV volume is low. Conversations between nurses and patients are barely heard. I've always thought that the hush over this room was just us patients collectively holding our breaths, waiting to see what would happen next, but every day I'm here, drug-free, I see the truth.

There's no air here.

We breathe in madness.

We exhale insanity.

And the people around me? They seem okay with it. No one fights the nurses or tries to escape through the windows. No one seems to mind that our movements are circumscribed, monitored every second so we never fall out of line.

They sit and walk around like this is normal.

Not so long ago I was just like them.

I close my eyes and rub my temples. Just one single memory and I'm already shaken up. How will I be when I get the rest of my past back? I'm almost afraid to find out.

"You're welcome by the way."

I jerk back so abruptly I almost fall out of my chair. Reagan pulls out the chair across from me and sits down. Today she's wearing black sweatpants but still has on a hospital gown. She crosses her arms. They look like two small sticks, barely supporting her. She looks so fragile. As if she could break in half at any moment.

"What are you talking about?" I ask.

Reagan rolls her eyes. "For yesterday. For being your shill. Decoy. Whatever you want to call it."

"That was for me?"

"More or less."

I narrow my eyes. The problem with Reagan is that she cloaks her words with layers of irony. I can never tell when she's being serious. Her subversive personality constantly has everyone on edge, including me.

Abruptly, she leans forward and her chair legs hit the floor loudly. Her dark green eyes widen with excitement. In spite of myself, I find myself leaning forward too.

"I just love pissing off that cranky old bat." Reagan twists in her seat and gestures toward Alice, who's outside the room, talking to another nurse.

Reagan turns back to me. "Because of yesterday I had to stay in the white room."

I suppress a shudder. The white room is every patient's nightmare. I haven't been there, but I've heard horror stories and whether they've been stretched and twisted for drama remains to be seen, but I'm not waiting in line to see if it's true.

"Well," I start out slowly. "Thanks for yesterday?"

Reagan smiles brightly, as though we're best friends. "No worries."

Just then Alice walks into the room. Reagan jumps out of her chair and points at her. "Oh, God. Attila the Hun's here!" Reagan shouts dramatically. "Everyone take cover! It's every man for himself!"

Alice glares at her. Even though her attention isn't directed at me, I shift my body away. "You're not supposed to be here."

"Why not?" Reagan challenges.

"Because of what you did yesterday. You lost a lot of points."

Fairfax has a point system. It's our form of currency. If you keep your allotted ten points per day you're regarded as a good patient. And if you lose points, you lose privileges. You're someone who needs to be monitored more carefully. People have been known to break down from losing a single point.

Reagan doesn't seem to give a tiny rat's ass about her points.

"What I did yesterday? What I did yesterday . . . hmm." Reagan taps one of her index fingers against her lip. "I did a lot of things yesterday. You're gonna have to enlighten me and tell me what I did."

"Get up."

Alice leaves no room for a reply and jerks Reagan up by the arm.

"Nuh-uh-uh," Reagan tuts. "If you keep grabbing patients like that, someone won't win Employee of the Month."

Alice lets go.

"Now, before I go back to 'my room,' can I have a quick smoke?"

"No. You lost smoking privileges."

"That's bullshit!"

"It's not. You know the rules, Reagan."

The two of them walk out of the room, but their arguing trails behind them.

My eyes flit nervously to the front doors. It's ridiculous, but I keep waiting for Sinclair to walk through them. I don't remember him. Not yet, at least. But I know that he can help me with my past.

His eyes are haunting me.

Last night I dreamed about those eyes, staring at me with the same heavy intensity as yesterday. But we weren't at Fairfax. I didn't capture my surroundings; I just remember the air smelling of flowers and a large table separating the two of us. His mouth moved, but I couldn't make out a single word he was saying. Then, very slowly, he reached across the table toward my hand. It inched closer and closer. It hovered over mine—and then I woke up.

I've never wanted so desperately to slip back into a dream.

A part of me thinks that if he comes by to visit, I'll be able to piece together the dream. But the clock moves forward.

Just then, my mother walks through the doors, like she does every Saturday at eleven sharp. Rain or shine, she's here.

She'll update me on everything outside of Fairfax: friends, family, events, gossip. Nothing is off-limits. Nothing except my husband. When I bring up Wes and his visits, she clams up and tries to change the subject.

I watch as she promptly signs in and makes a beeline for my table. She gives me a smile. It's incredibly different from the one on the woman who beamed at me as we looked through my wedding pictures all those years ago. This smile is wan, never quite reaching her eyes.

"It's good to see you, honey," she says.

Before she sits down, she moves in to hug me. The floral scent of her perfume surrounds me. When she pulls back she gives me a thorough once-over. Nothing has changed about her. She's impeccable. From her black bob, pressed black slacks, and dark blue dress shirt, all the way down to her heels.

"How are you?"

I give her my routine answer: "I'm fine."

Inside I'm dying to tell her about today: the pictures, the memories. All of it. But if our past has taught me anything it's that she thinks I'm lying too. She doesn't believe me when I tell her Wes is alive.

She nods, clutching her purse for dear life, as if the patients around us will steal it from her hands. "That's great," she replies mildly.

She scans the room, and watches a slight female patient playing checkers. The girl catches my mother's gaze and jumps out of her seat, the hem of her hospital gown brushing against her knees. She stands directly in front of my mother.

"Boo!" the girl shouts.

My mother jumps and a nurse instantly guides the girl away, telling her to quietly play checkers or she will get points taken away. The girl starts to cry. Deep, heavy sobs that make even my heart ache. They're the kinds of cries that carry out into the hall, slip through the cracks of the doors, and carry into the wind. They're the cries that give psych wards a bad rep.

"I didn't see her there." She brushes the sleeves of her shirt as if she's trying to wipe the crazy off her.

"How have you been?" I ask.

Instantly she perks up. "Great! There was a ladies' luncheon yesterday. It was just beautiful. You would've loved it."

"That's good," I say, but inside I'm questioning whether I really would have enjoyed it.

For the next few minutes she updates me on everything in her life. You'd think that not much would change week to week, but with my mother, it always does. She's always bouncing around from one event to the next.

I shift in my seat. "Listen, I wanted to talk to you about something."

"What about?"

"Just something about my past."

"Okay . . ." She draws it out slowly.

"What was my life like before Fairfax?"

A soft smile appears. She reaches across the table and covers my hands with hers. "It was beautiful. Absolutely beautiful."

The sincerity in her voice can't be faked.

"I had a visitor yesterday."

Her shoulders stiffen. Her back becomes ramrod straight. "Who?"

"Sinclair Montgomery."

His name hangs between us. The look in her eyes shows that she knows that I know about the list. But she never speaks up and offers up an excuse.

"Does the staff have a list of who can and cannot visit me?"

"Well, yes, but—"

"Who else is on the list?" I cut in.

My mother blanches. "Excuse me?"

"Who else is on the list?"

"Sinclair and Renee."

I let out a deep breath and try to rein in my temper. "Shouldn't you have told me that? Shouldn't you have told me that there even *was* a list?"

She closes her eyes and rubs the bridge of her nose. "Victoria, I was just trying to help."

"How was that trying to help?"

Her eyes flash with irritation. "You said you came to Fairfax to rest and I wanted to make sure that nothing or no one would get in your way."

"You should've let me decide that."

"I know, I know. I apologize. I thought I was doing what's best for you."

From the pain in her eyes, I think she's being sincere. I *want* to believe she's being sincere.

"So." She smiles. "What else can we talk about?"

"We can talk about Wes."

"Why?"

"Because I'm trying to leave Fairfax?"

Her face lights up. "That's wonderful news, but what does this have to do with Wes?"

"Because no one believes me. You always tell me that you want me out of here. So here's your chance to help me *get* out of here."

She leans back in her seat as if I've just asked her to donate a kidney. I can see her mind racing. She wants to help me. That much is easy to see. But will she agree? That's the real question.

"Victoria," she says slowly. "I don't know if I can do that."

I glance down at Evelyn and gently stroke her hair. My heartbeat is staccato and erratic. "Why not?"

"Because he really is dead."

All I can think is, *Here we go again*. Why did I think that this time would be different? I rapidly blink my eyes, trying to push back my tears.

I lift my head and look her straight in the eyes. "No, he isn't," I whisper fiercely.

"Yes, he is. Honey . . ." My mother licks her lips and glances down at the table. "I identified his body."

This isn't the first time she's said that. I didn't believe her then and I don't believe her now. "No, you didn't."

Her hand reaches across the table toward mine. I jerk back. She sighs loudly. "You won't even listen to me."

"Because what you're saying is a lie." I lean forward. "I see him all the time."

"Let's stop and think about what you're suggesting, all right?"

"You mean, asking for your help?"

My mother pointedly ignores me and continues. "If I give in and tell the doctors that Wes is alive when he isn't, then I'm just encouraging you to believe it."

I slam both hands onto the table. On my lap, Evelyn starts to fuss. "I will continue to believe it whether you want me to or not." My mother gives me a sympathetic look and that just fuels my anger. My voice starts to rise. "He comes every night at eleven. He tells me—"

My mother looks around, as if we're under surveillance, then interrupts me and says quietly, "You need to calm down, okay? I'm not trying to upset you."

Have you ever had someone treat you like you're less than, even though you know you aren't? It's a terrible feeling. It makes my heart thump furiously against my chest. I bite the inside of my cheek and chant in my head, *I'm right, I'm right, I'm right, I'm right, I'm right . . .*

My mother and I become quiet. There's nothing else that I can say, and nothing she can do to erase the tension. She finally speaks up. "Do you want me to leave?"

Part of me does. And a bigger part wants her to stay; if she stays longer than an hour, if she stays for the whole day, then maybe, just maybe, she'll see Wes.

"You don't have to if you don't want to."

"Very well." She ducks her head. "I'll stay."

Evelyn continues to fuss so I hold her against my chest, knowing that she is picking up on my frustration and anger. I take deep breaths and slowly but surely, she calms down.

"I have another question."

"Victoria, if this is about Sinclair again . . ."

"Of course it's about him. I have this man who shows up and claims to know me. And then I find out that you've been keeping him away . . ." I take a deep breath and watch my mother carefully. "What do you know that I don't?"

"I know that this man is nothing but bad news."

"But—"

"No, you need to listen to me." She leans in, desperation and fear in her eyes. "All the progress that you have made at Fairfax will disappear if you continue to see him. Do you understand?"

"Who was he to me?" I whisper.

My mother hesitates. "He was and is your trigger point. The root of all your problems."

"Quit talking cryptically and just tell me," I plead.

"Victoria, I'm not doing this right now." She stands up and I follow her, beyond frustrated that she won't help.

"I can handle whatever you have to say. It won't break me."

All right, all right. I've stretched the truth a bit, but I'm desperate.

My mother smiles and walks around the table. She reaches out and brushes her fingertips over my cheeks. She puts my hair behind my ear. "Oh, Victoria. Look around you, honey. You're already broken and there's not a single part of me that wants to watch you shatter even further."

There's nothing but silence between us.

"I'll see you later," she says finally. Kissing my cheek, she hurries toward the door as if Hell is nipping at her heels.

"Will you ever believe me about Wes?" I call out.

She stops and turns. "How can I? I know the truth."

I swallow loudly, dreading the words I'm about to say. "If you don't believe me, then don't come back."

She flinches at my words and so do I.

"You don't mean that."

"I really do. Almost everyone else in this place thinks I'm lying and the last person who should feel that way is you."

She holds her head high, looking as regal and self-composed as she did when I was a kid. Her lips pull into a thin line. The only tell that she's pissed-off is the white-knuckle grip she has on her purse strap. "Very well, if that's what you want, then consider it done."

Without another word she turns on her heels and walks out the door.

8

"Everyone needs to quiet down!" one of the night shift nurses shouts.

She's standing in front of the TV, holding a clear bowl above her, filled with small, folded pieces of paper with our names written inside. All but two lights are on in the day-room; the curtains are closed. The tables are pushed to the sides and the chairs are in three rows of eight, all facing the TV. The screen is blue with a DVD logo slowly traveling around it. For the past ten minutes I've been watching the word, waiting for it to hit the corner perfectly.

It's sad that something like this completely makes my day. Every Thursday is movie night. If you ask a nurse or doctor, they'll say that most patients are "encouraged" to go. But *encouraged* is just a dressed up word for *forced*. Unless you're bleeding from the eyes or convulsing on the floor, you're in the dayroom for movie night.

Everyone around me hushes up and watches Susan.

"The person who gets to choose tonight's movie is . . ." Susan pulls out a name and lowers the bowl. ". . . Louise!"

When it had been Reagan's turn, she'd chosen *Girl, Interrupted*. They made her choose again. Her next choice was *Sybil*.

Needless to say, Reagan never got to pick another movie again.

"Louise, what movie do you want to watch tonight?"

The older woman furiously rubs her hands together, thinking over the question as if this were the most important answer of her life. "*The Sound of Music!*" she finally says.

In the midst of soft claps and squeals of delight is Reagan loudly groaning. "That movie again? We've seen it, like, ten times! We get it. Julie Andrews can sing."

The nurse rolls her eyes. "Doesn't matter. It's Louise's turn to pick."

"Then can I go to my room, please?"

"No."

"I said please."

"And I said no."

Reagan slouches in her seat. Out of all the chairs to pick from, she chose the one on my right. For reasons beyond me, she seems to have latched on to me. Truthfully, it's not all bad. It's kind of nice to have someone to talk to in here.

You have your daughter! my mind hisses.

Instantly, I feel guilty and rub Evelyn's back. Of course I

have my daughter but sometimes it's nice to speak to someone and have them talk back. I love Evelyn's beautiful smile
and chubby cheeks. I love how she looks at me as if I'm the
center of her universe. I love it all, but I need to have just a
small amount of adult interaction.

The nurse loads the DVD. While the beginning credits
roll, she starts to hand out Styrofoam cups of popcorn. The
lights turn off and obnoxious shushing sounds die out. Finally, everyone settles in to watch, but nothing, not even Julie
Andrews and her lilting voice, can pull me out of reality. I
feel Reagan's eyes on me, but I also feel another set. Multiple
times I've twisted in my chair, only to see no one.

"What are you doing?" Reagan asks.

I turn to face the TV. In my arms Evelyn makes a fuss. I
give her a quick kiss on the cheek. "Nothing."

Reagan tosses a piece of popcorn in the air. She tilts forward and catches it with her mouth. "Oh, come on. If you're
going to lie, lie good. You could've said you were stretching."

"If I did, would you have believed me?"

"No, but I would've admired you for your quick thinking."

I smile and go back to watching the movie.

"How old are you?" Reagan asks bluntly.

Never have I seen someone jump so quickly from one subject to the next. I get whiplash having a conversation with
her.

"It's rude to ask someone how old they are," I point out.

She throws another piece of popcorn, only this time it
hits Amber, the girl sitting in front of us. She's an anorexic

who's been here probably just as long as I have. She's skinnier than ever and shows no signs of getting out of here.

"It's only rude when the person is ancient," Reagan shot back. "So . . . age?"

"Twenty-seven. How old are you?"

"Eighty-five," she says deadpan. "I'm like the *Curious Case of Benjamin Button*."

That makes me smile.

"I'm twenty-three," she says seriously.

Her reply shocks me. Reagan doesn't look a day over eighteen. Maybe it's her build. Pale skin stretched over incredibly small bones. Or perhaps it's her laugh. It's a genuine sound, as if she steals from life all its pleasure and uses every last drop.

Without a doubt Reagan is crazy, but sometimes I wish I could have her personality. Just for a few seconds.

"Does the baby like the movie?" She throws another piece of popcorn. It ricochets off Amber's head. Her skinny shoulders twitch and I know she's seconds away from blowing up.

Cautiously, I stare at Reagan. "Quit calling her 'the baby.' Her name is Evelyn."

Reagan holds her hands out in supplication. "My bad, my bad. Evelyn it is."

I still don't believe her and hold Evelyn just a bit tighter.

"Does 'Evelyn' like the movie?"

"She's a baby. She doesn't know what's going on."

"Now that is something I completely agree with you on," she remarks.

She throws more popcorn and a few times it actually

lands in her mouth. "You don't have a lot of friends here, do you?"

"No."

"Stick with me, Mommy Dearest. We can be the folie à deux of Fairfax."

"What's a folie à deux?"

Reagan turns and smiles deviously at me. "A madness shared by two."

Before I can answer, Amber turns around and shoots Reagan a glare filled with hatred. "Can you not talk so fucking loud?"

"Of course I can *not* talk so fucking loud but where's the fun in that?"

Amber makes a grab at Reagan's popcorn, prompting one of the nurses to stand up. "Girls," she warns.

"We're good, we're good," Reagan says. She gives the nurse a charming smile.

The nurse sits back and for the first time tonight, Reagan's quiet for a few minutes. I think it's a personal best for her. For all her hate of this movie, her eyes never stray from the screen. But I still can't focus on a damn thing. I keep thinking about my conversation with my mother today. When I told her not to come back I really hoped she would relent and tell me that she does believe me. That she'll stick by me as I slowly replay my past.

Did I expect too much from her? Maybe. But I think that maybe I thought too little of myself. Automatically, I want to assume that this burden is impossible for me to handle.

"Why are you scared? You're the bravest person I know."

Gasping, I turn around. Truly expecting to see Sinclair behind me. But he's not.

The movie drones on. Evelyn is fast asleep and soon I'm starting to nod off, when behind me I hear voices. One female, the other male. Within seconds I'm sitting up straight and twisting around. I know that voice. It strikes a chord in me.

My heart is beating like a drum as I take in Sinclair. He's standing next to the front entrance, talking to one of the nurses. He's quickly talking. Kate's face is set in a grim line, but she's not completely shutting him down. I requested for Dr. Calloway to take his name off the restricted list, but did she follow through? God, I hope so.

"What are you looking at? You're sup . . ." Reagan's voice trails off as she turns around. "Ah. Tall, dark, and dangerous. No need to explain."

"His name's Sinclair."

There's really no reason to say that, but I like his name coming from my lips. It feels right.

My eyes slide to Reagan. "Have you seen him here before?"

She nods. "A lot of times."

I try to hide my smirk by kissing Evelyn's head. The thought of someone seeking me out, of wanting to see me, makes me feel less alone. Gives me more hope to continue forward. But there's something else attached to this feeling. Something I don't recognize and can't explain.

Susan steps into the dayroom and gestures for me to come over. I stand up, suddenly feeling awkward. I can feel multiple sets of eyes, but I feel Sinclair's the most. His stare makes my skin feel like it's about to go up in flames.

"You have a visitor," Susan whispers. "But make it quick. Visiting hours are over at—"

"At seven. Yes, I know."

She shrugs and walks back to the nurses' station. I follow behind her; the bright lights of the hall make me squint. Once my eyes adjust, I look over at Sinclair. The hallway's empty, leaving the two of us all alone.

I have no idea what to say. I may physically react to him, but that doesn't make up for the fact that this is the second time we're meeting.

He smiles. Just smiles and yet it does something to me. This smile isn't the same smile he gave the nurse a few days ago. And it isn't a friendly smile. It's intimate, as though years of my life are behind that smile. It all seems ridiculous. Inconceivable. Impossible.

"How are you?" he asks quietly.

Psych Ward 101: Everyone and anyone will ask you how you're doing. It's up to you to find a go-to response that will satisfy them all.

But I don't want to use that response with Sinclair so I say: "I've been better."

A look of pure concern covers his face. "What's wrong? Is everything okay?"

A male patient in the dayroom twists in his chair and shushes us obnoxiously. I glare at him.

Sinclair gestures to an area right next to the front doors. "Want to go over there?"

I nod and he lets me walk in front of him. Sinclair slips up beside me, his arm pressed against mine. Warmth shoots down my arm, straight to my fingertips. I fix my eyes forward even though I can feel his eyes on me.

My mind is racing a mile a minute.

Ask him about his sister!

No, ask him about you. Maybe he can fill in the blanks of your past.

Did he know Wes?

Where did he meet you?

These are all viable questions and I don't know where to start. I lean against the wall, my shoulder brushing against the bulletin board with flyers announcing movie night, special game night, or the next special event or holiday. There's a few dull motivational posters stapled in the midst of the brightly colored flyers.

There's an appropriate distance between us, allowing my pulse to slow down a bit. I quickly take him in. He has a good six inches on me. The crown of my head meets his shoulders. I kind of like this height difference, how he completely dwarfs me. Standing next to him, I feel like no one can get to me. Hurt me. And that makes my heart practically sing.

He's wearing jeans. His brown jacket conceals his shirt. Flecks of snow cling to the tips of his black, mussed hair. I'm tempted to reach up and brush the snow away. Déjà vu hits me as if I had done that once before.

"Is everything okay?" he repeats.

It's bad enough that I'm stuck in a psych ward. If I tell Sinclair that I feel eyes constantly watching my every move, he might never come back.

I don't want that.

"Everything's fine." I brush my fingers against the back of Evelyn's hand.

His shoulders relax as he leans against the wall. "I can't believe I'm talking to you right now."

"I had you and your sister taken off the list. If I knew that you were restricted I would've tried earlier to—"

Sinclair quickly cuts in. "I know."

From the look in his eyes I know he means it.

A silence descends around us, but it's not that awkward silence that lingers between strangers. His presence is so achingly familiar, making the silence and speaking of past moments that we once spent together comfortable. A part of me thinks that if we stayed like this for a few more minutes, I might remember something about him.

But I can't keep quiet. The second I saw him walk into Fairfax tonight, my curiosity rose to the surface, asking questions and demanding answers.

"Will your sister ever visit again?" I ask.

Sinclair rubs the back of his neck. "Renee wants to but . . ." He frowns and stares at Evelyn, a faraway look in his eyes. Evelyn stares right back him. "A lot of things have happened since you've been here."

I straighten up. My brows furrow together. "Like what?"

Sinclair sighs and drags his hands through his dark hair, making the strands stand straight up. "I'm not here to make things confusing for you."

"Why are you here then?" I can't help the hint of desperation that slips into my words.

"To help."

I look away, glancing toward the dayroom, filled with patients. I don't want to spend my days looking forward to breakfast, lunch, and dinner. I don't want to spend my days in the dayroom, slowly wasting away. If I don't reach out to Sinclair now, I never will. "I'm . . . I'm trying to remember my past," I confess.

Sinclair's eyes bore straight into mine. He has bedroom eyes, watching everything with mild interest. People like him are dangerous because they may not be bold and loud, but they see everything going on around them.

"Is that a good or bad thing?" he asks.

"Remembering my past?"

He nods.

"It's . . . good. At least I think it is." The feeling of being watched never really disappears and just then, I quickly look around. Susan and Kate are behind the nurses' station. There's no one watching us. "I'm ready to leave Fairfax," I confess.

A myriad of emotions flash through his eyes but happiness is the only thing I can see. "That's great."

I nod and carefully construct my words. "The last time you came here, you said that you've tried to visit me every single day."

"I have," he says fiercely.

"I know . . . I checked the sign-in sheet." Nervously, I lick my lips. One of his arms brushes against mine. Electric currents shoot through me. I flinch slightly.

My body is going haywire and it's all this man's fault.

"What do you remember about me?" I ask.

"Everything. I remember everything about you."

I look at him from beneath my lashes. "Then tell me."

Sinclair frowns and says, "When I visited you last time it was obvious that I shocked you. I don't want to pile any more information on you."

"You're not piling information on me. I'm asking you to tell me."

Sinclair barks out a laugh and rubs his upper lip. He almost looks nervous. "Yeah. Okay. I can do that." He clears his throat, and leans in. Just an inch. Even though there's still an appropriate distance between us, it feels like he's mere inches from me, almost touching. "You love outdoors and gardening. Your favorite flower is hydrangeas and you hate orchids. Spring is your favorite season. You're addicted to chai. You love gossip magazines and when you read a good book you can never pull yourself away. . . ."

On and on the lists goes. Sinclair rattles off information like he's a walking encyclopedia of Victoria Donovan.

What he says sounds beautiful but I can't remember any of it. The helplessness that rushes through me threatens tears to pool in my eyes.

There are no words I can say. Nothing.

Sinclair pauses. "Do you want me to keep going?"

I think, if I ask him to, he can still keep rattling off information. But my head feels heavy, weighed down by all his facts.

"It's enough."

He's still staring intently at me. Somehow I don't think his question is meant to be answered. Even if it is, I have no response to give him. "It's enough." The air has left my lungs and my stomach is twisted so tightly it feels like it will never uncoil.

"Mr. Montgomery?"

Our heads turn toward Susan at the same time. She glances between the two of us and gives me a small, apologetic smile. "Visiting hours are over."

He gives her a brisk nod, looking calm and controlled, but I see the way his lips go into a straight line. It's crazy, but I feel a slight thrill that he's not ready for this conversation to end.

"I guess I should be going."

There's a moment when it looks like he's going to say or do something else. His eyes never leave mine. They speak to me, saying, *Just try. Try to remember me.* I brace myself, but he just says goodbye and walks toward the door.

"Wait!" I place a hand on his arm. The warmth that transfers from his body through mine feels like a lightning bolt. And it's all from one touch. I swallow. "Are you going to visit soon?"

Sinclair smiles the kind of smile that women dream about. One that makes your pulse speed up and your cheeks flame. "Of course I will. I'm not going to leave you here."

"Even though I can't remember who you are?"

"Especially since you don't remember. But you will remember," he says confidently.

"How do you know?"

Sinclair shrugs. "I just do." A ghost of a smile plays at his lips. It holds a memory behind it that I want to steal as my own.

His reply gives me more pleasure than I care to admit.

He says goodbye again and leaves. As I sit there, something deep down inside me, something dark and dormant, tells me I need Sinclair Montgomery to reconstruct my past.

Later on that night, I pull the photographs out of my pocket and stare down at the happy couple. Wes hasn't come to visit in two days. It's almost as if he knows I have thousands of questions for him, and he enjoys keeping me in suspense.

My door opens slowly and ominously and I know without looking that it's Wes.

Finally.

His shadow stretches across the floor and over half my face. My entire body stiffens and I turn my head his way.

"How is my queen?" he asks. There's an edge to his words.

My body is in the present. Yet my mind lingers in the past, holding on to the glorious memory for as long as it can.

He crosses his arms, his hands hidden behind his biceps. "Aren't you going to answer me, Victoria?"

I can't look at him. Those memories were so bright and vibrant. The two of us together took my breath away and now this? It's a letdown of epic proportion.

"No," I mutter.

"Why not? Did you have a bad day?"

Everything he says is filled with condemnation and sarcasm.

He crouches next to me and stares at the picture. The cologne that drifted behind me in my flashback is the same scent that circles around me now. It makes me suck in a sharp breath. "You remember that moment?"

I nod.

Wes sighs. "We were happy."

The blinds are open and silver light cuts through the room and slashes across his face. I see sincerity in his hazel eyes mixed with pain.

"How happy?"

Wes doesn't answer and my desperation makes me abruptly turn to him, until our faces are inches apart. "I'm sorry," I blurt out.

What am I sorry for? I don't really know. But I know something bad, something really bad had to have happened to bring us to this point. From the devastating expression Wes gives me, I think I'm the cause for all the bad things.

Did the bad happen all at once? Or was it a slow decline? Was Sinclair part of the bad? My first instinct is to say no, but I can't count anything out.

"Just tell me what happened to us," I whisper.

Wes shakes his head. "I can't."

"Can't or won't?"

"Both."

I drop my face into my hands and fight the urge to scream out my frustrations.

"Why?" I finally ask.

I lift my head and find Wes staring at me. The sincerity dissolves and turns into agitation. "Ask Sinclair."

My shoulders instantly stiffen.

Wes laughs bitterly. "What? You didn't think I'd find out he visited you?"

I didn't reply.

"I've known all about him."

"Tell me. You know I don't remember."

Wes jumps up, towering over me. I take a step back. "If you're dying to know, ask him." He laughs at my shock, but it's forced, as though he's doing everything in his power not to let his pain show.

Guilt clutches my heart at the thought that maybe I'm the person behind that pain. I have no sense of who I was and what I did, but I'm a good person. I know I am. No matter what happened, I would never deliberately go out of my way to hurt Wes.

"How do you know him?"

"Does that matter?" he shoots back.

No? Yes? I'm not sure. Lately, every single thought of mine is dissected, pulled so far apart I can see through them to the truth and lies on the other side. Even then I question myself. But if Wes knows anything about Sinclair, even the smallest piece of information, maybe it will trigger my memory.

"I know everything about him."

"You're lying," I whisper.

"What do I stand to gain by lying?"

We stare at each other. Wes means every word he says. I just can't tell if it's the truth or not.

Evelyn cries out and I'm pulled back to the present. I jump up and rush over to her bassinet and pick her up.

"I need to take care of Evelyn." Stubbornly, I hold her in my arms, hoping that he'll get the hint and leave. There's a beat of silence and I think he's going to stay. Just to torture me. But he finally nods. He kisses the top of my head. I want to believe that it's a gesture filled with love. I really do. But I can't. I close my eyes and bite the inside of my cheek.

"Victoria?"

I look over my shoulder.

"Don't believe a thing he says."

A comment like that can't be said in parting. I want to know why he said it, but Wes is already backing out of the room before I can ask.

"Just stop while you're ahead," he says. "Nothing good can come out of you turning around and staring at your past."

"Of course there's good."

"Like what?"

"Like my freedom. Like Evelyn and me getting out of here."

Wes doesn't glance at Evelyn. Not once. Just keeps his sharp eyes on me. He shakes his head sadly. "If you think that, then maybe you really are crazy," he says.

The door shuts behind him and I'm left in silence, weighing his words.

9

Just because one group of pictures triggered memories, it doesn't mean a new set will.

I'm too nervous to invest faith that this method will be the one that works.

My heart thunders in my ears as I make myself comfortable across from Dr. Calloway. Even Evelyn stops her fussing long enough to peer at Calloway.

My file seems to have taken up permanent residence on Calloway's desk. It sits at the very top on a small stack of file folders. I know it sounds petty and ridiculous, but I like that I'm at the top. That means that this is important to Calloway too and that, in her eyes, I'm not just some crazy person.

"Ready for some more photos?"

Nervously, my left leg bounces up and down. Dr. Calloway instantly catches the action. She laces her fingers together and leans in. "What's going through your mind?"

I try to take a deep cleansing breath. "That this time the pictures might not bring any memories."

Dr. Calloway shrugs. "That may be the case. We don't know. We've only just begun to start the process. I don't expect every single photo in your file to evoke a memory. I hope so, but if they don't then they don't. As long as the photos spark something, even down to the most minor memory, then we're on the right track. How does that sound to you?"

Some of the tension releases from my body. The nerves don't but I really don't think that feeling will ever fade. "It sounds good," I reply.

We immediately get to work. As she pulls out a new batch of pictures, I nervously adjust Evelyn in my arms.

Photo number one: It's of Wes. He's staring into the lens, brows slightly raised, eyes wide with shock as if someone just called out his name. He's dressed down in sweats, hair messy. It's a shock to my system to see Suit-and-Tie Wes so casual. I peer at the surroundings, but they don't look familiar.

Photo number two: me. My hands are in the air as I smile widely. Behind me is a massive house in the middle of construction. With scaffolding lining the brick. Wes is in the background, standing in the doorway. He stares right into the lens just like I do, but the hatred brewing in his eyes is enough to make the hairs on the back of my neck stand up.

Photo number three: me and Wes together, with our arms wrapped around each other. We're standing in the entryway of our house. Light curves around us. I can see the boxes lined against the wall inside the house. Wes's smile is genuine. But mine is not. I look dead behind my eyes.

The process speeds up, just like the first time.

Then, I hear them. The voices. They start out so quietly that it feels like someone's whispering into my ear. The volume slowly increases and so does the number of voices. I try to block them out; it's all becoming too much.

Right before my eyes the image of Wes seems to rise from the picture, until he's standing right in front of me, his face a mask of frozen shock. The room starts to spin. I feel like I'm on a carousel, spinning around and around. Soon everything around me is nothing but one big blur. I see a diaphanous array of lights all around me. Very slowly they are closing in on me.

I hum to block out the past, but it's stronger than I am. It squeezes past my barriers and hugs me tight. It sucks me down, away from the present, until I transport back into my past. . . .

The last thing I remember is my pleading for the past to be nice to me.

Please, please, be on my side.

10

Our first anniversary snuck up on us like a thief.

One second we're walking down the aisle, going on our honeymoon, and the next we're in May. If every year of marriage is like this, then we're golden.

Instead of celebrating with a nice dinner at a fancy restaurant we were staying in. Our townhouse had quickly turned into our cozy getaway from the stress of work and life.

We ordered Chinese takeout. The small boxes were scattered around the table. This entire week at work had been brutal. Likewise for Wes. The only thing that kept me upbeat was knowing our anniversary was waiting for us that weekend. The two of us were wearing sweats. The atmosphere was laid-back and casual and I wouldn't have had it any other way.

"Goals for this year?" I asked.

Wes leaned back in his chair. "Make partner."

"Of course, of course." I finished the last of the orange chicken and pushed the box aside. "Anything else?"

"To always be happy. With you." He took a drink, tilted his glass in my direction, and gave me a cheesy wink. "What about you?"

My throat suddenly became dry. Without a doubt we were happy. Every day I seemed to love him more and more. I wanted to extend that love. I wanted to start a family. How Wes felt about starting a family remained to be seen. In the beginning of our engagement, kids were brought up, but always in the distant future. For me, the distant future was upon us. For Wes, it might still be years away.

This urge, this desire, didn't come out of nowhere. It had been brewing in me for months. Every time I saw a mother pushing a baby in a stroller, holding a child's hand in the grocery store, or watched a mom or dad hold their child's hand or whisper comforting words in their ear as they got stitches or shots, a part of me cried out for that.

I'd always thought that I would never love anyone else in the world the way I loved Wes, but something told me being a parent would easily trump that love. What would it be like to have that much love for another human being?

"I was thinking . . ." I started out slowly.

Wes lifted a brow and waited patiently for me to continue speaking.

"I was thinking that maybe we should try for a baby."

"A baby?" he asked bluntly. His question was said with no emotion, almost as if I were asking if he was going to do the dishes or take out the trash.

It threw me off guard for a second. I hadn't known what his reaction would be, but deep down I'd hoped that he would be a little interested in the idea. Just a little.

"Well, yes," I replied.

He sat back in the chair heavily and frowned at me with confusion. My stomach dropped; this was not how I expected this to go. At all.

"Look," Wes began slowly. "We've always vowed to be honest about everything, right?"

I nodded. Suddenly it seemed that that vow was biting me in the ass. Dread and apprehension clashed together and danced down my spine.

"I don't want kids," Wes finally said.

He shrugged and gave me a half smirk, as though it was a decision that could never be reversed no matter how hard I tried.

"Never?"

"Never."

I was shell-shocked. I blinked rapidly "Why not?"

"Do I need a reason?"

"Yes."

"Come on, Victoria." A laugh escaped him. He raised his hands. "What do you want me to say? I don't want kids."

"I want you to tell me why. I don't want kids because . . ." I trailed off. "Fill in the blanks, Wes."

Abruptly he stood up from the table, taking his plate with him. I followed him, not ready to lay this conversation to rest.

"Tell me why," I persisted. "I want to talk about this."

"We already did."

"No, we kind of did and then you flipped out."

"I didn't flip out!"

He dumped the remaining food into the trash. "Why are we even talking about this?"

"Because it's important to me. Because you asked me what my goals were for this year and I told you and now you're angry with me. That's why we're talking about this."

Wes turned around, his hands curled around the lip of the counter. All happy anniversary vibes had disappeared, replaced with anger.

Like every normal couple, we'd had our arguments. We'd disagreed. But those moments never seemed to last long enough to make a dent in our relationship. One of us always caved.

But in this case, I was willing to make an exception; this was something that I really wanted.

"You need to let this go," Wes said, a slight edge to his words. "You're like a dog with a fucking bone."

"Then just give me an answer!"

"I don't want kids because I don't want the responsibility," he said like an explosion.

Silence. The TV blared in the living room, but in the kitchen it was so quiet you could hear a pin drop.

"I have too much on my plate right now to think about having a child, Victoria."

"There will always be too much on our plate. There will never be a right time to start a family."

"If there's no right time, then why try?" Once again, he shrugged. That gesture was seriously starting to piss me off. It seemed lazy to me, as if he saw my frustration and anger and just didn't really want to take the time to fix everything.

I took a step back. His words had struck my heart. "Well," I breathed, "there you have it."

"I would ask if that's a problem, but clearly it is."

"Of course it is! I want kids!"

Wes crossed his arms. "All right, say we have a baby. What are you going to do when it's born? Continue to work and abandon it?"

His words were said with such venom and hatred I flinched.

"What are you talking about? I would never abandon my child."

Wes rejected my words and shook his head. "We're not having a baby."

Wes was shutting the conversation down. I turned and walked away.

"Victoria! Come back." He caught up with me and wrapped his arms around me from behind. "I'm sorry. I want our child to have the best. I want it to have all our attention. My caseload is getting heavier by the minute and I'm afraid that I couldn't give a child the love and affection he or she deserves. That's all. I didn't mean to make you cry, all right? Even if we tried for a child, look around. Right now it's just the two of us and yet we're outgrowing this townhouse. We need a home—a place to settle down."

Wes painted such a beautiful picture. It was so alluring, so perfect that I found myself agreeing.

"Then I'll give my two weeks' notice to the hospital." The words slipped out of my mouth before I could really think about them.

Wes's eyes brightened. "You're sure about that?"

"Yeah," I said anxiously. The more I thought about it, the more sense it made. "Absolutely."

Wes stopped in front of me and held my face between both hands. He smiled as he leaned in and gave me a gentle kiss. One filled with promises and hopes for our future. When we pulled apart I rested my head against his chest.

"So we're going to do this?" I whispered into his shirt.

"We're going to do this. But I don't want to rush. I want us to get a house and settle into the perfect home that we can call our own."

There was so much excitement brewing inside me. It was impossible to wipe the beaming smile off my face.

Together we cleaned the kitchen, exchanging secret smiles every few minutes. I was wiping down the counter when I looked in the direction of the living room. I did a double take at the large, framed photo of the two of us on our wedding day. Hopefully, in a year, there would be a framed photo of our baby right next to it. I swiped my phone from the counter, turned, and looked at Wes. "Hey! Look over here, Future Father of my children."

Wes whipped his head around and I snapped a photo. If I had to title this photo, it'd be one simple word: *Before*.

Before kids.

Before exhaustion.

Before that perfect family I wanted us to be.

This chapter of our life was coming to a close. A new one was waiting to be written and I knew it would be unforgettable.

11

August 2013

"Well, what do you think?"

Wes removed his hands from my eyes and stood next to me, a big smile on his face. In front of me was the beginning of our house. I'd been here once when we were looking at property and when the foundation was being poured.

Since then, it had come a long way. But it was still the bare bones of the home it was to be. The house had been framed, with some areas covered with plywood on the outside. Even from here I could see the special framing for where the rooms would be and the cutouts for windows.

"I think it's certainly different from our townhouse."

"Before you start to freak out, remember it can normally

take up to eight months for a custom home to be built. But before you know it, you, my queen will be living here."

I smiled at his promise.

Excitement surged through me as I pictured the life and family that Wes and I could have here. It was a beautiful dream.

"Want to go inside?" Wes asked. He looked so happy. The sleeves of his light blue dress shirt were rolled up as he looked up at the house. This house was his creation. All of it. I couldn't say no to him.

"Of course," I replied.

"We couldn't have chosen a better spot," Wes commented. "I was talking to the contractor and he said that *Senator Carradine* was thinking about buying the property to our right."

I nodded idly, barely paying attention to what he was saying. In my mind, I was adding items to the to-do list for this house.

Since May we'd looked at nothing but properties, trying to find the perfect place for our forever home. Instantly I fell in love with the property on Bellamy Road. It was attached to a newer subdivision, with maybe four or five homes on the street. It was peaceful and quiet, surrounded by nothing but acres and acres of woods. It was a far cry from living in town, where there was always something going on.

Hand in hand the two of us walked across the road. There was no sidewalk, or even a front yard for that matter. Any grass that remained was matted down or covered with dirt. Construction workers toiled around us, completely focused on getting the job done. There was no front porch. Two thick pieces of wood were turned into a makeshift ramp that led into what would be the foyer. We stepped inside. Just this space alone was larger than our kitchen and living room combined in the townhouse.

I turned in a circle, looking at all the wooden beams and plywood. To the right I looked at the U-shaped staircase with two landings. I pictured them finished: mahogany steps. White risers. The banister would match the steps and the wrought iron spindles would complete it all.

Even though it was just the two of us, we were very slowly outgrowing the townhouse. The spare bedroom was Wes's office, and that was putting it loosely.

One of the first things he wanted in this house was an office, with built-in bookshelves.

My wants were simpler. I wanted an open floor plan. In my head I could picture each room having multiple windows. French doors that led to the deck. A bay window in the master bedroom. Most of all, I pictured a beautiful backyard, with flowers everywhere. I didn't have much of a green thumb. The last time I tried to "garden," I was a little girl helping my mother out. A few flowers wilted away. After that I stuck to plants and fake ficus.

"Straight ahead is the living room and kitchen," Wes said. "Now, I talked to the contractor and he said that the type of flooring you want in the kitchen is on back order and it may take a couple of months. He left other options for you to look at." I nodded, overwhelmed by everything I was seeing but smiling in spite of myself. Wes's enthusiasm was contagious. How could I not be so happy when that was all he was feeling?

"Let's look around some more," he said as he guided me deeper into the house.

We moved from room to room, quietly watching the people work around us. We walked up the stairs to the second floor and the whole time I pictured what it would be like to hear the sound of kids' feet running up and down the halls. The idea made me smile and gave me hope; I still wasn't pregnant.

In the back of my mind, I knew there was no reason to be down on myself. We'd only been "trying" to get pregnant actively since the beginning of the summer, but almost immediately my imagination kicked in and started to reach for all the things that could possibly be wrong.

Wes showed me the spacious master bedroom, with a massive walk-in closet with separate racks for my dresses and shoes and purses. "Do you love it?"

"Who wouldn't love this? It's amazing."

"This is all for you."

I gave him a grateful smile and made a slow circle around the room.

Up next were the two spare bedrooms. It was the bedroom next to ours that caught my eye. I could picture soft white carpet beneath my feet and the walls painted a soothing yellow. There would be a rocking chair in the corner. A white armoire filled with baby clothes with a changing table right next to it. A wicker basket of toys would be on the floor. And placed right in front of the large window would be a white crib. I walked over to where the window would be and looked out into the backyard. The grass needed to be mowed but I could picture flowers in a wide range of colors planted along the white picket fence that was being put up. I saw a hammock hanging between the two large oak trees. I would put brown wicker furniture on the deck. It would be my own personal escape.

I turned back to Wes. He was watching me with a hint of a smile.

"This would be a nice nursery," I said casually.

Wes leaned against the doorframe and cocked his head to the side. "You think so?"

"Yeah," I said softly. "I do."

"You're not pregnant, are you?" he asked bluntly.

My smile slipped. "No, I'm not."

What kind of question was that, and why did he look so relieved? His reaction clashed with my pain, instantly putting me on the defensive.

Without a word, I walked out of the room. In such an empty space, the sound of my footsteps echoed all around me. I hurried down the stairs with Wes hot on my heels.

"Victoria!"

I stopped and whirled around. "What?"

Wes stopped two steps above me. He gripped the wall and banister for support. "What's wrong with you?"

"What's wrong?" I stared at him with disbelief. "You looked so happy when I said I wasn't pregnant. And you know how much I want a child."

He looked genuinely confused and hurt by my actions. It was as though we'd never discussed the idea of kids. It was as though my efforts to quit my job had all been in vain. "Getting pregnant isn't going to happen in a flash. It might take time."

"I know that," I said through gritted teeth. "But you looked so relieved back there!"

In this empty house, my words echoed all around us, slamming home my point.

His lips moved into a thin line. In my eyes, this shouldn't be an argument. Money and things should create arguments. Not children. He dragged his hands through his hair. "I'm still coming around to the idea of it, okay?"

"But just two months ago you said we could start trying for a baby. I didn't put the words in your mouth!"

"In a way, you did. You wouldn't let the topic go."

There was nothing I could say to that. It was clear that we had each taken different things away from the baby conversation. On the first floor, workers discreetly tried to get out of the eye of the storm. I didn't blame them one bit. I wished I could walk out with them.

Wes walked down the steps until he was right next to me. "Isn't it enough that I'm open to the idea of a baby?"

"No. It's not enough. Having a baby is not like buying a car. You can't trade it in if you don't like it. That's not how it works."

Within seconds, his face morphed into anger. I saw rage in his eyes. His fist flew, only inches away from my head, and hit the plywood next to me. I covered my head as I hurried down the rest of the steps and looked at Wes in shock.

He stared at the now-cracked piece of wood and at his fist, looking just as shocked as me. When his eyes met mine,

I saw a wild, frantic, terrified look on his face. He hurried down the stairs. I stopped myself from taking a step back, away from him.

A hush descended across the house. Even the construction workers were staring our way.

"I'm sorry," Wes whispered. He pulled me to him. His arms encircled my shoulders. My body was rigid.

Wes pulled back, his hands cupping my face. He smiled, but it didn't have the same effect it usually did. "I'm so sorry, Victoria. I exploded. You know I love you. I love you."

Slowly, almost robotically, my arms wrapped around him. Wes calmed down instantly.

I didn't know what had just happened. It unnerved me. It terrified me.

"We can make memories in this house. Memories that will last us until we die. Do you trust me?" Wes asked.

I nodded, but it was a knee-jerk reaction.

"We will. We will," he repeated over and over into my hair. "That beautiful garden you want? I'll call a gardener and have them start working on the backyard. We'll make the room next to ours the nursery. Anything. Anything you want."

The promises continued, but my confidence that I knew my husband like the back of my hand was shaken. I had no idea what the hell just happened minutes ago and I had no idea how to make sure it never happened again.

12

"Don't break that! It's fragile!"

Wes glanced over at me. "It's a flowerpot, Victoria. If I break it, we can go buy another one."

I bit down on my tongue. We? Why did he say "we" when we both knew it would be me to go buy another? That's how it had been since we started construction on the house. I thought we would decide on details together, ranging from things as simple as knobs for the kitchen cabinets to the number of bookshelves he wanted in his office.

I really thought this house would be *our* project. It was supposed to be our dream home, so why wasn't he as invested in it as I was?

That was the least of my problems, though. Wes and I

used to crave our time, spend every possible moment to-gether, but now there was this impatience about him. A stiff quality, as though he was counting down the hours until he could leave my side. I was quick to blame his workload and the stress that he put on his own shoulders.

He told me it was because of work. A lot of hours. A heavier caseload. When I suggested that maybe he cut back, he gave me a dirty look and said: "How do you suppose I support this picture-perfect life you want?"

The house was supposed to be for our family. At least, that's what I thought.

But finally, here he was, helping me with all the gardening supplies. It was the first time we'd been alone in a while and I didn't want the time to turn sour.

The backyard was nothing now, but I saw what it could be. In my mind I saw a brick path with flowers and neatly trimmed hedges lining it. The oak trees clustered at the very edge of the property would have patio chairs beneath them. But the best part was that it was in clear view of the cherry blossom tree. Right now it was in full bloom. The pale pink colors of the buds popped up in a sea of green. In the midst of a construction zone, it was a beautiful sight.

I couldn't wait until the gardener arrived.

While I resented Wes for hardly participating in any of the house decisions, I happily jumped at the task of finding a gardener. There were many choices, but ultimately I settled on Renee Davery. Her business, Fairhaven, was a florist shop and landscaping business wrapped into one. Taylor once mentioned that Renee had the most beautiful floral arrange-ments.

Wes gently placed the flowerpot underneath the cherry tree. He dusted his hands off and stood up. "I have to go," he said. "What are you doing today?"

"Probably work on the backyard with this Renee lady."

"That's it?"

"That's it," I repeated.

"All right. Love you." He gave me an absentminded kiss on the cheek. Gone were the days where one goodbye kiss turned into two, then four.

I watched him walk away. Five days ago we got into an awful fight. Wes came home later than usual. I ate dinner by myself. I called him and it went to voicemail. Every second he didn't come home, I was seething inside. A hatred filled my heart. Black and heavy, it covered me. The emotion took me over and when Wes walked through the front door, I jumped out of my seat, demanding to know where he had been.

We argued, but instead of me backing down, like I always do, I stood my ground. He screamed at me to leave him alone and when I didn't he promptly turned right back around and left the house. He didn't come back. The next day he came home and apologized. He told me that he had slept at his office. I didn't know what to believe. It was the first time we'd ever gone to bed angry and apart.

I squeezed my eyes shut and took a deep breath.

When I opened my eyes again, I watched as a small woman walked around the side of the house with her hands filled with shovels and supplies. She moved forward like a woman on a mission. And when she reached me, she abruptly dropped all the supplies. I waited for her to look up and say hi, but she walked briskly back to her truck.

I watched as she moved back and forth between her truck and the backyard. Normally I was very quiet and contained but I wanted to talk to her and introduce myself.

I cleared my throat and she finally lifted her head. Her head was covered in a baseball cap, with the bill shading the upper portion of her face. Her skin was caramel from being out in the sun, her black hair pulled back in a ponytail. I knew without seeing all of her face that it was makeup-free. She seemed the polar opposite of the ladies I spent most of my time with. For that reason alone I was intrigued.

"Hello," I blurted out.

She lifted her hat and gave me a quick once-over. "Hi."

"I know you're the new gardener but I thought I should introduce myself." I approached her as she knelt beside a flower bed.

"I know who you are," she cut in. She plucked her gloves off and dropped them onto her jean-clad thigh. She smiled and shook my hand. "Mrs. Donovan."

I nodded slowly and gestured toward the derelict, vast space behind me. "Looks like you have a lot of work cut out for you."

"It's not as bad as you think. It seems like a lot but I think I can get the flowers planted and shrubs trimmed within a week."

My eyes widened. "That's impressive."

She shrugged. "It's my job, Mrs. Donovan."

"You don't have to call me that." Confusion clouded her gaze. "Mrs. Donovan," I supplied. "My name is Victoria."

"Victoria it is then." She looked at the boxes of flowers lined up neatly next to her.

"So here are some flowers that I think you would love."

I glanced down at them. I had no clue what their names were; I just saw a wild array of bright colors. I didn't know where to start. "What are those?"

Renee shielded her eyes and looked to where I pointed. "Orchids," she replied.

I kneeled next to her. She seemed taken off guard. "I don't like those."

"I don't care too much for them either," she confessed with a small smile. She held her hand out to me and even though we had shaken hands just moments ago, this hand-shake was offered with meaning, as if I had earned her re-spect. "I'm Renee."

Up close, I could see the small bump on the bridge of her nose. Wrinkles surrounded her coffee-brown eyes and ap-peared on the edge of her lips whenever she smiled. She seemed practical and levelheaded—like the kind of person who'd say what she needed to say and go on her way.

"You don't have to stay in this sweltering heat. I have things covered." To back up her words, she bent her head and got to work.

If I was honest with myself, there wasn't much I had to do. I looked over my shoulder at my work-in-progress house. The sound of hammering and sawing rang in my ears. Just like my future garden, I saw my future house: The back porch would have a brown wicker furniture set. The French doors would have lace curtains billowing in the wind. And a basket of petunias would hang from the wooden beams ex-tended above the deck.

The truth was, I was lonely, and even though Renee wasn't

exactly the most talkative of people, I liked the vibe she put off.

"I . . . I can help you," I said. She lifted her head, her eyes sharp like a cat. "If you want me to," I added quietly.

Renee hesitated. Finally, she motioned a gloved hand in the direction of her truck. "Go get some gloves and I'll teach you a thing or two."

I followed her directions and found an old pair sitting out on the back of the truck bed. Was I that transparent? Did I have a blinker above my head that said, *Look at me! I need a friend!*

I must have because she gave me menial tasks, like helping her pull out weeds along the oak trees and around the neighbor's fence. The time passed in silence. Renee seemed to go into a zone when she worked. Her lips spread into a thin line and her eyebrows formed a tight V. But she did hum, very quietly to herself. So quietly that I couldn't hear her unless I was right next to her.

When I finished watering the flowers I stepped back and looked them over. "I love those lavender-blue flowers," I said, pointing to my right.

Renee lifted her head for only a second. "Those are catmint."

"Catmint," I repeated blankly.

"Funny name, right? The nepetalactone in the plant lures cats in, giving them a temporary bliss. Think of it as cat weed."

I smiled. "Impressive." I scanned the rest of the flowers and pointed in front of me at the flowers with petals that were golden at the tips, with the color slowly bleeding into red to the head of the flower. "What about those?"

"Blanket flowers," Renee threw out within seconds. "They're also called gaillardia. They're pretty now, but in a few weeks, when they're in their prime, they'll take your breath away."

For the next hour I pointed to this flower and that. Renee rattled off the details so easily. I smirked and nodded approvingly. "You know quite a lot about flowers."

"It's in my blood. I lived in my backyard while my mom was always tending to her garden."

"What's your favorite flower?"

Renee was bent over yellow tulips. At my question she leaned back and stared at the ground thoughtfully, lost in her own world. "Hyacinth," she announced and reached out in front of her to brush a single finger against a pale pink petal. "I think they're elegant and uplifting—a garden must-have. Every time I look at them they instantly calm me."

The two of us didn't say much after that. We slipped into a comfortable silence and eventually, Renee resumed her humming. It wasn't annoying or loud. It was very soft and soothing to me, making the tension from my shoulders fade away.

"Do you hum a lot?"

Renee jolted, as if she had forgotten I was there. "Sorry. I didn't know I was doing it."

"It doesn't bother me."

Renee shrugged and continued to pull out weeds. "It's something my mom does all the time. I guess it kind of rubbed off on me when I'm lost in my own world or whenever I'm stressed. It relaxes me."

I nodded. I thought there was some merit to what she said.

She glanced at me out of the corner of her eye. "You should try it sometime. It works. Trust me."

"In that case I will be humming twenty-four/seven."

The words came out of me so quick. I covered my mouth. It was the first time I had ever told anyone that maybe my life wasn't as perfect as it appeared. There was no way to take them back.

Renee didn't lean forward, with a hungry look in her eyes for gossip. She just smiled. "In this backyard, there should be no stress. Not a care in the world. This is all yours."

"My haven."

"Exactly." She gave me a warm smile. "Now if you want, you can help me water the rest of the plants."

13

I slammed the car door and hurried up the pathway. I was late. About a good fifteen minutes. Part of me wasn't sure Wes was going to be able to make it. As usual, he was held up at the office. We were supposed to meet the contractor working on our house. Wes kept reassuring me that things were progressing, but I was skeptical. I swear, every time it felt like we were taking two steps forward we ended up taking four steps back.

Coming here was the last thing I wanted. Like the little bitch she was, Auntie Flo had arrived this morning. She was never a welcome guest and especially not this time. Seeing red on the toilet paper was like a giant fuck-you from my

body, saying, *Oh, hey, about that baby . . . It isn't happening.*
Better luck next month!

I had to admit, though, that in the past few months, the
house had really progressed. It had taken on the appearance
of a European-style home, with bay windows flanking the
front door and a portico supported by two white columns.
The exterior was covered in a light gray stucco.

A worker was laying the bricks down for the front sidewalk. The double front doors were open. A few workers
walked in and out carrying supplies. Sounds of drills and
hammers traveled behind them and into the open air.

I scanned the area, looking for the head contractor. Wes
said his name was Sinclair Montgomery. Over breakfast Wes
had told me, "He's a nice man. I think you'll like him."

"Doubtful," I'd replied.

Even though I had no clue who I was looking for, it didn't
take a genius to figure out which one was Sinclair.

A tall man stood next to the front door, deep in discussion with a construction worker. He was dressed in black
slacks and white dress shirt with the collar unbuttoned and
the sleeves rolled up, revealing tan forearms. Stitched on the
right side of his shirt, in block letters, was MONTGOMERY
CONSTRUCTION.

His hair was coal black, cut short on the sides and styled
on top. His skin was the color of honey. He was tall—even
taller than Wes. I imagined I would come up to his chest.
And such a big chest at that, muscled and well defined
enough to make his biceps strain against his shirt.

The man standing there was the last thing I expected. He

didn't look like he built houses for a living. He looked like he graced the world with his mouthwatering smile and had scores of women dropping at his feet. He didn't have to work for anything because everything was given to him by a single crook of his finger.

I cleared my throat loudly and stepped forward. His head snapped in my direction. "Are you Mr. Montgomery?"

"Call me Sinclair." He held out a large hand, rough and calloused. A hand that swallowed mine whole. If he tightened his grip even a little he could have easily crushed every bone in my hand.

Regardless of my judgments, my manners kicked in. "I'm so sorry I'm late. I lost track of time. I was—"

"No worries. You're fine." He looked behind me. "Believe me, you're not late. I've had clients who have been almost two hours late. Now that's late." He peered over my shoulder. "Is your husband coming?"

"He'll be here soon. I'll catch him up to speed."

Sinclair took a step back and gestured to the giant monstrosity looming above us. "Do you see an improvement?"

"Improvement is an understatement. It looks practically done."

"Not quite. But we're definitely getting there."

"How about we take a look around? I'm sure you've done this multiple times already, but at least now we can go through a detailed list of what's been done and what still needs to be done."

We stepped through the doors and entered a construction zone. Drywall was up. It didn't seem like any progress had happened since the last time. The wrought-iron banister was being installed. We were so close to being done. "It looks amazing."

We went from room to room. Sinclair went through a detailed list of everything and the longer he talked, the more I found myself staring at him. All of my frustrations that I carried with me into the house seemed to fall off my shoulders. He had a natural way of speaking that instantly put me at ease. When I asked a question, he looked at me. Not through me. Directly at me.

We stepped into what I referred to as the baby's room. I made a direct beeline to the window. Brand-new windows had just been installed. With my arms crossed I peered into my backyard. I smiled. The yard was beautiful, looking more and more like the perfect haven I'd always dreamed of. I wished I could take credit for it, but it was Renee's hard work. Along the fence was landscaping, with a few flowers planted here and there.

"It's a pretty view."

I turned and saw Sinclair leaning against the door. It sounded like he was referring to the garden but his eyes were on me. My heart quickened but I didn't look away like I probably should have. Instead, I held his gaze. There was a faint stirring in me. Warning bells went off in my head.

I gave him a brief smile and returned my attention to the backyard. "My big plans for the backyard are finally starting to take shape."

He came up beside me. "What are your 'big plans'?"

I crossed my arms and tilted my head to the side, staring thoughtfully out the window. And told him everything. All the decisions that I normally kept to myself, I revealed to him. By the time I was done talking, I was slightly out of breath, shocked at how easily and willingly I'd spoken.

Sinclair whistled. "You have it all planned out."

Out of the corner of my eye, I saw Sinclair staring at me. Heat rose to my cheeks and I tried to pretend that it was nothing. "The house is going to be beautiful, but this garden? This garden is going to be *beautiful*. No offense."

He smiled. "None taken."

Silence circled around us. Sinclair didn't move from my side. He gazed out the window. "You know," he said slowly, "I didn't peg you for a garden-type person."

"What did you peg me as?"

"A pool person."

My eyes widened and my body shifted, just a small bit, in his direction. "A pool person?"

He nodded and continued to stare outside, knowing full well that he had my attention. "The ritzy person who wants an immaculate yard and an inground pool with a grotto. They'll spend all this money, but they'll never use it."

I nodded. "Ah, I understand."

He looked skeptical. "Do you really?"

Leaning in slightly, I said, "The person you just described is my mom."

He laughed and I just smiled.

"Have you lived in Falls Church long?" he asked.

"Born and raised here." I glanced at him. "You?"

"I moved here two years ago. I grew up in a small town. Farmville, Virginia."

"I've heard of it."

"Well, you might be the only person that's heard of it. My parents still live there."

"You left them all alone?" I teased lightly.

"Don't feel bad for them. Two of my siblings live around the area. And then I have a sister who lives in Falls Church . . . actually, she's your gardener."

"Renee?" My eyes widened, but my mind was running, putting Sinclair and Renee next to each other and seeing if there were any similarities. Now that I was looking closely at Sinclair, I could see it: the olive skin, coal-black hair. High cheekbones.

Sinclair simply nodded and a hint of a smirk played at his lips.

"She never mentioned it."

"Renee isn't exactly the most talkative person."

"I gathered that. At first I thought I was annoying her."

"Oh, believe me, if you were annoying her, she'd let you know. Renee comes off as aloof, but as you get to know her she'll come out of her shell."

"Good to know."

Was it wrong of me to want this conversation to never end? Probably.

Out of the corner of my eye, I snuck another glance at him. Sinclair caught me red-handed. He smirked, and two parentheses appeared at the corners of his mouth.

My heart started to thump like crazy and I had to remind myself that I had a husband. Husband. Another man I was supposed to spend the rest of my life with. A man whom fate and the world had led me toward.

So why was I reacting this way?

"Did you start without me?"

The sound of Wes's voice made me jump. My head whipped to the left as Wes stepped into the room. He was dressed in a black suit. His navy striped tie was loosened. He draped an arm around me and gave me a quick kiss on my head and shook Sinclair's hand. Even though there was a healthy distance between Sinclair and me, Wes's eyes narrowed.

"I thought you had a case to work on."

Wes waved his hand in the air. "I left early. Couldn't let you tour the house by yourself." He gave me a smile but it didn't reach his eyes. Wes directed his attention to Sinclair. "How is everything?"

"Just fine. We were just finishing up the tour."

"I was telling him my plans for the garden," I said quickly.

"She loves that damn garden." Wes's abrupt words were scathing, almost cold, completely taking me by surprise. Where was this coming from?

"It sounds like it's going to be stunning," Sinclair replied. The friendly smile stayed on his face but I saw his eyes dart between Wes and me.

"So, Sinclair, how long do you think it will be until we move in?" Wes asked.

Sinclair's brows furrowed in concentration. "If you want the honest truth: about another month."

"*Another* month?" Wes asked curtly.

I gave him a look, but he ignored me.

Sinclair rubbed his bottom lip, staring between the backyard and me. "If you want, I can have my men working overtime to get it done faster. Maybe a few weeks?"

"And we're still on budget?" Wes snapped.

Sinclair crossed his arms and smiled. "Still on budget," he said smoothly. But the friendliness was gone from his eyes. Wes stiffened beside me. There was a beat of awkward silence. Wes cleared his throat and glanced down at his watch.

"I think we should be going."

"Right. Right." Sinclair swept his hand toward the door. "Sorry for holding you up."

We had nothing planned for that night. Nowhere to go. I had no clue why Wes was so anxious to leave.

We walked down the stairs with Sinclair behind us. The hairs on the back of my neck stood and I knew he was staring at me.

Sinclair followed us out the front door and stopped at my car. Before I got in, he held out his hand. "It was nice to meet you, Mrs. Donovan."

Manners dictated that I shake his hand. But I was hesitant; Wes was watching me too closely.

Finally, I took his hand and the minute I did, I felt a zing that hit me straight in the heart. "Likewise, Mr. Montgomery," I managed to say.

Once again he shook my hand. Those butterflies that I had when I first saw him swarmed in my stomach, begging to take flight. I shoved all unwanted feelings down as much as I could.

"Please, call me Sinclair."

I nodded. "Sinclair it is."

He held on to my hand longer than necessary. Long enough to make Wes stare between the two of us with suspi-

cion. I would be the biggest liar if I told you my heart didn't
speed up. Quickly, I snatched my hand away and opened up
the driver's-side door. Wes caught it with his hand.

"I'm driving."

"But your car—"

"I'll pick it up later."

There was a deadness in his eyes. As if all the emotions
and life had been snuffed out of him. He was angry and the
last thing I wanted was to get into another fight with him.
People were all around us and I'd rather fight in private than
in public.

I got in on the passenger side. The door slammed behind
me, the sound ricocheting. Wes stared straight ahead, saying
nothing.

He started the car. For a few blocks there was silence. No
radio. No conversation. I went to roll down the window, just
to hear the wind rush by. Anything.

But he locked my window.

We stopped at a red light and Wes finally turned toward
me. "What the hell was that back there?"

"What are you talking about?"

"Have you met Sinclair before?"

"What?" I frowned. "No."

Wes laughed darkly. It sent chills up and down my spine.
"Don't lie."

"I haven't!"

The light turned green. Wes took off, his foot pressing the
gas pedal to the floor. The engine revved. I glanced at the
speedometer. He was up to 55.

"Are you cheating on me with him?"

My jaw dropped. What in the hell was he talking about? "No!"

I looked at the speedometer. He was at 65. I feared he was going to do something really stupid.

"Liar."

I gripped my seatbelt with both hands. "I'm not! That's the first time I've ever met him."

"Could've fooled me." Wes turned his eyes on me. "You know how he was looking at you."

"Wes," I said very carefully. "Eyes on the road."

"Don't tell me what to do!" he screamed.

He was not rational or in control. I had no idea what was running through his head. I just knew that in this state of mind he was capable of anything. Up ahead was a bridge. I could see us driving straight off it.

Self-preservation made me react. I swallowed loudly and touched his arm. In my sweetest voice I said, "I love only you, Wes. So slow down. Okay?"

He clenched his jaw and I thought he was going to keep ignoring me. But then, out of nowhere, he pressed the brake pedal. The tires squealed. I jerked forward, my face inches from the dashboard before my seatbelt jerked me back.

I panted heavily and looked around. A car behind us honked and drove around us. I wanted to get out, flag the car, and ask the driver—a random stranger—to help me. At this point it felt safer.

Wes laughed. A loud, genuine laugh, as if my reaction was hilarious. I stared at him in disbelief.

And then his laughter faded and he smiled as if I was the

most important person in his life. "You want to get something to eat? I'm starving."

I blinked at him rapidly. How could he go from zero to sixty and then right back to zero?

"What just happened?"

"What are you talking about?"

I hooked a thumb behind me. "Back there. The accusations. The cheating."

"You mean a conversation? That's what you're talking about?"

That wasn't a conversation. That was mere seconds away before a murder-suicide. How he didn't recognize that was beyond me.

My emotions were reeling. One second I was defending myself. The next I saw my life flash before my eyes. And then . . . nothing. My heart continued to pound at a rapid pace, showing no signs of slowing down. It was as though Wes's stunt had left it in a permanent state of fear.

"So? How 'bout it?"

Slowly, I turned toward Wes. "What?"

"Dinner?"

I swallowed loudly and looked out the window. "Dinner sounds great."

I wasn't hungry, but I wasn't about to tell him that.

Wes did a U-turn and headed back into town. I couldn't stop shaking.

He reached across the console, his hand curved around my kneecap. He gave me the same smile that had made me fall for him.

"I love you," he said.

I think he believed what he said. I think he thought this was love.

At a red light, he shifted in his seat to look at me. "But don't play games with me, Victoria." His other hand curved around my jaw. When the pad of his thumb brushed against my cheek I shivered. He moved even closer so our lips were practically touching. His next words were soft but deadly. "You'll lose every time."

Then he kissed me. And I let him because my heart refused to believe that I could be married to a monster.

14

December 2013

Sinclair made good on his word and a month later, on an early Saturday morning, we were moving into our dream house.

I spent the weeks before the move packing up everything. They say moving is one of the most stressful things to go through, but the chaos around me—packing up boxes, going through everything—kept me distracted. There was no time to focus on the blemishes slowly appearing in my marriage.

No time at all.

Instead, I concentrated on what I knew to be true: Every couple has flaws. No one is perfect. Put two people together and it's normal for those flaws to become even more apparent. Yes, that's all this was.

We were a completely normal couple. Besides, Wes had

been perfectly fine these last few weeks: no outbursts, no anger. He was back to being the same man I loved. He had just had a bad few moments. I kept trying to tell myself that, but at the end of the day I still had my doubts.

Wes parked the car on the opposite side of the street. As the movers backed the truck into the driveway, I stared at our house. Even though it was the middle of December, the weather seemed to be on our side, with not a single cloud in sight. I had my North Face zipped up and a black beanie to keep myself warm. Wes was dressed just as casually. It might have been the first time in a while I'd seen him without a suit and tie.

Wes smiled at me and held out his hand. "Welcome home, Mrs. Donovan."

It was hard to believe that this day had finally arrived. A car drove by, causing leaves to scatter across the road. A few skipped under the car and flew up in the air before they slowly fell to the ground.

"You ready for today?"

"Absolutely."

Hand in hand, we hurried across the road and got to work. Wes helped the movers and when I tried to help, he smiled and told me to do nothing but tell the movers where I wanted everything. So I did. I stood in the finished foyer, with the walls freshly painted. The windows sparkled and the sun shined in. The front door stood wide open as men walked in and out, carrying dismantled furniture, boxes, rugs. I watched as the first floor slowly began to fill up with items. A rush of excitement danced down my spine. I couldn't wait to cut open every box and make this house our own.

In the middle of the afternoon, everyone took a break and Sinclair arrived. His car pulled up behind ours and a slow tingle spread across my skin. He stepped out of his car and I stood up and leaned against the doorframe and watched him. He was dressed casually in jeans and a black polo shirt. Sunglasses concealed his eyes and gave him an aura of danger. Wes shook his hand and spoke to him briefly, then gestured in my direction.

When Sinclair saw me, his lips pulled up into a grin. He waved. I waved back, but my gaze instantly traveled to Wes, who looked completely nonplussed to see Sinclair around me.

"It's finally moving day," Sinclair said as he walked toward me with quick, confident strides.

"Finally," I said with a smile.

"Let me guess . . . you're telling the movers where to put everything."

"How did you know?"

"You're the queen of this palace. What else would you be doing?" We stood there, a small slip of silence creeping around us. I cleared my throat and quickly stepped aside to let him through. Sinclair slipped off his sunglasses and hooked them on the collar of his shirt. I saw a peak of his collarbone and olive skin that led to his shoulder.

My pulse didn't quicken. It soared. It pounded against the base of my throat, begging to burst free. All because of a fucking collarbone.

I quickly looked away.

Sinclair was completely oblivious. He circled the foyer, staring at the walls and floor with a critical eye. "What do you think?" he asked.

"It's beautiful," I replied and I meant it. This home was truly my dream house.

Sinclair moved down the hallway, toward the kitchen, but I stayed put. I wanted to follow him yet I was terrified of Wes seeing us together.

I went back to my spot at the front door and a few minutes later Sinclair walked back down the hall. He stepped outside the house and looked around. "How are you doing?" he asked casually, not looking at me once.

"I'm good."

"Just good?" He grinned.

Every time I talked to Sinclair I felt he was searching for something. I stayed perfectly straight when all I wanted to do was relax and slip into an easy conversation.

"What are you doing here on the weekend?" I asked him.

"I thought I would take a day off."

"It's not a day off if you're visiting a client," I pointed out.

"Since the house is finished, you're no longer a client." He lifted a brow. "We're friends."

Friends.

No, that didn't sound right. Friends shouldn't look at each other the way we were doing.

Nothing between us was friendly, but I nodded and gave him a weak smile. "Don't you have a family?"

He smirked. "No. No family."

I already knew that, but I wanted to hear him say it.

Since I'd found out he was Renee's brother, I'd casually asked her about him. I wanted to find out all I could. It was wrong, but I couldn't ignore my curiosity. He was the middle child out of three. He was single. No ex-wives. No children. No nothing.

And all my mind could think was, *How? How was this incredible man not taken?*

"Why not?" I said before I could think twice.

"Why don't I have a family?"

I nodded.

Sinclair chuckled and shrugged. "Haven't found the right person."

"You will."

"You think?"

"Of course."

And then he looked me straight in the eye. His face was serious. "Maybe I've already found her."

I gulped at the intensity in his eyes. "Maybe."

Heavy pause. Tension crept over us. A handful of unspoken words hung between us.

"I should be going," Sinclair finally said. "I'm glad you like your house."

"I love it."

"I'll see you later."

There was no masking the innuendo. I heard it loud and clear. Here was my chance to clear everything up. With a simple shake of my head the looks and sexual tension would vanish. But instead I nodded. I heard him, heard his request, and agreed.

At the end of the day, my mother stopped by. We all had dinner together and then she and I got to unpacking.

She was a woman on a mission, quickly reverting to the mom I grew up with. When the kitchen was unpacked, she immediately moved to the living room.

A few times she made Wes come and help us. He looked completely drained, but he didn't say a word.

"Mom, we're beat."

She placed her hands on her hips and exhaled loudly. "What time is it?"

I glanced at my watch and groaned. "Eleven forty-five."

"Oh, I had no idea it was so late." She looked around the living room. The sofa and overstuffed chair were angled toward the TV. The carpet was rolled out in front of the sofa. Lamps were plugged in and pictures were on the end tables. All that was left were the curtains and pictures.

My mother grabbed her purse and coat. Wes and I walked her to the door, afraid that if she glanced around at the bare space she'd make a run for it, find a drill, and start hanging up curtain rods.

I leaned heavily against Wes as I stepped out onto the porch. In the distance I could hear a dog bark. Across the street the neighbor's lights were on. Their blinds were shut, but I saw the shadows of bodies moving around. Streetlamps ran the length of the road. This small community was just as I had pictured it.

"Well, I'll let you two get some rest." She gave me a big hug and pulled back. "I'll be back bright and early for round two of unpacking."

"Goodie," I teased.

She was walking to her car when I quickly thought of something. "Mom!" She turned around. "Hold on one second. I forgot something." I grabbed my phone from the kitchen and ran back to the front door.

"Before you go, can you take a picture of the two of us?"

She grabbed my phone but playfully rolled her eyes. "You and your pictures . . ."

She walked to the middle of the pathway. Wes draped his arm across my shoulder. My hand snaked around his waist.

"Smile in one . . . two . . . three."

I smiled.

I'm pretty sure I did.

15

Everything I remember, Dr. Calloway writes down. Her hand moves quickly across the paper. I talk rapidly and I know that doesn't make it easy for her, but part of me is so afraid that if I don't say it right at that second, then I never will. She keeps up with me, never telling me to start over.

When I'm done, she sets the pen down and looks over at me. "So things were difficult between you and Wes."

Here it is. I knew we would have to have a patient-doctor chat. With anyone else, I would try to change the subject. But I feel the smallest amount of loyalty to Calloway and answer: "It seems like it."

My hands shake as I brush back Evelyn's hair from her

forehead. She picks up on my nerves and tilts her head back to look at me.

"Two outbursts that came out of nowhere . . . I think that would make anyone nervous."

I stare down at the floor, trying to handle the rush of memories slamming into me. "I was scared."

Dr. Calloway remains silent.

My eyes close. "It just didn't make sense. I didn't understand what was going on. I felt like I was—"

Abruptly I stop speaking. Because if I admitted that I felt like I was going crazy, it would just be used against me.

I stand up. "Can I go now?"

Dr. Calloway doesn't appear shocked by my request. She shrugs. "If you want to."

"I want to."

I can't move fast enough to the door. I'm almost out when Dr. Calloway says my name. I turn even though I don't want to.

Calloway smiles at me. "It's okay to be scared."

And it's okay for her to say that because she's not the one revisiting her past. She doesn't have to live through it. The door clicks shut behind me. Evelyn's fussing in my arms. Her head is moving left and right. I quicken my steps, to my room, completely ignoring Alice. The second I'm in my room, I grab the bottle on the end table. Most times, I give Evelyn the bottle and she's back to being the calm and sweet angel that I love. Today she rejects it as if it's poison. I change her diaper. I swaddle her. I give her a pacifier. I gently rock her.

Nothing seems to work.

My patience is starting to wane. Her cries ring until my eardrums feel like they're going to burst. I can't focus on a thing. I can hardly breathe. Everything feels like it's closing in on me.

"Stop crying!" I shriek.

My outburst only makes her cry louder. It's not her fault. None of this is her fault. I take a deep breath and place my daughter in her bassinet and hurry to the bathroom. If the door had a lock, I'd be using it right now. I want a minute alone. Just a single minute where I don't have to worry about nurses knocking on the door.

Just a single minute to think everything through.

My hands curl around the lip of the sink. My shoulders droop as I take a deep breath. Turning on the water, I watch the clear liquid circle around the drain and take another deep breath before I cup my hands beneath the water and splash my face with it. Blindly I reach out for the towel always hanging to my left and pat my skin dry. When I look in the mirror I see myself but it's all wrong. I'm wearing the clothes I did when we first moved into the house. My eyes, which normally look completely blank, are now filled with fear.

I'm staring at Young Victoria.

She's so beautiful that when she smiles at me, I lean against the sink for support.

She knows her fairy tale isn't how she pictured it would be, but she holds out hope. I can see it in her eyes. Young Victoria believed in love. She didn't know that she would become one of the many souls who were left behind.

She didn't know.

I reach out and trace Victoria's features across the mirror. My heart is breaking.

"What happened to us?" I whisper to her.

She leans in and I brace myself for her to reach out and pull me into her life.

But she doesn't.

I blink and the image of her is gone, and I'm back to staring at my present self.

There's a sharp rap on the door. I turn around just as a nurse peeks her head in. Thank God, it's not Alice, but a much nicer day shift nurse. "Just checking on you."

I'm not ready to leave the bathroom. I'm not ready to face my daughter. If I could hide out in here all day I think I would. "I'm going to take a quick shower," I blurt.

The nurse nods. "Okay."

"But can I have a razor? I need to shave my legs."

I'm a woman in my late twenties and I'm asking for permission to use a razor. The past aside, that might be the saddest thing I've heard.

The nurse looks doubtful, considering whether I'm a suicide risk. "I'm not going to kill myself or anything," I hastily add.

She finally nods. "I can give you one, but I have to be standing right outside the door."

She leaves and returns seconds later with a pink razor. I wonder if they have a storage closet filled with pink razors.

I close the door behind me and turn on the shower. It blasts out cold water that slowly becomes warmer. I quickly shed my clothes, hanging them on the hook on the wall. The cold air causes goosebumps to appear on my skin.

I step into the shower and slide the curtain shut. The warm water beats against my body. My muscles instantly relax. I close my eyes and tilt my head back so the water reaches my hair. When it's good and wet, I turn in a slow circle, letting the water reach every inch of my skin.

It's a crazy thought but I can't help but think that if I stand here long enough maybe all this darkness around me—stuck inside me—will wash away.

I'm beginning to see that truth has its price.

It's your sanity it wants and craves more than anything.

It lures you in under the stipulation that it can make you free, but if you look at the fine print you'll finally see that it will leave you alone with your doubts and fears until it makes you feel like you're going crazy. Sometimes it comes in and saves you. Sometimes it doesn't.

And everything I'm reliving just piles on the pain.

It seems like the more memories that come back to me, the louder the voices become. But sometimes I think they'll get louder until I discover every last detail of my past. Then they'll go away.

16

During lunch the next day, I hum quietly to Evelyn, more to block out the voices in my head than to soothe her. If I hum long enough, all the noise fades away. But I know it's just a temporary reprieve.

They'll be back. They always are.

All around me, patients are either eating or just shifting food around on their plates. There's a quiet murmur of conversation. A few patients, like me, sit at the same table for all three meals. The rest sit wherever; they'll talk for a bit, but never long. Most of the time we all eat in silence; forever friendships aren't exactly created at Fairfax.

Reagan sits across from me today. During meals, she

hardly says a word. "Oh, will you stop the fucking humming!" she snaps.

If she could hear the noises inside my head, then maybe she'd get it. I just stare at her, and if anything, I hum a bit louder.

"Seriously, you gotta stop. I'm this close to chopping my ears off and throwing them at you!" For dramatic emphasis Reagan picks up her plastic fork and holds it threateningly to her left ear.

"Don't listen to her. I think it's a pretty tune. What song is that?"

Gasping, I lift my head and see Sinclair standing beside my table. Reagan drops the plastic fork and boldly looks him up and down. I can't blame her. Wearing black dress pants and a white dress shirt with the collar unbuttoned, he looks mouthwatering.

"Hi," I say dumbly.

"Hi." Sinclair smiles and points to the empty chair across from me. "Can I sit down?"

I nod anxiously, feeling like a bobblehead doll.

As he scoots his chair in, his legs brush against mine, causing a bolt of awareness to shoot through me.

This is Sinclair's third time visiting me. Warmth surrounds my heart. My guard lowers. My body relaxes.

"What were you humming earlier?" he asks.

I shrug, suddenly feeling embarrassed that he witnessed that. "Just a little nursery rhyme that Evelyn likes."

His smile slightly fades but I choose to ignore it because my daughter turns her head and looks in Sinclair's direction.

She smiles at him, and when she likes someone, I like some-one.

"Do you want to hold her?" I offer.

Sinclair sits back in his chair, looking shell-shocked. His face drains of color as he stares thoughtfully at Evelyn.

Reagan whistles loudly. "Don't take this offer lightly, Tall Dark and Brooding. Mommy Dearest never lets anyone hold the baby."

Sinclair doesn't reply and apprehension kicks in.

"You don't have to hold her if you're not comfortable with it," I blurt out.

"She looks content in your arms," he replies quietly.

I paste a smile on my face to hide my hurt feelings. It didn't occur to me that Sinclair just might not be a kid per-son. That's okay, right?

It should be. But for me, it's not. I want him to like Evelyn. I want him to see her brilliant smiles and hold her in his arms.

"I think she likes you," I confess.

He shifts uncomfortably in his seat. "Does she not like a lot of people?"

I shake my head emphatically. "Oh yes. She hardly lets anyone hold her."

Reagan spits out her water, spraying little drops across the table. "You're kidding, right?"

When I dodge her question and glare at her she rolls her eyes and stands up, holding her tray in both hands. "As al-ways it was a pleasure, Mommy Dearest."

She walks away and harasses another patient. I take a deep breath and focus my attention on Sinclair.

He's shaking his head. "Is that your friend?"

"Reagan?"

I nod. "I wouldn't really call her friend."

"Do you have any friends here?"

Before, I would have gestured to Evelyn and told him that with my daughter with me, I don't need a friend. But that reply doesn't hold up like it used to. I need someone to lean on, and to help me as I untangle my memories.

"No," I finally say. "No friends here . . . but you're here now. And you're a friend, right?"

"I've always been here, Victoria." His hand reaches across the table. It hovers over mine for a second, but at the last second he pulls back. He laces his fingers in front of him.

He's becoming less and less of a stranger. Feeling and emotions are taking root in me, slowly growing. I see a flash of the memory I unearthed about him: the two of us walking around the house on moving day. The awareness that I had of him when I knew I shouldn't.

I want to feel guilty. A good person feels guilt. But it's like trying to force yourself to cry or to care. If it's not there . . . it's not there, and that makes me the shittiest person alive.

I sneak another glance at Sinclair, only to have my gaze collide with his.

"I remember you," I say so quietly, I'm afraid he can't hear me.

But he does. His face goes a little pale and I can't tell if he's happy or scared.

I have to speak up before I lose the courage. "I remember meeting you at the house. The walk-through that I was late to?"

"You weren't late. Believe me, I've had clients who—"

"—who have been almost two hours late. Now that's late," I finish for him.

A small slip of a smile appears on his face. He swallows loudly and drags both hands down his face. "Holy shit," he breathes. His hands fall heavily to the table. With his elbows resting on the surface, he leans in. "Do you remember anything else?"

"I remember the day we moved in."

"That's it?"

"That's it."

He looks momentarily disappointed and I have to stop myself from asking him to tell me what's running through his mind; he's thinking about a memory of the two of us. I can see it in his eyes, how they take on a faraway look. There's a chance it's the moments I just mentioned. Or maybe not.

Nervously, I lick my lips. "There's more to us, isn't there?"

"Of course there is; hasn't there always been?"

My eyes blink rapidly, trying to push back the tears as much as possible. "I remember your sister too. . . . We had a good friendship, didn't we?"

"You did. Which I'll never understand because she's bossy, and a loudmouth. You two were the complete opposites of each other, yet somehow it worked." He pauses for a second. "Are you scared to remember everything?"

"Sometimes no. A lot of times, yes. I don't know how I'll react to the truth." My eyes slam closed. I rub the bridge of my nose and take a deep breath.

"Is this all too much?" he asks.

"No."

Yes.

But I'll never tell him that.

Sinclair rests his elbows on the table and dips his head closer. I find myself doing the same thing. Those green eyes that border on being a burnished gold stare straight into mine. They're enthralling, pulling me in when I have every reason to stay far, far away. My gut starts to twist again and my body starts to tingle.

"Tell me something I can't remember," I say quietly.

Sinclair looks me straight in the eye. "The very first time I kissed you, I got a taste of your soul and it was everything that I'm not; it was light to my darkness; cheerful to my worries. That moment will always stay with me. You may forget the story of us, but I'll always remember."

I think my heart just dropped to my stomach.

I cradle Evelyn just a little bit tighter and ask a question that I know I have no right to ask. "Sinclair, did you love me?"

Very slowly, he drops his hands and stares at me so intensely, so completely my hands start to shake. "I loved you then and I love you now."

17

Maybe Wes is right.

Maybe I have no business digging up the past. The beauty at the beginning of our marriage was slowly fading away, leaving in its wake a relationship that was slowly starting to sour. And if I was just reaching the middle of our story, what was the ending like?

I shudder at the thought.

Time may have dulled the pain and covered the wounds, but now I have been cutting them back open, forced to feel the pain tethered to my heart. I'm reminded that my heart doesn't beat. It lives through words.

It's bruised and fractured and sometimes I think it's going to fall apart, but it's alive, saying:

I ache.

I ache.

I ache.

But no matter the pain, I know I have to find out. I've gone this far. I can't turn back now . . . right?

Evelyn's screams go up an octave, making me flinch. I place her head on my shoulder and soothingly rub her back as I walk down the hall. "It's okay," I whisper. "It's okay."

Alice shoots me a dirty look but doesn't say a word.

All Evelyn seems to be doing is crying. No matter what I do, she won't stop. I even hum a nursery rhyme in her ear—a surefire way to get her to calm down. Still screaming.

Endless questions run through my head: Am I not giving her enough love or attention? Is she sick?

It seems the more pieces of my memory that I get back, the bigger this strange and horrifying disconnect becomes, as if the wires that connect us have been tampered with. The distance between us just seems to keep on growing. I have no idea how to stop it.

Before I go into Dr. Calloway's office, I stop and stare helplessly into my daughter's eyes. "Please, please stop crying," I plead with her.

She blinks, her light brown lashes fluttering against her cheeks, and stares at me blankly. The wailing stops, but she fusses and squirms in my arms, as if she'd rather be in anyone else's arms but knows it won't happen.

Before Alice walks away, she mutters underneath her breath: "Fairfax is no place for a baby. . . ."

Taking a deep cleansing breath, I knock once on the door before I walk in. Dr. Calloway greets me and I make a beeline for the same chair I always sit in. Very quickly, I'm starting to see Fairfax as a transition stop between my old life and the one waiting out in the world for me.

We go through routine questions and I give her my routine answers. There's this anxious energy swirling between us.

"Ready for a new batch of photos?" she asks with a smile.

As afraid as I am of seeing the rest of my past, I'm addicted. I need to know the rest. "Ready."

"Excellent."

My file is already open in front of her. She pulls out only three photos.

First up: Wes and me. We're sitting across from each other. The wineglass in front of my half-filled plate of food is full. Wes's is empty. He's leaning into the photo, a smile on his face. But it's all wrong; there's no feeling behind the smile, just a darkness that makes goosebumps trail across my skin. My expression is something altogether different. There's no smile. Not a trace of happiness on my face. I look shell-shocked and there's fear in my eyes.

"Next picture," I say a little too loudly.

The second photo is older. The edges are curling inward and there's a slight yellow tinge to the overall picture. It's of a little baby girl. A typical studio background is behind her. She's wearing a blue and red plaid dress with black lace trimming the hem. Her chubby legs are in black leggings. A big, red headband with a bow bigger than her head is on her face. She gives the cameraman a big toothy grin. I find myself staring back.

"That's me."

Dr. Calloway doesn't reply. I'm breaking our routine, but

it feels good for once to finally recognize something before the memories take me over. My mother had a larger photo of this one framed in our house, right next to one of my brother. She would stare at it lovingly, a whisper of a smile on her face. Growing up, I never understood the meaning behind the smile, but now that I have Evelyn, I get it.

The third photo: me and Sinclair. Blood roars through my veins as I stare at the image of the two of us. The setting is a party of some sort. Balloons and streamers are in the foreground. Happy smiling faces that I can't put names to are around us. It looks like Sinclair and I are dancing. His hands hold mine in the air as I spin around. The hem of my dress lifts and twirls around me. My free hand is palm up, fingers stretched out, as if I'm trying to grab on to the moment. Strands of my hair block my vision, but I'm still staring at Sinclair, the biggest smile on my face. All I can see of him is his profile, but I see the small dimple etched into his cheek and know he's smiling too.

Dr. Calloway starts to speed up the process. The pictures start to flip back and forth, over and over and over. I may remember the photo of me as a baby, but my memory latches on to the one of Sinclair and me. I feel the crisp air. I hear a car door slam. Voices trailing behind me.

Slowly, I'm sucked back into that memory.

I go willingly. . . .

18

A fresh new year of marriage should always come with arguments, tears, and frustrations. But a new batch of happiness, smiles, and laughter should always outweigh the bad. Always.

I tried to tell myself that, but as I sat across from Wes in the restaurant I knew it was all a farce. Gone were the days of making toasts and promises to each other and talking about what the future might hold.

There was this wall between us. It was transparent. Never noticeable to the public eye. Just to us. Sometimes I would forget it was there. Sometimes there were moments where I missed the Wes I fell in love with, reached out for him, only to be blocked.

This distance wasn't instantaneous. We didn't go from being in love with each other one second, to being virtual strangers the next. The more time passed and I wasn't pregnant, the more resentful and frustrated I became. Making partner at the firm may have been Wes's dream, but it wasn't mine. Lately he'd been getting home later and later. I had more of a relationship with his voicemail than him. I kept trying to figure out how we got here, how we let it get to this point. Was it because of my desperation to start a family? Wes's ability to go from zero to one hundred within seconds?

I didn't know and it drove me crazy.

Our partnership that used to be so strong was now dismal. I remembered when we were engaged, how I would shake my head at the couples around us who were divorcing, separating, splitting. There were nasty spats. I would always think to myself: *That will never be us. We will never let things get that bad.*

But here we were.

Here we were.

Slowly, I moved my food around the plate and shot Wes a glance. His attention was on his food and it was as though today were an average day for him.

No happy anniversary. No nothing.

I didn't expect a huge celebration, or any materialistic things. I just wanted an acknowledgment. A "Hey! We've made it through another year together. Next year will be even better!"

But we were almost done with dinner and I didn't see that acknowledgment surfacing anytime soon.

He wiped his mouth and dropped his napkin on the table.

There was a combative look in his eyes, as though I was his prey and he was the predator. It made me squirm in my seat. "Aren't you going to finish?" he asked.

"I'm not hungry."

He chuckled. "Victoria, Victoria . . ."

"What?"

He moved his arm away and stared at me. "What do you mean, 'what'?" he said, his voice rising an octave. "Can't I say your name?"

For a good second I looked him in the eye and tried to find a piece of the Wes that I loved. I couldn't find even the smallest one.

"What?"

"God, we're fucked-up." I dropped my face into my hands.

His eyes flared up with anger and hurt. "That's a shitty thing to say."

"It's the truth." I lifted my head and stared into his emotionless eyes. "Do you even love me anymore?"

"Of course."

"Can you tell me that you love me just as much as you did at the beginning?"

"No. I can tell you I love you more." He said his words earnestly and with such apparent conviction that I almost believed him.

Almost.

Love is three-dimensional. So deep and vast. So powerful that you can't say the word without the emotion splashed across your face and displayed in your eyes.

Wes's eyes were dull and flat.

"I think our definitions of love are different," I said quietly.

He barked out a laugh. "You live in a fucking garden. 'Let me tend to this flower!'" He mimicked my voice. "'Oh, this flower needs water.' 'And this one isn't getting enough sunshine!'" One more mocking laugh. "If you get away from those flowers you might realize what love is."

I shook my head.

"Are you mad at me?" he asked gruffly.

I wished I was mad. Mad was an emotion. An emotion that kick-starts your heart. I had nothing to give.

"You're mad," he announced.

He shifted. "I'm sorry. All right?" Wes's voice lowered. It was gentle and imploring.

"I'm sorry," he repeated.

"Fine," I said. I put my fork down across my still-full plate, trying to think of how I could tell him the next thing I had to say as gently as possible. Yet I didn't see any easy way and this needed to be said. It had been a long time coming.

I took a drink of water and cleared my throat. "I was thinking about going back to work."

Finally. I had told him.

His reply was instantaneous: "Why?"

"Well, do you see a baby crawling around?" I replied. "There's no reason for me to stay home."

"Of course there is."

"Wes, I'm miserable."

He blinked, staring at me with confusion and anger. "You're miserable in your dream house. What else are you miserable about? Are your diamond shoes too tight?"

"There's nothing for me to do! I'm going out of my mind."

"You have your garden."

"Which you just mocked me about."

"I was joking. You seem happy enough to me."

And therein lay the problem. Nothing about me was happy.

In public I was a good wife. I volunteered at a soup kitchen. I gave money to charity. I was in a book club that met the last Friday of each month. I hosted brunches where my friends would come over and we'd sit around my dining room table and gossip, all under the guise of concern. Wes and I would go to dinner with friends and family and he was the perfect gentleman.

The second we were alone, however, the varnish rubbed off and my sadness became visible. If he looked my way once he would notice.

"You're not going back to work," Wes said. His voice was firm. Final. Leaving no wiggle room for discussion.

"You can't tell me what to do."

"Um . . . I think I just did."

I felt a hate so powerful it was overwhelming. It clouded my vision until everything was shrouded in a black haze. I wanted to kill him. At that moment there was nothing that would've made me happier than to watch him take his last breath, and know he could never hurt me again.

To be honest, it was scary to feel that much hatred for one person. I felt no remorse for wanting to hurt Wes. I just felt remorse for *thinking* those thoughts.

I wadded up my napkin and tossed it onto the table. "I'm going to the restroom," I muttered as I walked away.

"Victoria. Wait!" he called out behind me. I made a quick right toward the restrooms. The hallway was narrow, with dim lighting. I stopped and turned around, knowing that I couldn't avoid him forever even though I wanted to.

He moved toward me like a predator and didn't stop until he had me caged between him and the wall. I stared up at him, while he stared down at me. "Why did you just run off?"

There was no change in his expression and his voice was deceptively soft, making the hairs on the back of my neck stand up.

"You can't control me," I repeated, my voice shaking.

"Don't whisper it!" He slammed his palm against the wall behind me. "If you have something to say, you fucking say it," Wes said viciously.

"You can't control me!" All vestige of self-control disappeared.

It was the only time I had ever lost my temper. I have to admit, it felt good.

Wes stepped back from me. He laughed erratically and stared up at the ceiling. "You think I control you. . . . That's hysterical." As Wes continued to laugh, I shifted to the left, trying to remove myself from his line of fire.

But his laugh died down and his attention instantly became locked on me. "I build you a beautiful home. I provide for you. I give you everything and you think I'm controlling? Any other woman would kill to have your life."

"Yeah, they might want our first year of marriage. But not the one we have now."

He shot a look at me filled with so much hatred, I flinched.

Wes started to pace back and forth. He finally stopped walking and stared at me with determination, as though he had it all worked out. "I'm keeping you," he announced.

At first I didn't think I had heard him right. But he stood there, not cracking a smile, and I realized he was dead serious.

Now it was my turn to laugh erratically. "I'm not an object! You can't own me."

His head tilted to the side. "Isn't that what love is? Owning someone?"

"No!" I said in disbelief.

"It is, though!" The wild, crazed look in his eyes was back. "Don't look at me like I don't get it. You're the one who stares at the world with rose-colored glasses, Victoria!"

I couldn't figure out which one of us was more fucked-up: me for staying or him for thinking love equals ownership.

I raised my hands in the air. "I give up. I give up, okay?" I had exhausted every option and there were no more left. I walked down the hall. I didn't know where I was going but I knew I had to get away before things got worse. "I'm leaving."

"Like hell," Wes said behind me.

The next thing I knew, two hands were wrapped around my shoulders. I was spun around and backed up until my head slammed against the wall. My skull started to pound. I saw nothing but black spots dancing in front of my eyes. I went to push Wes away but it was like trying to push a boulder. There was a sadistic look in his eyes, as though he took pleasure in causing pain. His fingers curled around my wrists and held them between us.

I stood there scared, trying to figure out the quickest way to escape. A dark smile spread across his face as he removed his hands, only to curl them around my neck and start to choke me. All the air left my lungs. I wanted to collapse. I slapped at his hands, wheezing to take a breath. My actions just made him laugh. I wanted to curl up in a ball. Shocks of pain ran through my body. Desperately, I slapped at his hands.

He pressed harder, and the edges around my vision started to fade.

This isn't happening.

It can't.

Then he dropped his hands and took a step back.

My hands curled around my knees as I hunched over and sucked in all the air I could. My lungs felt like they were on fire. So much pain. I wanted to cry but no tears formed. My mouth opened. There were no words. Just small gasps.

My head lifted and I found Wes staring at me, a blank look on his face. "Find someone who can love you better than I do. Find him! Where is he?" he whispered urgently. His fingers curled around my biceps, digging into my skin.

The hallway was starting to grow dim. Wes was swaying, multiplying all around me. I thought I was going to pass out.

"He's standing right in front of you, Victoria. I am him. I am the only man who will love you."

His hand landed on the crown of my head. For a second, I thought he was going to slam it against the wall and kill me. Right then, a part of me didn't care. But all he did was pat my head, like I was some unruly pet.

"I'm not letting you go." His thumb and forefinger curled around my jaw, making me look up at him.

We stood there, looking at each other. I was fighting to breathe. He was fighting for control of me. The whole time I was bracing myself.

He held me for a moment longer and then I finally panted out: "You're hurting me."

"Good." His hands lowered at the same time his forehead touched mine. "Now you can see how much you hurt me. I love you, Victoria."

With a husband like mine, I'll never need an enemy.

I woke up the next morning slightly disoriented. The sheets were stiff, and freshly washed. Sunlight was blaringly bright, shining on my face. That was all wrong; I always close the blinds at night. But then I realized that I was still in the guest bedroom. There was no way in hell I wanted to sleep in the same bed with Wes the night before. That was like sleeping with the devil.

Wes knocked on the door sometime around two this morning, but I never let him in.

I sat up. Across the room a mirror was mounted on the wall. Even from here I could see my eyes were puffy from shedding so many tears. Surprisingly, there were no bruises on my neck. If it weren't for my sore muscles, I would have thought the entire horrific scene had never happened.

I dropped my face into my hands and groaned. What happened last night was grounds for leaving someone. I knew that. Yet I was petrified. Scared to live with him and scared to run away from him.

I didn't know what he was capable of and that was the most terrifying thing of all.

I pulled back the covers and went to get up when I saw something out of the corner of my eye. On the pillow next to mine was a navy blue box with a small white bow on top. A note was folded up next to it. I opened the gift first. It was a beautiful diamond bracelet that I'd seen in a jewelry store a few months ago. I had mentioned to Wes that I thought it was stunning. He didn't comment and I simply forgot about it. The happiness this thoughtful gift would have brought me just a year ago wasn't there now. I felt nothing. I carefully put it back in the box and picked up the folded note. My name was written on the front in Wes's hurried handwriting.

The note was simple:

V–
I'm sorry about last night. I love you.
—W.

I traced the loose scribble of his initial, wishing that I could capture the husband I once loved. But I could feel that part of him slowly fading away.

My tears dropped onto the note, slowly traveling down the paper, melding with the ink, smearing "sorry" and "love you."

Rip it up! my mind chanted.

The urge to do just that was strong, but I found myself holding on to it.

I slammed the lid on the velvet box, got out of bed, and grabbed the photo album on the dresser. I sat on the edge of the bed and pored through my wedding pictures.

I was shocked to see the woman I once was. It seems impossible, but I vividly felt her happiness.

I continued to flip through the pages.

My body was here, keeping me alive, but my soul was somewhere far away from this house, this marriage, this life.

19

June 2014

I didn't want to leave the house.

I didn't want to do much of anything. I just wanted to lie in bed, draw the sheets above my head, and press REWIND on my life.

As Wes's routine went, there were no more outbursts. No punches thrown. No pain. The only time he ever said he was sorry was in the card the day after our anniversary, but that was it. He pretended that everything was okay and we should move on with our lives. But it wasn't that simple for me. I lived in a constant state of fight-or-flight.

I had quit my job for the sake of our future and what did I have to show for it? Nothing.

There was no baby. For the past few months, I'd resigned

myself to the fact that there would never be one. Months ago, I had suggested to Wes that he and I see a fertility specialist. He shut that conversation down quickly. He said that there was no reason to force it. That we've hardly been trying. I didn't tell him that if he really gave our marriage the attention he did at the beginning, he'd realize that we'd been "actively" trying for more than a year.

Maybe being childless was a blessing, though. The thought of bringing another life into the environment I lived in made me feel sick.

Lately, I found myself sucked into a bottomless black hole where I'd see the good moments with Wes. I'd see us sitting at a dinner table with friends and laughter all around us. He'd look over at me, a gleam of happiness in his eyes, and it made me see that there was still a sliver of good left in him.

When Wes was at work, the house felt incredibly empty. I became a master gardener with the help of Renee. Our friendship seemed to get stronger as time went on. I had multiple friends in Falls Church but they were climber friends—the ones that latched on to you for a while but had no problem dropping you as they moved on up the ladder.

Renee was a forever friend and I was treating her dismally. She had texted and called me multiple times this week. I answered once and replied to two of the texts. She said that if she didn't see me face-to-face she was going to knock on my door until I answered. I'd much rather go to her shop, say a quick hello, assure her I'm fine, and go.

I was afraid that if I stayed too long she'd see the residue of my angry fight with Wes. The abuse. The shame. And that was the very last thing I wanted.

Just stay home. It's better to be alone, my mind whispered.

The desire to give in and hole myself away in my house was strong. But I'd been home for almost a week and knew that if I didn't force myself to get out now, I never would.

It didn't help that the weather forecast was dreary. Clouds had settled in, creating a silver sky. The heat was suffocating, making sweat form at my temples and my clothes cling to my skin. I found myself hoping that the sky would open up and let the rain fall.

I parked right across from Renee's shop. At that time of day, it was pretty quiet. Most people were at work. As I slammed my door the sounds of children's shrieks of laughter pierced the air. I slowly walked toward the park. It was one of the nicer ones in Falls Church, with new playground equipment, secure fencing, and a pavilion for picnics and parties. Large oak trees peppered the area, with benches directly beneath them shielding people from the bright sun.

I found myself stopping, staring wistfully at the moms sitting underneath the tree. They were all lost in their own world. Here and there they'd glance at their kids and then go straight back to their conversations. One mom had a stroller next to her. She moved it back and forth and every so often would pull the stroller close and smile at the toddler squealing and laughing inside it.

Was it so horrible that I wanted that? Wes seemed to think so. I could think of a thousand different scenarios that could break up a relationship. I just never thought children would be one of them.

One of the moms glanced at me. Her eyes narrowed at me

with suspicion and realized that I looked all wrong: me lingering around a park like a creeper.

Quickly I turned around and hurried across the street, hoping to escape their stares, yet I felt them on my back. I crossed my arms over my chest. My shoulders were hunched and if I could have folded in on myself, I would have. Even though it was cloudy, I pulled my Ray-Bans out of my purse and put them on. It sounds crazy—and probably pathetic— but my sunglasses felt like a small barrier between the outside world and myself. With my sunglasses on, no one that walked past me would be able to see my eyes or my pain.

That was an ingenious idea. Why didn't I think of it sooner? I smiled down at the sidewalk and promptly slammed into a wall. I stumbled back and lifted my head, quickly realizing that the "wall" was actually a man.

"Sorry," I muttered. I gave the man a quick glance and did a double take. I knew him. He was the contractor who built our house.

He smiled and I felt my stomach drop. "Victoria, isn't it?"

I pushed my sunglasses up into my hair. Sinclair Montgomery. How could I forget him? He was still as tall and imposing as ever. Summer had treated him better than me, and his skin was the color of honey. His black hair was shorter than I remembered. He was dressed casually in jeans and a black T-shirt that strained across his wide shoulders.

"It's good to see you," he said.

I found myself smiling back. "You too."

Sinclair gestured to the flower shop. "You here to see Renee?"

"Yes. I've been meaning to see her, but I've been busy."

"It's best to bite the bullet and see her or she'll pester you until she has her way."

Of that, I had no doubt.

He held open the door and swept a hand toward the doorway. "After you."

When I walked past him, my shoulder brushed his chest and the scent of his cologne circled around. It smelled woodsy. Like nature. Or hard work. I ignored the rapid beating of my heart. I didn't have to look in the mirror to know my cheeks were red.

"Victoria! One of my favorite people!" Renee exclaimed as she walked from behind the counter.

"I'm not included in the list?" Sinclair asked.

"That depends. . . . Do you have the keys to my car?"

He tossed a set of keys at her. Renee caught them with one hand. "Done and done."

"Then let me start over: Victoria! Sinclair! Two of my favorite people!"

"That was good," Sinclair replied. "But next time, put some more feeling behind it." Sinclair rested his huge arms on the counter and glanced at me. "Victoria, would you treat your brother this way after he so kindly took your car to the shop to get a tire patched up and the oil changed?" He didn't ask me the question to be nice and include me in the conversation. There was genuine interest in his eyes. I was struck by the fact that it had been almost a year since I'd seen this man but somehow he made it seem as if no time had gone by.

Little by little I found myself relaxing. "I never think of treating my brother so badly," I teased.

"Liar," Renee said.

Sinclair gave me a smile that I felt from the tips of my fingers all the way down to my toes. I quickly looked away.

"So where have you been?" Renee asked me.

Sinclair pulled out his phone and turned his back to us.

"Oh, doing nothing really," I said evasively. "Just relaxing at home."

Even to my own ears, my explanation sounded weak and just plain sad. Renee frowned and stepped closer, peering at me very carefully.

She was getting way too close. I needed to leave. Right away. "Hey, you know we're not outside, right? You can take your sunglasses off."

I took a step back. "I know. But I just wanted to stop in and say hi real quickly."

"Stay," she said solemnly. "I just have to get a few things done, but I wanted to talk to you." She glanced at Sinclair. "We'll go in the back room and talk. Okay?"

"Okay," I said a little too loudly. It sounded wrong. I felt like a parody of the person I used to be and now I was going above and beyond to prove that I was fine.

Renee drifted back over to the cash register and I took the opportunity to really look around. I'd been here a few times before, but it seemed like every time I stepped into Renee's flower shop, something was different. She had an eclectic decorating style and I loved it. Renee didn't believe in throwing anything out. She would scour antiques stores and flea markets looking for anything that would fit her shop. The walls were painted a dark teal. On the wall in front of me was a whole array of mirrors, all different shapes and sizes. A long wooden table ran the length of the wall and was flanked by two broken ladders, leaning against the wall. Most of the white paint was chipped off, but the steps were sturdy, holding a wild array of flowers.

"All right," Renee said behind me. "Let's chat. I'll be back in a few minutes," she said to Sinclair.

He threw his hands in the air. "What am I supposed to do?"

"Just do what you do best: Sit there and look pretty, Sin."

As I followed Renee, I glanced over my shoulder, directly at Sinclair. His gaze clashed with mine and I quickly looked forward.

The back room was a small area with a desk shoved up against the wall. An outdated laptop was open with Post-its stuck around the screen. A small, framed photo of Renee and her husband was next to the stapler. Angled perfectly for Renee to look at. A small mini fridge was plugged in next to the door. Renee gave me the office chair and grabbed a water from the fridge.

"Thirsty?" she asked.

I said no and sat down.

For a while, Renee and I talked about mundane things, nothing too heavy, but soon we had covered every easygoing topic until there was nothing left.

Renee sighed and tossed her empty bottle in the trash can. "So where have you really been?"

"At home. Busy."

Renee quirked a brow. "Yeah. Busy. Is everything okay with you?"

"Everything is great." I gave her a bright smile, but it was starting to quake because inside, my soul was screaming, pleading, begging for me to tell Renee the truth. It was taking all of my power to keep quiet.

"All right, all right. Everything's okay with you. . . ." Renee pushed away from the wall and stared down at her hands as though she were working out a complicated math problem. She raised her head and looked me in the eye. "Is everything okay with you and Wes?"

I hesitated. It was only a second, but it was enough for Renee. "What's going on?" she prodded.

Now it was my turn to stare down at my hands. "We're just going through a rough patch."

Renee nodded empathically. "That's normal. Couples go through tough times. Sometimes my husband drives me crazy and other moments I can't get enough of him. But most of the time he drives me crazy," she said teasingly.

I smirked, appreciating her attempt to lighten the mood. "How long does he usually drive you crazy?"

Her brows formed a tight V. "That depends on how stressed out I am. The same for him. The longest time though?"

I nodded anxiously, waiting for her reply like it was manna falling from heaven.

"I'd say probably around the time that I opened up this business. We'd been married for only two years. He was worried that the business would fail. Honestly, so was I. But I wanted to at least try and see if it had a chance. We were snapping at each other for a good two months and then one night he didn't come home and that was our reality check. We made a conscious effort to work through the stresses of life, trying not to take it out on each other."

Two months. To me, two months seemed like a walk in the park.

"From the devastated look on your face, I assume that's not exactly what you wanted to hear," Renee said wearily.

I slumped in the chair. "Things are much worse than that between Wes and me."

"Like how?"

"If I tell you—"

Renee held up both hands. "I won't tell a soul. And I mean that."

I nodded and took a deep breath. "Things have been stressful lately for Wes. He's trying to make partner and it's taking longer than he anticipated. He works crazy hours. We hardly see each other and it's just . . . rough. Last year, I thought having a baby would really round us off, make us happier than we could even imagine. But that didn't happen. I quit my job . . . I gave up a part of my identity for Wes. He didn't want a baby, but I pressured him into it. . . . He's lost his temper a few times. It happens out of nowhere, when I least expect it." I exhaled loudly. "Each outburst is becoming worse than the last and I don't know what to do anymore."

I always thought telling the truth would be akin to pulling teeth. But in a way, I felt free.

"These outbursts," she said, starting off slowly. "How bad are they?"

Renee presented the question calmly, not completely coming out and asking me if the relationship was abusive. Instead it was silently implied.

I was repressing every bad thing that had happened to

Wes and me and it was slowly eating me alive. I knew I had to confess the truth to someone, but it was the last thing I wanted to do. No one wants to come out and reveal their pain and humiliation. It's like standing naked in front of a group of strangers.

But Renee was no stranger and deep down I knew that if I was to confide in anyone, Renee should be the person.

I stood up from my chair. Renee gave me a confused look as I turned and gave her my back. Sometimes words fail you. Sometimes there's no adequate way to describe a situation or your feelings. Sometimes you have to show them.

Staring at the wall, I reminded myself that I could trust her, then I raised the hem of my shirt up to my shoulders.

I knew the moment she saw it from the way she gasped. Most of the bruises from the night of our second anniversary had faded. But what Renee saw wasn't a bruise. It was a cut. When Wes slammed my back against the wall in the restaurant, I hit the edge of the mirror. It left a nasty cut of about five inches.

Only a few seconds passed by, but it was long enough for me. I dropped my shirt and quickly turned back around.

Renee wore a look of horror. "What was that?"

"That was a brief look into my marriage," I mumbled.

A pained expression crossed her face. "Has this been happening the whole time?"

Leaning against the counter, I shrugged and stared at the floor. "Not the whole time."

"Then how long?"

"Just . . . recently," I confessed, not bothering to admit the times where he'd acted completely erratically.

"This just doesn't sound like him. I can't believe this," she replied in a half daze.

"Well, it is."

A tense silence swirled around the room. Renee started to pace back and forth. "This is not okay," she said fiercely.

"I know that."

She whipped her body around, eyes wide. "So you're going to leave him."

I hesitated and her face fell. "Oh, Victoria. No. . . ."

"It's complicated," I mumbled, but even to my own ears my reply was weak. I might have revealed a small portion of the truth, but I wasn't ready for it all to come out into the open. I couldn't explain to her that my fear was a large, powerful beast living inside me, controlling everything I did, to the point where I felt paralyzed in my own body. Choices and decisions that I would have easily made in a heartbeat were now uphill battles that I could never seem to conquer.

I couldn't tell her that I felt like the biggest hypocrite. So many times I had seen people in and out of the ER with suspicious-looking bruises, and watched carefully as excuse after excuse rolled from their tongues. I always thought that if I was in their place I wouldn't put up with it. I would leave, because I was strong. I knew my self-worth and knew I deserved better.

But here I was.

If I could track down every patient whom I silently judged, and just tell them I was sorry, I would.

"Look, you don't need to tell me that it's wrong. I know that. And you don't need to tell me that I need to leave. I promise you, whatever you're thinking about right now, I've already thought about a thousand times over."

Renee's lips went into a flat line and I knew there were thousands of things she was dying to say, but didn't. For that I was grateful.

I pushed myself away from the counter abruptly and straightened out my shorts. "Can we drop this, please?"

"Sure."

I grabbed my purse and walked toward the door, anxious to leave this conversation behind us.

"Victoria?"

I slowly turned.

"This isn't your fault," Renee said quietly.

I lifted my head and blinked back my tears.

"And you ever need anything, I'm one call away."

"I know," I replied.

She stopped me by grabbing my arm gently. But it still made me flinch. "I mean it. I'm there. For anything."

When people reach out and try to help, I truly believe it's done sincerely. But also with naïveté. It's so easy to make declarations while being far away from the situation and even easier to run away when everything gets rough. But from the look in Renee's eyes, I knew she meant it.

"Thank you," I whispered gratefully. And I meant it.

The second we emerged from the hallway, Renee put a small smile on her face as if nothing was wrong.

"We're back," she announced.

Sinclair tapped his watch. "You do realize you've been back there for almost thirty minutes, right?"

"We were talking."

Sinclair's eyes veered between his sister and me. "About?"

"I'm sorry, did you grow a vagina while I was back there and I didn't know it? Why do you care what we were talking about?"

He held his hands up in surrender. "Just asking. No need to rip my head off."

"I should be going," I announced.

"All right. See you later," Renee replied breezily.

Sinclair stared at me for a long second, making me feel like I was under a microscope. "See you later," he finally said.

His words weren't empty, just said to be nice. No, his words sounded a lot like a promise.

20

July 2014

Nobody should be ringing the doorbell at eight in the morning.

It's just wrong. A cardinal sin.

I belted my robe as I hurried down the stairs. "I'm coming. I'm coming."

Quickly, I peered through the peephole. My mother was on the other side.

I flipped the lock and opened the door.

"Good morning." My mother breezed past me, looking bright-eyed and cheerful as though it were the middle of the day instead of early morning. She carried a box with VICTORIA'S STUFF written on the side. She balanced two coffees and a carryout bag on top of it.

I didn't know where to start so I took the food and coffee. Then I pointed to the box. "What's that?"

My mother dropped her purse and the box on the table against the wall. "Oh, I was cleaning out the attic and found some of your old things. I thought you'd like to see them."

I really didn't, but I shrugged. She took a deep breath and grabbed one of the coffees out of my hand. She still hadn't explained why she was there and it didn't look like she was going to do so anytime soon.

"What are you doing here?" I asked as I shut the door.

"I just wanted to spend some quality time with my only daughter."

"At eight in the morning?"

"Is it a crime to want to have breakfast together?"

There was so much wrong with this impromptu visit. I didn't know where to begin. My mother liked planning things in advance. No surprises. She applied that theory to everything.

Something was up.

I followed her toward the kitchen. "I told them to give me two decafs but I think they messed up the order. There was a long line so I didn't bother getting it fixed."

"It's fine. I have some creamer."

As I grabbed two plates, my mother sat at the kitchen island and took two large bagels out of the bag.

Coffee and carbs. Dear God, was she here to tell me she was dying and had three weeks to live?

"Is everything okay?" I asked cautiously.

She linked her fingers together and placed them on the

counter. "Of course." She waved her hand in the air as if scattering my words away and stared at the French doors. "I always seem to forget how beautiful your garden is."

"Is that what you came here to talk about? My garden?"

My mother frowned at me. "Of course not." She took a small bite out of her bagel and wiped her hands with her napkin. "How are you?"

She gave me a meaningful look. The same look she gave me as a teenager when she knew I'd fucked up and wanted me to confess.

I took a sip of my coffee. "I'm good," I replied slowly.

"Are you really?"

"Mom . . . what's really going on?"

"Wes spoke with me," she confessed.

"About?" I asked a little sharply.

"He's concerned about you."

"He's concerned about me," I repeated back dully.

"Well, yes!"

Impatiently, I waved my hand in the air. "Mom, just tell me what he said."

"He says you've been acting erratically and unpredictably. He says the two of you have had terrible fights and he tries to work through things with you but you're inconsolable."

I was in a state of shock. I'd seen a dark side of Wes. But never in a million years did I think he'd try to turn my own mother against me. This was a new low.

"And you believe that?" I sputtered.

"Of course I do. I mean, you've clearly been unhappy for a while."

"How would you know?" I snapped.

"Well, I have a pair of eyes that work perfectly fine. It's clear something is wrong with you!"

"For legit reasons that you don't even know about!"

"Tell me," she urged. "Maybe I can help."

"It's none of your business and no, you can't help."

My mother crossed her arms. "Now calm down. I didn't come here to get into a fight with you." She stood up and walked around the island, her hands outstretched for a hug. I took a step back. My heart was thumping so hard, I could barely breathe.

"He told me you expressed to him that you weren't happy in the marriage."

Of course he did.

"He loves you dearly. My God, he was a wreck when I talked to him."

I dragged my hands through my hair and took a deep breath. I felt like I was in the Twilight Zone. Everyone else around me saw this wonderful man. No one ever saw the side I did. He hid it so well that I looked like the liar. I looked like the villain.

"You have to give your marriage a chance."

"You shouldn't hand out advice when you don't have the full story."

"Enlighten me, then. Fill in the blanks."

"Will you believe me?"

She hesitated. Just for a second, but long enough to show that she probably wouldn't. She saw my life, my marriage as a trophy she could tote around and show off to her friends, and if I told her just a small bit of how I was feeling, she'd do everything in her power to talk me out of it.

"I'm beginning to think I married a complete stranger."

"Victoria, that's ridiculous. You—"

"Can you let me finish?" I threw my hands up in the air. "You're so quick to correct me when you don't even know the full story."

"Fine. Keep going."

"As I was saying, I think the man I married isn't what he seems."

"It doesn't matter!" She couldn't help herself. She had to give her opinion. "You stop at nothing for the people you love the most."

Wes would stop at nothing until he captured my soul and put it in a glass jar.

"And I know you love Wes," she said.

"I love the side of him that's good," I admitted slowly. "Yet, unfortunately, even when that side is out, I can't help but wonder when the bad will creep back up."

"Victoria, you are a married woman. You made *vows*."

Based on how my mother said the four-letter word, it sounded sacred. A consecrated moment of promises you should never try to escape.

"So do you want to tell me what's going on inside that mind of yours?" she asked.

Seconds ticked by. My mother waited for an answer while I stared at my half-eaten bagel as though it held all the secrets to my problems. I thought of the brief note he left on my pillow the next morning. I thought of how Wes and I lived at cross purposes, where he assumed "sorry" made the slate clean and his long hours provided me with comfort that made me happy. And I thought of how I had moved out of the master bedroom and into the guest bedroom, refusing to let Wes touch me or be in the same room as him, all in a last-ditch effort to protect myself.

"He's been stressed with work, hasn't he?" my mother prodded.

"Yes."

"Honey, everything is okay. Arguments are going to happen. It's inevitable. But that doesn't mean you should run and hide. You have to face each problem head-on and you have to do that together."

"It's not that simple. None of this is." Nervously, I licked my lips. "There's something wrong with him, Mom. I mean, something seriously twisted," I said.

"Victoria, that's just your imagination. You've—"

"It's not my fucking imagination!" I dragged my hands through my hair and fought the urge to tug at the strands. God, I really felt like I was going crazy. "You haven't seen him when he gets all angry. It's beyond anything I can explain. He turns into a different person!"

"Victoria," she said calmly. "Listen to me, okay?"

Slowly, I met her eyes.

"It's a constant battle to keep your head above the water. If you try to work past this, the two of you will make it to the other side."

My mother has always believed that every challenge has a solution if you try hard enough. But this wasn't a challenge. It was a living, breathing nightmare.

"And what happens if we don't?"

She looked me in the eye. "Then at least you know you tried."

There was nothing I could say to that.

"I have to get going." She stood and gave me a weak smile as she hugged me. I was in such a state of shock that I stood frozen, like a block of ice.

When she pulled back, she looked me in the eye. "Why don't you look through the box I gave you?"

I frowned. "Old memories aren't going to help me."

"You're wrong," she said softly. "They help all of us."

We walked toward the front door. My mother opened up the box she had brought over. She pulled out a photo album, looking ready to take a trip down memory lane. I had no desire to join her; I was still reeling from our conversation.

She flipped through the first few pictures before she pulled out a photo and handed it to me. It was of me as a little baby. "Why are we looking at this?"

My mother plucked the picture from my hands. "Maybe you two should consider starting a family." She brushed her thumb across the glossy surface of the picture. "Having you and your brother was the best thing I'd ever done and brought your dad and me closer than I ever thought possible."

She had no idea that we'd been trying for a child for a while. I had no desire to tell her either. So I nodded my head and followed her to the door, yet all the while, my heart was breaking apart.

When the door closed behind her, I leaned against it and closed my eyes.

Deep down I knew there was no amount of sorrys, no gifts or child that could ever bring Wes and me back together again.

21

July 2014

"What do you think about this one?"

Sinclair peered at the flower. "The black rose?" He shook his head. "Too dark."

I brushed my fingers against the deep purple petals. "I kind of like them."

"You're supposed to be helping Renee make a bouquet for a wedding, not a funeral."

We were in Renee's flower shop. It was downtown, in the heart of Falls Church. It was a quaint little place with a green and white striped awning that had seen better days. The front door was painted black, with chips of paint flaking off around the doorknob. A bell was looped around the door handle. People seemed drawn to its exterior, and curious to

step into a place that looked like it had been there for de-
cades. When the weather was warm, plants and bouquets
would be displayed right outside the store.

The shop was Renee's pride and joy, and the fact that she
trusted me enough to let me run it, even for two hours, was
shocking. The first thirty minutes I fidgeted behind the cash
register, completely clueless about what to do. Sinclair
showed up an hour ago. He was just as clueless as me and we
made a useless pair.

The weather was bleak. Rain clouds came in and thunder
rumbled in the distance; only one customer had walked in.

"This could be for a wedding." I gathered the long-
stemmed roses and held them out to Sinclair. "Here's your
bouquet. I wish you well in your future failed marriage."

Sinclair lifted a brow. "I don't know how she does this
shit. I'm getting high off all these flowers."

"She has a talent, that's for sure."

"Apparently you do too if she lets you help her create her
bouquet masterpieces."

I shrugged and went back to trimming the stems of some
black roses. Sinclair was still dressed in black pants and a
white dress shirt with the sleeves rolled up to his elbows. The
logo of his construction company was on the left side of his
shirt. He'd been here for an hour and showed no signs of
leaving soon. It was fine by me. I loved when he was around,
which lately was a lot.

We started talking on the phone just days after Wes and I
moved into our house. They were quick conversations that
became steadily longer. Soon we started to email each other.

He never came to my house. Instead I would spend time

with him at Renee's shop. It was our meeting place and I cherished every second; without him something malignant lived in me, slowly killing me. Around him, though, I came alive. I could breathe.

I could *be*.

It was hard to believe that I had met Sinclair only nine months ago. It felt like it had been longer. We talked to each other with such ease. He never looked uninterested in what I had to say. It felt amazing to know someone was listening to me.

During all this, we never did anything inappropriate. We knew there was an invisible line between the two of us that neither should cross. But I was inching closer and closer to that line and it was getting harder and harder not to cross it.

"Why are you all dressed up?" I asked him.

"I had a meeting with a potential client. A huge house out on Bellamy Road."

"I could be getting a new neighbor?"

He grinned and my stomach twisted. "You could, but nothing's set in stone."

I bit down on my lip to hide my smile. I loved that Sinclair was confiding in me. When I asked him how his day was going, he didn't shrug his shoulders and slam his office door. He didn't narrow his eyes and ask what my angle was. He told me the truth. Someday, in the near future, I hoped I could do the same with him.

Gathering the stems, I tossed them in the trash. "How did you live with her growing up?" I asked over my shoulder.

"Oh, it was a nightmare."

"Really?"

Sinclair nodded and grinned devilishly. Already I could see the mischievous brother he was to Renee. "Her room was always spotless. Every single thing had a place. Everything. If anything was ever moved from its designated area the world was over."

"And your room?"

"Fucking disaster. It drove her crazy. When she got in trouble, she never got grounded or had things taken away. No, our mom would make her hang out in my room."

Resting my elbows on the worktable, I smiled and leaned in closer. Both Renee and Sinclair had this . . . spark about them. Instinctively, people were drawn toward them, anxious to hear the next words that slipped from their lips.

"Poor Renee," I commented.

"Not poor Renee," Sinclair quickly replied. "More like poor world. Or poor Sinclair!"

I grabbed the broom leaning against the wall and swept the floor for the millionth time; honestly, this place was immaculate. "It's probably a good thing that we met as adults then," I said.

"Why?"

"She sounds like she's always had her life put together. Whereas mine has been . . . scattered."

"Really?"

I nodded. "I was the youngest. I was carefree and wild. If things got done, they did. If something was wrong, then just figure out a way to fix it. I switched my major so many times in college I lost count. I wanted to dip my hands into everything, ignoring the fact that it was impossible. It drove my mother crazy how relaxed I was. It still does."

"You sound more like a free-love hippie than the 'youngest child.'"

I gave him a look over my shoulder and continued cleaning up. "All I'm saying is that she would've taken one look at wild Victoria and run in the other direction."

"Doubtful. You probably looked beautiful then, just as you do now." He said the words so quietly that at first they didn't register. Kind of like a whisper—it took a second to process.

My head lifted and I found Sinclair looking me straight in the eye. I didn't see regret or embarrassment. He meant every single word. My stomach twisted tightly from the intensity in his gaze.

We were quickly veering past the normal bounds of conversation into a place we had no business being in.

It was then that I realized Sinclair had listened to every word I said. Better yet, he seemed interested. My husband didn't. Even from the beginning, conversations always circled around Wes. He would listen to me talk but it always came back to him in the end. And maybe I'd known that all along. Maybe I'd told myself I was okay with that.

But I had to admit, it felt amazing to be heard.

Sinclair cleared his throat. "Can I ask you a question?"

"Of course," I replied as I set the scissors down.

"Did you work before you got married?"

I paused, my hands hovering over the vase. "I was a nurse."

"But not now," he stated flatly.

I nodded. "Wes and I wanted to start a family."

Wes and I? What a joke. The more time that passed, the

more I realized that Wes could spend the rest of his life child-less and be perfectly fine.

"But not anymore?" Sinclair asked.

"Not anymore."

Sinclair leaned against the table, watching me carefully, as if I were a puzzle piece he couldn't seem to click into place. "Do you miss being a nurse?"

"I do." My voice was quiet even to my own ears. This should have been a moment where I quickly changed the subject, but my lips parted. "I worked mostly in the emergency room. It was crazy most of the time. Sometimes I would be so exhausted at the end of the day I would lay my head on the pillow and pass out. But there was always something new each day. It was never dull."

"You really loved it."

I smiled very faintly. "I still do."

"Then go back."

I lowered the scissors and looked at Sinclair beneath my lashes. "I wish it was that simple."

"Of course it's that simple."

"No, it's not. It's—" Abruptly I stopped talking. Frustration was starting to creep into my words. It was impossible to explain the situation to him. He wouldn't understand. No one would understand.

"I'm not trying to make you angry," Sinclair said after a beat of silence.

I slumped over the table and rubbed my temples. I wished I could tell him the truth. "I know you're not."

He stood up and walked around the table. His shoulder brushed against mine. Heat. All heat. It was enough to make me feel like I was going up in flames. Or maybe that was my body reacting to him. Not even with Wes did I respond that way. I wanted to shift my arm away but I couldn't. It was amazing to have all these feelings brewing inside me.

"I would say I'm trying not to pry into your life, but that's not true."

Instead of answering, I kept my head down, staring at the oak table.

"I've watched how he is with you. . . . It isn't right."

Sinclair rested his elbows on the table and looked into my eyes and leaned in so close, our faces were mere inches apart. The guise of friendship slipped from his eyes, only to be replaced with blatant desire. Goosebumps broke out across my skin.

"You deserve better," he said gruffly.

I nodded, the only thing I could do. I couldn't breathe. I couldn't speak.

What was this between us?

I've loved.

I've liked.

I've lusted.

But none of those feelings came close to right now.

I knew that Sinclair felt this . . . this connection between us too. His brows slammed together as his gaze made a game of going between my lips and eyes. On his tan neck, I could see the fluttering of his pulse.

It was beating just as hard as mine.

Sinclair moved closer. And I did the craziest thing: I leaned in too. But I didn't feel like I had a choice. I couldn't remember the last time a man actually looked at me and didn't see me as his to own. I wanted to be honest with Sinclair and tell him just that. My mouth opened.

"Sinclair, I—"

Right then the shop bells sounded as the door opened. I jumped away from the table like it was on fire.

"Okay, I'm back," Renee said, out of breath. She carried two large brown bags. Her steps were quick as she made a beeline to where Sinclair and I now stood with a healthy distance between us. "That took much longer than I anticipated."

I crossed my arms and then dropped my hands to my sides. I crossed my arms again. I couldn't stop fidgeting. I couldn't stop sneaking glances at Sinclair. He had stood up. His hands were on his narrow hips. He stared at me, his gaze unflinching.

"Don't worry about it," I said to Renee just a little too loudly. "Everything was fine."

She dropped the bags onto the table and glanced at me curiously. Her eyes flitted between Sinclair and me. "Was it too crazy here?"

"One customer."

Renee whistled. "Sounds like it was a packed house," she replied dryly.

I could feel Sinclair's eyes on me. But Renee was already on to me. There was no way I was looking in his direction. I pointed to the bags. "What did you get?"

"Oh!" Renee clapped her hands excitedly and reached into the bags. "After my appointment, I went to the farmers' market. I found this beautiful flower that I know you'll just love. . . ."

She continued to talk. Her mouth moved up and down but I couldn't latch on to a single word. I looked over her head, to where Sinclair stood. With my eyes I pleaded for him to not push what *almost* happened.

". . . I think I'm going to try and make it a weekly trip," Renee said. She flipped through her calendar, and stopped short. Her face turned pale. Her elbows landed on either side of the calendar as she stared down at it. "Shit, shit, shit, shit." Renee dragged her hands through her hair.

I tried to peer at the schedule but her arms covered it. "What's wrong?"

"I forgot to drop off flowers."

"For?" Sinclair asked.

"A client. I completely forgot. Jeff and I had a date night all planned out for tonight."

"I'll do it," I blurted out.

Renee looked visibly shocked. "What?"

The words came out before I could think them over, but now that they had settled, I realized it might be fun. And if not fun, at least interesting. "Yeah," I said as I walked around the register. "I'll do it. No problem."

"I'll go with her."

My eyes widened in shock. I whipped my head around and stared at Sinclair. He shrugged as though it were nothing, and never once met my gaze.

"You're going to deliver flowers," Renee stated skeptically.

"Yeah," he replied.

"You're going to deliver flowers."

"Yeah."

"For me."

"Yes!"

"Not once in all our entire childhood, teenage, or adult years have you ever wanted to help me out."

"Well, I'm helping you out now."

"Yeah, that's it," Renee said dubiously. They said nothing but gave each other that "sibling stare" of silent communication.

A moment went by and I cleared my throat. Renee pulled out her keys and tossed them to Sinclair. "Now, don't go too fast. And the brakes are sensitive."

"Renee, relax. Believe it or not, I have driven a car before."

Renee snorted dismissively at her brother. She glanced at me, thousands of questions in her eyes. Sinclair was going to deliver the flowers. There was no need for me to go. Yet I found myself creeping closer and closer to the door.

"I'll see you later," I called over my shoulder as I rushed toward the door. Within seconds he had caught up with me and held the door open. When we were both outside, I stared straight ahead. "I think I'll drive there in my own car."

"Are you sure?"

When I glanced up at Sinclair I saw that all the intensity brewing in the shop had followed us outside. The two of us going anywhere together was a really bad idea.

Delivering flowers isn't as cut and dried as you'd think. The fact that we arrived five minutes before the party should have worked in our favor, but people were already sitting at the tables. Kids ran zigzagging between tables, trying to beat their brothers, sisters, or cousins with balloons plucked from the tables. The birthday woman—who we found out pretty quickly was called Barbara—was picky. She had Sinclair move the flower arrangements from one table to the next. Once that was settled, she'd have him turn it to the right, no, to the left. Can you move it forward a bit? Yes, right there is perfect.

I leaned against the wall, watching more and more people filter in. The tables were covered in red, disposable tablecloths, with black foldout chairs tucked beneath them. Every time someone moved a chair around, the legs would scrape against the floor, creating a noise that had me cringing.

This looked less like a birthday party and more like a homecoming dance.

But it was nice to watch the members of this woman's family come in. They were are all hushed words and talk about the weather, yet when they saw Barbara, they smiled and laughed as if no time had passed since they'd last seen one another. I tried to remember the last time that Wes and I had visited extended family. Probably during our wedding.

Unease trailed down my spine as I realized that other than my mother, I had made no effort to keep in contact with anyone on my side of the family. I hardly saw my brother or his family. A few cousins were scattered around the country.

Was that my fault or Wes's? I didn't want to dig any further into our relationship's past. My gut told me that if I did, I'd see things clearly. I'd see things for what they were.

Sinclair walked over to me and I shoved away all dark thoughts of Wes. "That took longer than I thought."

He dusted off his hands and leaned against the wall. His body was mere inches away from me. He looked so at ease, as if we always stood this close. As if we didn't have my husband, my humiliations and fears and shame between us.

"I have a newfound respect for my sister now," he said.

"As do I." I pushed away from the wall. "All set?"

Sinclair nodded and pulled out his keys.

I grabbed my purse and we walked toward the front doors, Sinclair behind me. "No, no, no. Where are you two going?"

Sinclair and I turned around at the same time. Barbara had a margarita in one hand, holding it above her head as she moved in and out of the crowd. The dictator was gone, replaced with a brand-new, happier person. "You two should stay!" When we said nothing she grabbed my hand and swung it back and forth. "Stay and have fun."

Sinclair and I exchanged glances.

"You want to?" I asked.

Sinclair looked at me with shock. True, spending a Saturday night at a party for a virtual stranger wasn't at the top of the list but it beat going home to a cold monstrosity, which instead of being filled with good memories was holding all the harsh words Wes and I threw at each other.

Maybe my thoughts showed, because Sinclair gave me a small nod and smiled at Barbara. "We'd love to."

"Excellent, excellent!" And then she was gone, shouting at someone clear across the room.

Sinclair dipped his head and whispered in my ear. "Do you really want to stay here or were you just being nice?"

I swallowed hard and kept my eyes glued on the crowd. "It doesn't seem so bad." I looked at him from the corner of my eye and found him staring at me. "Unless you already have plans tonight."

He held my gaze and tried to fight the pull between us. "I have no plans. Did you?"

Wes had said he was having another night at the office. Lately, that was more of his home than the one he shared with me. I looked away.

"Nope. No plans."

There was no time to be bored or think about the problems swirling around in my life. As it turned out, Barbara's family was outgoing. More friends of the family showed up and from our table in the corner we watched everyone. Drinks and laughter were all around. It was impossible to be in an environment like that and not have it rub off on you.

I drained my fourth cup of fruit punch, wishing that it was some form of alcohol instead. "Is it possible to get drunk off fruit punch?" I mused.

"If by drunk you mean sugar high, then yes, it's possible."

I glanced at Sinclair and smiled. "This night isn't as bad as I thought it would be."

Sinclair scanned the people around us. "It'd probably be better if we stopped hiding in the corner."

"That's the difference between you and me: I'm okay sitting in the corner, whereas you love to talk to everyone." I nudged him in the arm. "It's killing you sitting here next to me, isn't it?"

All humor vanished from Sinclair's eyes. His stare was so acute, I had to fight the urge to look away. "It's not killing me at all," he said gruffly. "I like being with you."

Greedily, my heart scooped up his words when it had no right to. But Sinclair did that. He made me want things that I had no business reaching for.

I cleared my throat and looked back at all the laughing people together.

Sinclair stood, his chair screeching loudly. He loomed above me and held out his hand. "You wanna?" He nudged his head toward the people dancing.

I like to have fun in different ways but dancing in front of people was not one of them. I shook my head. "I'm good right here."

"Something tells me you'll be good wherever you are, but come on, it'll be fun."

Sinclair said it with a small smile. He didn't know how his words struck me straight in the heart.

"Come on," he urged. "Just let go, a little."

I nodded and released my tension and grabbed his hand.

The song was something from the eighties, one I vaguely remembered my mother listening to when I was little. The people around us, they didn't care. They were locked in their own time, reliving happy days. Their energy was infectious, making it impossible for me not to smile.

Yet I still hesitated, and moved awkwardly from side to side.

Sinclair tilted his head. "You didn't strike me as someone too shy to dance."

"It's not that I don't want to dance. It's the fact that we're surrounded by strangers."

At that he lifted a brow.

"And you know . . ." I flung a hand in the air. "It's awkward."

"Not really. The fact that these people are strangers should be the one incentive to dance."

I smiled; he had a point.

"You look like an idiot? Doesn't matter. You'll probably never see these people again."

"Except for you," I pointed out.

"Except for me," he agreed, a devilish look in his eyes. Sinclair reached out and grabbed my hands, swallowing them whole with his own. "And you better believe I'll tease you mercilessly."

Our hands were the only parts of our body touching, yet there was this electric charge between us. He kept them in the air and wildly moved them left and right until I had no choice but to follow his lead.

Then he spun me around. My skirt twirled and I smiled so wide. I couldn't remember the last time I had had so much fun.

Two, then three songs went by. My feet started to ache. Yet we continued dancing, having fun in our own little world.

When we finished, my cheeks were red.

"Was that so bad?" Sinclair asked, his eyes gleaming with energy as we walked back to the table.

"It was fun," I replied, but the truth was more than that: Dancing with Sinclair was the most alive I'd felt in months. Maybe years.

My smile faded as I realized that I needed to find things bad about Sinclair, to keep my distance. Not more and more redeemable qualities that imperceptibly pulled me closer to him.

But maybe it was always going to be this way.

Maybe this attraction would always be inexorable.

"You really can dance. I knew you were holding out on me."

Moments later an older woman asked Sinclair to dance. I let her take my place and sat down at the empty table, just watching everything around me. Such happy, joyful people—and all I could think about was whether Wes and I would ever be like them.

I pulled out my phone. It was 10:43. My eyes widened, though not because of the time. It was the fifty missed calls that had me on edge. Every single one was from Wes.

"You okay over there?"

I gave my phone one last look and dropped it back into my purse. The smile I gave Sinclair was one of my weakest. "I'm great."

He crossed his arms and I knew he could see right through my words.

Abruptly I stood. "You ready to go? It's getting late."

"Sure. Let's go."

Side by side we walked out of the building. My mind was racing a mile a minute, trying to think of what I would say when I got home to Wes. Most times I could never predict when he would snap, but I felt it this time. I'd been careless. I had let go of my worries and now I had to deal with him.

"It wasn't as bad as I thought it would be," Sinclair said.

"I actually had fun too."

"I know; it was the most I've ever seen you smile."

"I smile all the time."

"No, I mean really smile. A true smile."

My grip on the strap of my purse tightened. If I looked at

Sinclair right then, I knew I'd never want to look away, so I stared straight ahead. I could feel his gaze on me.

"Where are you parked?" I asked him.

Sinclair gave me a frustrated look and pointed toward the opposite side of the parking lot, toward the back entrance. "Over there."

I nudged my head to the opposite side. "I'm over here. So I'll see you later. This was fun." My words were rushed and disjointed. I turned around before I made a bigger fool of myself.

"Victoria, wait," Sinclair said, and grabbed my arm.

I turned around willingly and stared into his eyes. "What are you running away from?" he asked.

You, I wanted to say. But I didn't. I couldn't. The truth was the last thing that needed to be said. I took a step back. "I'm running away from nothing," I said as I started to rifle through my purse for my keys. "It's late and I have to get home."

"You're lying."

I frantically moved my wallet out of the way. Where in the hell were my keys? I was a disaster. My brain was on the fritz, jumping from one thought to the next. And it was all Sinclair's fault.

"Victoria, come on. Talk to me." Sinclair took a step closer. I looked over my shoulder, scanning the area for anyone who might be watching us. When I turned back around I bumped straight into Sinclair's chest. The very tips of my breasts brushed against him. I sucked in a sharp breath.

"Victoria," he said gruffly. My name rolled off his tongue perfectly, sending chills up and down my spine.

A surge of longing ran through me. For a brief second I let my forehead rest against the solid wall of his chest. His body enveloped mine and if anyone had walked by, they could never have seen me. So I tilted my head back and met his gaze. His face was inches from mine. He was closer than he'd ever been and yet I wanted him even closer.

It all happened so slowly. There was plenty of time for me to pull away. Yet I stood there, motionless as his lips touched mine.

There are hundreds of ways to be kissed, but this?

This transcended them all.

From his soft lips, to the angle of his head as he held my face between both hands—it was perfection.

Anyone could come outside and catch us, but that didn't matter to me. Sinclair Montgomery's lips were on mine.

His tongue slipped into my mouth and a small gasp escaped me. I leaned into him until there was no more space between us. His strong arms wrapped around me.

I had to get home. My husband was waiting. But that didn't matter to me; Sinclair Montgomery was touching me.

Stop right now, my mind screamed. *You have to stop.*

But I really couldn't; this kiss was bigger than me. This kiss was the kind that had the power to intricately weave my and Sinclair's lives together.

My hands reached out and curled around the hem of his shirt. I wanted this to keep going, to never end. To never stop feeling this way. My tongue moved against his and his hands dropped away from my face and firmly gripped my hips. A groan rose from the back of his throat.

My palms were splayed against his stomach, my fingers

stretched apart to feel every cut of muscle hidden beneath his shirt.

It could've gone further. In fact, a few minutes later and I think it would have, but laughter sounded in the distance. It wasn't loud, but it was just enough to jerk the two of us back to reality. We broke apart at the same time.

My lips tingled. I had to stop myself from brushing my fingertips across them. I wanted that kiss back. I wanted to hold on to it and never let it go. Sinclair took a step back, as if he could read my thoughts. I held up a hand. He stopped in his tracks. His hands hung heavily at his sides. My heart whispered that it was all wrong and those hands should be wrapped around me once again.

"Don't say sorry. Don't say that can never happen again," Sinclair said, his voice a ragged whisper.

He ate up the distance between us until it was mere inches.

"I don't have a choice," I replied. "I'm *married*."

"You're married . . . but does that mean you're in love?"

Once upon a time, I could've answered that question within seconds. Love seemed to be the only thing keeping Wes and me together. Love used to be what we lived for. But now? Now it was gone and I didn't know how to get it back.

I didn't answer Sinclair. He looked into my eyes for a long moment and then stepped away. He gave me a brief nod. "Good night, Victoria." The look in his eyes showed that this conversation was far from over.

"Good night, Sinclair."

I watched him get into his car and drive away. I watched the taillights until they completely disappeared.

When I turned around, I walked directly into Wes.

I gasped and placed my hand over my heart and took a deep breath. He had that dead look in his eyes and it sent fear rushing down my spine. "What were you doing?" His voice was calm and so deceptively soft that I knew he saw the kiss.

"Wes—"

"What were you doing?" He advanced slowly.

I took a step back and quickly looked around. The parking lot was filled with cars but everyone was inside. If I screamed loud enough, though, they might hear me. Might.

"I tried calling you tonight and you never fucking answered me."

My throat constricted. Suddenly it was getting harder to breathe. "I was busy."

"Busy with Sinclair? Busy fucking around behind my back?"

My mouth opened but Wes beat me to the chase. "I need to know where you are!" he shouted. "At all times!" He took a step back from me, laced his fingers behind his head, and laughed up at the black sky. "I called and called and you didn't answer."

He wasn't making sense and because of that, I was too afraid to speak. Rationally, I knew I wasn't dealing with a sane person. Whether I comforted him or angered him didn't matter; he would snap regardless. I was stuck between a rock and a hard place.

"Okay, okay," I said soothingly, as if I were talking to a child. I needed to calm him down. To try to defuse the situation and then make a run for it. "I'm sorry I didn't answer your calls, Wes."

"Don't say sorry, Victoria! You're my wife. Mine! I shouldn't have to question what my wife is doing each fucking night!" he screamed.

"Wes—"

"Stop talking!"

Suddenly he was in my face, the anger pouring off him in sheets. I could see that the alpha quality I had found so alluring at the beginning, the one that used to pull me in, had two sides, and now the ugly side was rearing its head. There was nothing attractive about it. It was scary and dangerous and I couldn't get away fast enough. I took a step forward but Wes blocked me.

"First you talk about divorce. Second you mention going back to work. And now you're going behind my back, turning into a fucking whore. What else are you doing, Victoria?"

His fist slammed into my stomach so fast I had no time to protect myself. I wheezed, my hands instinctively moving to my stomach. Wes shoved me back until I hit the car and his fist connected with my ribs this time.

When I was sixteen and first started driving, my brother teasingly said that if I needed protection, to put the length of my keys on the key chain between my fingers and use it as a weapon. I laughed off his comment then, but now it wasn't a bad thought. My eyes opened. I blinked through the blinding pain, only to see my keys on the ground, daring me to pick them up.

"Victoria?" Wes grabbed my chin and jerked my head up until I was forced to look him in the eye. "If you leave me, I'll go after every single person you love." With his other hand he brushed away my tears. "Renee. Your mother. Even Sinclair. All of them gone."

"Why are you doing this?"

He frowned at me in confusion, as if I should already know the answer. "Because if you leave my world, what else do I have?"

Without another word, he walked away.

A hideous image comes to mind where Wes is eating my heart. He's ripping it to pieces and I can feel every single tear as if it's still attached to me.

I know it's horrifying. But the worst thing of all is that it's not too far from the truth. Wes and I were eating at each other instead of building each other up.

All we knew was distraction.

If we continued down this path one of us would be dead.

I don't remember grabbing my keys. I don't remember getting into my car.

I just remember ending up slumped over my steering wheel, crying over the memories of Wes and me during the happier times.

My heart saw all of this and whispered to me: *But Sinclair Montgomery kissed you. Sinclair Montgomery touched you. . . .*

22

November 2015

There's a stain on the ceiling.

It breaks up the fine-fissured surface and makes me re-count the perforated black dots spread across it. I've lain here for an hour, trying to focus my attention on anything but the fear building inside me.

Who am I?
  Who am I?
    Who am I?

I hate the person I'm seeing in my memories. It is excruci-ating, to look back at them. I compare it to being strapped down to a table while your skin is peeled back slowly. You sit there in pain, screaming for it to stop, and it never does. I want to reach through time and shake my past self. I want to tell her all the things she should be doing differently. But I can't.

I rub my eyes and take a deep breath.

This room is sterile and screams of loneliness. The sheets are stiff against my skin and the mattress creaks every time I move. The pillow is lumpy. My neck has a crick in it from a restless night of sleep. How did I ever allow this place to become my home?

Evelyn cries loudly and for the first time, I don't reach for my daughter. I let her lie in her bassinet.

Horrible mother. That's what I'm turning into. Yet even as I acknowledge the truth, I still don't try to amend my wrong. I let her lie there.

My heart feels frozen. Young Victoria, her pain feels so fresh. So raw. I push up my shirt and glance at my ribs, expecting to see bruises in shades of plum and blue. There's nothing. My fingers graze my skin and drift to the left until I find the exact spot where he hit me. I press down into my skin until I feel bone.

Nothing.

But it happened. *Oh, it did happen.*

"Have a good day, Victoria?"

Quickly I sit up in bed. Standing on the opposite side of the room is Wes, leaning against the wall and staring at me curiously. I'm still reeling from today's session. The last person I want to see is him.

"How did you get in here?"

"I've been here the whole time. You didn't hear me come in."

He's lying. He's lying and both of us know it. His words make me jump out of my bed. I tug at my hair and at the very last second stop myself from crying out in frustration. "You haven't been here the whole time." I start to pace, always counting to twenty-five. "I would've seen you."

"Technically, that's not true. There are so many things you haven't noticed."

I pause mid-step. Finally, something we can agree on. "You're right. I really haven't seen things for what they are."

Wes narrows his eyes. He takes a step forward. My first instinct is to take a step back, but I see past Victoria, flinching and cowering. Hiding in fear. I refuse to repeat the past. If he hurts me, I'll scream and one of the nurses will show up.

"I'm remembering things, Wes."

Wes stares right at me. He cocks his head to the side and gives me a blank look. "Like what?"

"How messed up we were." I swallow my fear. "How you hurt me."

He frowns at me. "I treated you like a queen."

"No, you didn't," I whisper fiercely.

"I"—he takes a step forward—"would never"—one more step and he's directly in front of me—"hurt you. Ever."

"That's not true. You hit me here." I point to my cheek. "And here." I lay a hand on my stomach.

"What is that doctor telling you?" Just for a second, part of the venom he threw at me in the past comes out. A flash of anger, his words dripping in hate. It's there for a second and then gone. But I saw it and that's all that matters.

"She's not telling me anything. She's showing me—"

Abruptly, I stop talking. Remembering has put a crack in Wes's masquerade. I can't see him in the same light anymore and that means I can't trust him.

"What were you going to say?"

"Does it matter? You're going to deny everything."

"Of course it matters! You're being fed lies."

"It's not lies!" I scream.

Walking around my bed, I put as much distance between us as I can and grip the edge of Evelyn's bassinet. "You need to go."

"Don't believe them, Victoria."

"Go."

"I've stuck by you when no one else has. Shouldn't that say something to you?"

"Go."

"Someday you're going to regret everything you've accused me of. Someday you'll realize that there's no one in the world who will love you like I do." He shakes his head, looking at me with anger and disappointment. As he brushes past me, my entire body locks up. "Instead of looking at me," he says, "perhaps you should consider looking at yourself. Maybe you're the villain in the story of us. After all, you're the one who's locked away. Not me."

The second he's gone I try to close the window. Aren't these windows impossible to unlock to begin with? It should be a breeze to lock back up. I put all my strength into twisting the lock but it doesn't budge.

I take a deep breath and tap my head against the wall.

This man used to be everything to me, but now I see he's my Achilles' heel. So I cover my ears and scream.

I wake up Evelyn. She screams in fear, but I scream louder.

A nurse runs into my room, looking every which way. "What's wrong?"

"Wes was in here."

Within seconds, her expression relaxes. I want to shake her, make her see the truth. "Victoria, he's not here."

"Yes, he was." Anxiously I rush over to her and grab her hand. She tries to pull away but I tug her close to the window. "He escaped from here and now the window won't lock."

She jerks her hand away from me, shoots me a dirty look, and inspects the window. Furiously, I rub my hands together. Evelyn's wails have died down. A good mom would be comforting her child right now, but this need, this obsession to have someone catch Wes has taken over.

"What did you do to this damn window?" Kate says between grunts. She tugs on the lock and just like me ends up failing to flip it back into place.

"I didn't do this. He jammed the lock!" I point at the lock smiling and she looks at me like I'm truly, positively insane, and I don't care. "Don't you see? This is my proof. He was here."

The nurse drops her hands to her sides and gives me a thorough once-over. I catch the fear in her eyes. "He wasn't here, Victoria."

"Yes, he was! And now he's probably right outside my window, waiting for you to leave just so he can sneak back in."

"I *promise* you, no one's out there, okay?"

She doesn't get it. No one gets it and it doesn't matter how many times I try to explain it to them; they're not willing to listen to what I have to say. She works on the window and after a few minutes, finally gets it to lock. She tugs on the cord and the blinds slam down onto the windowsill, blocking out the clear black sky and full moon.

"He was just there a few minutes ago," I say weakly.

Kate's face drops in pity. "Why don't I get you something to help you sleep?" She reaches out and pats my arm. "Would you like that?"

I jerk out of her grasp. "I don't need medication." It's on the tip of my tongue to tell her I haven't swallowed a single pill in months. "I need you all to believe me."

Kate tries a different approach. "Why don't you lie down? Maybe if you take a quick catnap you'll feel better?"

"I'm not a baby. You can't talk to me as a child."

"Victoria, lie down or I'll get the doctor."

Translation: Either listen to me or the doctor will knock you out with drugs.

Anger festers in me, running through my veins, begging for a way out. But I slowly move to my bed. I lie down in the exact same position I was in just minutes ago.

How? How is that even possible? Time trudges by but then it's gone in the blink of an eye.

I'm so tired of looking like the crazy one. I'm so tired of looking like a liar. As I lie there in bed I know I shouldn't back down to Kate, but I'm too tired to care.

Kate draws the sheets up to my chin like I'm a child and gives me a plastic smile. "Thatta girl."

Like a mummy, I lay there unmoving.

"I'll check up on you in a few minutes."

Tonight, I have no doubt she will.

"If you're still bothered by this tomorrow, maybe you should bring it up with your doctor," she says.

"Maybe," I reply dully.

Kate walks to the door, but before she leaves she looks over her shoulder. "Do you need anything else?"

"No," I whisper.

23

Last night's events trail behind me like a ghost.

I didn't get a wink of sleep and now I'm paying for it. My eyes feel heavy. They keep opening and closing, over and over again. Evelyn didn't sleep much either, but that's my fault. I held her in my arms all night, paranoid that Kate or the night shift doctor would stop by my room for an impromptu visit and either knock me out with medicine or steal my daughter.

The phone rings loudly. Everyone stops talking and glances at it. Reagan, who's been pacing in front of it for the past thirty minutes, pounces.

There are two forms of outside contact: visiting hours and the phone.

Everyone, and I mean *everyone,* vies for the phone. Besides board games and television this is the most coveted piece of entertainment here. It's a beige wall phone with a cord that has been stretched so much over the years it practically skims the floor.

Reagan cradles the receiver between her shoulder and cheek and leans against the wall looking like a teenage girl talking to her crush. In a sugary-sweet voice she says, "Thank you for calling Fairfax Behavioral Health Unit, where we don't condone murder, or thoughts of murder, but the doctors will shove enough pills down your throat to choke a horse. How may I help you?"

She stares down at the floor for a second and then rolls her eyes. She holds the phone away from her, not bothering to cover the speaker, and points to Alice. "It's for you."

Alice stands up. She turns pale. "Who is it?"

"Satan. He wants to know why you're not manning the portal to hell," Reagan replies deadpan.

Alice rolls her eyes and Reagan cracks up laughing until tears are streaming down her face. "Oh, that was good. I needed that. . . . I needed that." Then she glances at the new girl. "Stella!" she screams dramatically. "STELLLA, it's for you!"

A new girl jumps out from her chair and snatches the phone. "God. I'm right here," she hisses before she places the phone next to her ear and faces the wall.

Reagan shrugs and starts to make laps around the room. She's always mischievous, with a gleam in her eyes. But today she's edgy, staring everyone down, looking for a fight.

"I'm so fucking bored!" she announces dramatically as she weaves around the tables.

A few patients look up, but no one really pays attention to her.

She spins a chair backward and straddles it, sitting directly across from me, and points to the wall. "There's something wrong with that clock."

The nurse doesn't even bother to look in the clock's direction. "No, there isn't."

"There is! It was twelve fifteen when I walked in. I'm pretty sure hours have gone by and look. It says only twelve twenty!"

I have to agree with Reagan. If anything it feels like the clock is moving backward just to taunt us.

"I repeat, there's nothing wrong with the clock," replies the nurse. "And if you're really that bored why don't you go to art class. It starts in fifteen."

"Art class?" Reagan claps her hands and gives the nurse a mocking smile. "Enough with all the choices! I'm so excited I'm about to queef out a unicorn riding on a rainbow."

The nurse spins on her heels and walks away.

I keep my eyes glued to the page in front of me. I've been rereading the same page over and over for the past forty minutes, just waiting for the words to string themselves together and for me to slip into the beautiful world of the story. But it's not working; there's a black cloud over my head, leaving me in the foulest mood. I want to lash out at anyone who looks my way. It would probably be in my best interest—and that of everyone around me—if I stayed in my room today, but I can't sit still even if I try.

Normally when I'm this nervous, I have Evelyn to comfort me. To hold and to hug. But for the first time she's with one of the nurses and now I'm starting to regret my decision. It sounded great this morning. Evelyn had spent the entire night wailing in my ear. It didn't matter how many times I comforted her. It was as though she too understood Wes's parting words to me, and now doesn't trust me.

Susan, one of the kind nurses here, offered to watch Evelyn. She said that sometimes moms need a moment to themselves. So I agreed. Her shock was visible. Normally, I would never let anyone take care of Evelyn. But Susan held her arms out, and very gently I placed Evelyn in them. Almost instantly the tears stopped.

The silence was deafening and since then all I can hear are Wes's words echoing around me: *"Maybe you're the villain in the story of us. . . . Maybe you're the villain in the story of us. . . . Maybe you're the villain in the story of us. . . ."*

Reagan leans back until her chair taps against Xander's. His reason for being at Fairfax is unknown. I just know that he talks to pretty much everyone and he's been here longer than I have. Reagan says none too quietly, "What are you doing?"

"Quietly reading!" Xander shouts back. "You should try it sometime."

"You guys," a nurse warns. "Keep it down."

Reagan catches me staring. Her chair lands on all four legs loudly, making me flinch. She rests her chin on the back of the chair and stares at me. "Whatcha doin'?"

"Watching you talk to Xander."

"How long have you been here?" she asks out of nowhere.

"A long time," I reply tersely.

"How long?" she repeats. "Four years? Five? Two? Gimme a ballpark figure."

If this is her way of striking up a conversation she needs to do better. Anger simmers inside me, just begging to rise to the surface. I try my hardest to push it down. "Does it really matter?"

"Of course it does. One month in this place is the equivalent of a decade in prison."

I bite down on my tongue to keep from saying something I know I'll regret later. It's obvious I don't want to talk to Reagan. Yet she stays put, and stares at me.

"How's your daughter?"

"Fine."

"Where is she?"

I sit up straight and glare at her. "With the nurse."

"So not only is Fairfax a loony bin, it's also a fucking day-care center. How quaint."

I don't respond.

"We should have a sign made for outside. I can see it now." She spreads her hands in the air, as if a rainbow will appear between them. "*'Fairfax: Making your kids crazy one day at a time.'*"

Reagan's words run alongside Alice's perfectly: "Fairfax is no place for a baby."

The very thought makes my anger grow.

I should take deep breaths. Smile and pretend she's not there. But my world is in a downward spiral and I'd love to wrap my hands around Reagan's neck just to get her to shut up.

"I'm dying to know why you're here," she says.

Before I go, I place my hands on the table and lean in. "The cardinal rule at Fairfax is to never ask someone how they got here, why they're here, and how long they've been here. And something tells me this isn't the first time you've been to a place like Fairfax. Surely you know the rules of the game by now."

I know my words touch a nerve. Her eyes slightly widen before she smiles slowly. "That's a fucked-up thing to say."

I shrug. There's a good chance I might be sorry later, but not right now.

"Here's why I think you're here. You wanna know?"

I walk away and say over my shoulder, "No."

"I think you're here because you're weak!" she shouts. I stop walking. The blood drains from my face. I don't turn around but I can feel Reagan's smile on my back.

"Yes, that's right, you're weak. You walk around like you own this fucking place, thinking your facsimile life is perfect, but the truth is you're weak and spineless. You're a *victim*."

Victim. Reagan spits the word out like it's poison.

I can't take it anymore and whip my body around. "Shut up."

Reagan smiles and jumps out of her chair. She stands behind another patient. "Talks to her hand. Doesn't know the days. Crazy."

She runs to the next table, slides into an open seat, and points to a woman staring at the clock. "She thinks the year is 1993. Kurt Cobain is still singing and Clinton is president. She's a goner."

Then she slowly stands and looks me in the eyes. "But you? You see you. You speak. You are here. Yet you cower to everyone around you. A single challenge becomes a roadblock and you give up. All you do is carry that stupid baby around—"

Reagan is crazy. Reagan is loud, always making jokes and pointing out the problems with everyone else just so no one will look at her and take notice of her issues. I know all this and yet I rush back over to where she stands. I've taken the bait.

"Shut up!"

"You can change her stupid fucking diaper. You can feed her and sing her all the nursery rhymes you want. But it won't change a thing. You want to know why?" She leans in close. "Because you're a bad mom."

Xander swears under his breath. He's not laughing. Susan is in the nurses' station but she stands slowly from her chair, watching Reagan with a critical eye. Alice smiles.

Do not take the bait, I tell myself. *It's a trap.*

But I can't. Two words keep echoing in my head: *Bad mom. Bad mom. Bad mom.* They become louder until it feels like they're being shouted into my ear with a megaphone.

Reagan sees my turmoil. She laughs, slowly at first, and soon she's clutching her gut, tears streaming down her face she's laughing so hard.

The color red leaks into my vision. It's all I can see. The anger inside me, which has been simmering for days, finally comes to the surface. It bursts so abruptly that I have no time to think about my actions.

I climb over the table and tackle Reagan to the floor. I've taken her off guard and knock the wind out of her. I use it to my advantage.

Shouts and screams echo around me. Chairs scrape against the floor. There's the shuffle of people moving. Yet I don't stop. My hands wrap around her throat and I squeeze as hard as I can.

"What about you, Reagan?" I pant. "Tell me your fucked-up story."

Her face is turning blue. I keep squeezing, even when I see the fear in her eyes. I press my thumbs deeper into her skin.

"Tell me what you're running from," I demand.

I'm going to let go. I swear. I just want to show her that she's gone too far. But someone's hands land on my shoulders. "Victoria!" Sinclair shouts behind me. Where did he come from? "Let go."

He tries to pry my hands away from her, but I have the strength of twenty men.

"Tell me!" I scream at her. Reagan weakly slaps at my hands. Her legs kick beneath me.

It takes him two more tries before Sinclair finally pulls me back. He holds my wrists together, behind my back, like I'm a criminal.

My heart is pounding against my ribs. I can't catch my breath, and you know what? It feels good.

"You know nothing about me, you stupid bitch!" I yell.

Reagan sits up with the help of two nurses. Color slowly comes back into her face. She greedily sucks up all the air she can and then starts laughing uncontrollably. "Bravo! You've come alive, Victoria."

"You are a fucking psychopath."

Reagan looks wounded by my words. I smile breathlessly and open my mouth to say more. I have hundreds of insults lined up, just waiting to be said. Who knew I have so much pent-up anger?

I'm ripped out of Sinclair's grasp. Two nurses drag me farther away from Reagan. I kick my legs, trying to fight them. Sinclair stares at me with pain in his eyes and I know it's because of me. I brought that pain to him. I start to panic. He's seen me snap. He'll never come back. I'll be alone when I'm just now seeing what we were.

"Sinclair," I say. He says nothing. "Sinclair. I'm sorry."

The nurses push me down the hall, toward the women's ward.

"Sinclair, I'm sorry!" I scream.

The doors open, and with all my strength I turn to escape the nurses' grasp. But they have a firm hold on me. The doors slam shut and Sinclair's face is gone.

I go limp and let the nurses drag me into my room. They put me on the bed and I stare up at the ceiling. I feel numb.

Before the door shuts, one of the nurses tentatively asks, "Do you want Evelyn?"

I turn my head.

There should be a desperate urge inside me to see my child, there should, but there isn't. I picture holding her and every time I look down at her face, there's nothing there. What if she was there during the fight? In my dark haze of anger would I have still protected her? I want to say yes. But something holds me back. I've never had anger that strong and powerful that I become a completely different person.

Maybe I did the right thing by handing her over to the nurse. That's the only silver lining in this entire ordeal.

"No."

The door shuts behind the nurse and I curl into a ball.

I feel myself coming apart at the seams.

24

I still want to hurt something . . . someone. Anything I can get my hands on. At some point in the afternoon, the nurse brings Evelyn into the room.

She's been crying nonstop. I walk over to her bassinet. And stare down at her.

Bad mom, bad mom, bad mom . . .

I cover my ears, so desperate to get Reagan's voice to stop. I will take the medication the nurses give.

I'll do anything.

I start to pace the room, carefully counting my steps. My room is small. I never make it to twenty-four steps. I scared everyone in the dayroom. I know it. Angry outbursts are a dime a dozen, but they're never caused by me. If the others could just slip into my skin and feel the fear running through me, they'd understand.

"What did you do?" a voice says behind me.

I whirl around and find Wes sitting in my rocking chair. As he moves back and forth it creaks ominously. This is the last thing I need right now. I still feel like I'm back in the dayroom, reliving Reagan's words. I'm close to losing my mind and Wes might just take me over the edge.

I can't escape him. No matter where I go or what I do, he's there, always watching me. Always.

"Oh God," I groan and drop my face into my hands. "Leave me alone," I whisper over and over and over.

"I'm afraid that's not possible."

I lift my head. "How did you get in here?"

Wes stops rocking and stands up to his full height. He's not smiling. "How do you think?"

My fingers curl into my palms. I keep pressing, until I feel my nails digging into my skin. I don't back down when Wes looms over me. "You made me come here."

I take four steps backward. I close my eyes and remind myself to breathe. "No, I didn't," I say.

Suddenly Wes is in front of me. His hands are on my shoulders. "Yes, you did. Why do you think I come here?"

If someone came into my room right now, they would see a man in love. A man concerned and worried. But it's a role that Wes is playing. Trust me, you can't believe him. It's an act.

"You're messing with me again," I say.

"Why would I do that, Victoria?"

Too many words and voices are being thrown my way. And not one at a time. It's all at once and I can't think.

"I love you, Victoria."

I jerk his arms off me and hurry to the other side of the room. Wes doesn't follow me. He looks hurt that I want to get away from him.

"Tell me what's wrong, Victoria."

"Stop saying my name!" I yell. I'm losing my composure. Quick. "You're trying to make me look crazy." I point a finger at him. "But you're the crazy one here. Not me."

At first he doesn't respond, just stares at me with those empty eyes. And then he walks toward me. My body stiffens. I take a step back and another until my shoulders hit the wall. He keeps his eyes on me the whole time and doesn't stop until we're a hairsbreadth apart. No one else would cut through my personal space like this.

No one else but him.

He places his hands behind me. He ducks his head and leans in so we're eye to eye. "There's your side, my side, and the truth." He lifts a single brow and smirks. "Which one do you think your nurses and doctors will believe?"

I hate him. I hate him for being right.

"Why did you attack that girl?"

"You saw that?"

"Of course. She said you were a bad mom." His lips twitch and I know he's going to say more.

I can't bear it. I cover my ears.

Wes yanks my hands away. "I'm talking to you! Listen."

"You think I'm a bad mom too, don't you?" I whisper.

"Did I say that, Victoria?"

"No. But you're thinking it."

"I think you're losing it and you're lashing out at me." I open my mouth and Wes covers it with his hand. I instantly freeze up. "Victoria, I just want to make sure you're okay," he says. I don't believe a word that comes out of his mouth. All of it is mind games.

He moves toward Evelyn's bassinet. I try to intercept him but he's too quick. He peers into her bassinet and smiles. It doesn't reach his eyes.

"What are you doing? Leave her alone."

Wes ignores me and picks up a book from my nightstand. *Goodnight Moon*. It's Evelyn's favorite and always makes her fall fast asleep. Well, it used to. Back when she used to love me.

But still, I don't like Wes holding the book. It feels like he's trying to slip into a memory he has no business being in.

He opens the book and flips through the pages, reading aloud.

Goodnight . . . goodnight . . . goodnight . . .

He stops and smiles at Evelyn. *"Goodnight nobody."* His words hang in the air, swarming around my head, ready to choke me.

I snatch the book out of his hands. I'm shaking so badly I can barely move. "You need to go," I whisper darkly. "Now."

Wes doesn't move.

"Go." My voice gets louder. "Before I scream for the nurse to come."

Maybe he can see it in my eyes that I mean every word I'm saying; he takes a step back from me. "God offers to every mind its choice between truth and repose. Take which you please; you can never have both. Remember that, Emerson's words."

I flinch.

"I'll see you later," Wes says. But my eyes are closed, hands over my ears. The damage is done, though, and all my mind replays is: "Take which you please; you can never have both."

I slide down the wall, my knees curled close to my chest. Beside me Evelyn cries and cries and cries in her bassinet.

I can't make it stop and cry out in frustration, covering my ears. Soon my cries turn into groans.

Slowly but surely I feel myself splitting apart at the seams. I can't keep doing this. Staying here. Listening to Wes. Hearing my daughter wail.

It's all too much.

Doubt is starting to creep into my brain. It wants to take up residency. It wants to build a little town and invite all its friends: fear, paranoia, sadness, pain. I start to hum loudly.

This is how crazy begins. It creeps up on you very slowly, tapping your shoulder. It makes you turn around in fear. And then, when you think you're in the clear, it attacks. It grabs ahold of you and drags you down, down, down. . . .

25

"Knock, knock."

I lift my head just as Dr. Calloway walks into the room. She carries in a tray with food. Dinner. On the tray, in the corner, is a white paper cup with my medicine.

She gives me a tentative smile as she places the tray on the small end table next to my bed. I glance between her and the food, waiting for what she wants to say, but she doesn't say a word. Just sits on the edge of my bed.

The silence is going to drive me crazy. I want to shake her and ask: "Why are you here?"

I should tell her that Wes was in here, but I'm afraid I'm pushing it. I'm bracing myself for my "punishment," which could be anything from staying in my room, to taking away my points, or banning me from having visitors. But I'm ready to fight back. I didn't do anything wrong. I reacted just like any other person would.

Evelyn finally fell asleep. Her cries still rang in my ears. My nerves were shot and to the point of falling apart.

But all I can think about right now is where Reagan is. It seems unfair to me that I suffer in silence while she gets off scot-free. So I ask Dr. Calloway.

"Reagan's in her room too. The fight wasn't one sided. But—"

"But I'm the one who touched her first," I cut in.

Dr. Calloway nods and looks at me with concern. "Exactly."

"So am I in trouble?"

Please say no. Please say no. Please say no.

"Well, I'm not thrilled at what you did. Judging from the look on your face, I'd say neither are you. So you'll lose a few points."

I lift my head and when she says nothing else I lift a single brow.

"Library and outdoor time will be revoked for a week."

She and I both know that she's letting me off easy. I can't remember the last time I willingly went to the library.

"You'll still receive visitors and be able to go to the rec room."

My eyes blink fast. I keep waiting for the other shoe to drop, but that's it. I think my disbelief is written across my face because Dr. Calloway quickly speaks up.

"If I thought you were a danger to yourself or anyone else, I wouldn't be this lenient."

"My life is dislocated," I confess. "Memories are ripped apart and scattered. I'm so scared that you might not be able to fix me."

"The second you let your pain become your identity is the moment you should be scared. What I saw in the rec room was not a broken person. But maybe you're right. Maybe I really can't fix you, but that doesn't mean I'm going to stop trying. Victoria, I can't think of a single person in this world not crushed beneath the weight of life. You're going to be just fine. I know it."

It's so incredibly easy in this place to feel locked up and alone, but I finally feel as if I have someone on my side. I swallow back my tears. "Thank you," I whisper.

She smiles and shrugs and points to the tray. "You should eat up. Dinnertime ends in fifteen minutes."

I devour everything on the tray. I don't even look at what I'm eating; it's just the action of it. So normal and routine. The whole time, Dr. Calloway remains seated. All that's left is the pills. I don't take them, and I hope Dr. Calloway doesn't notice it.

I know she's not sitting here because she wants to. She has something else she needs to say. I drop my spoon onto the now-empty tray and stare at her expectantly.

"Before I leave I wanted to know if you'd like to see more photos." My mouth opens but Dr. Calloway quickly adds, "You don't have to say yes. If you're not comfortable because of what just happened . . . I understand."

I answer without a second thought. "Yes."

After what just happened, this might be a really bad idea. My mind is already being stretched and pulled apart. My emotions are at an all-time high. My relationship with my daughter seems to weaken by the day. I should probably stop right now.

Stop it all.

But this, seeing my past, is like a drug to me. Very slowly, I'm feeling the ties between Young Victoria and the Present Victoria tightening, bringing us closer together.

Dr. Calloway pulls out another stack of photos and my pulse picks up. It's part fear and part excitement. I wasn't expecting this at all. There's no time to brace myself.

26

There's no handbook or guide on how to leave your husband. No tips. No "Five Easy Steps." I felt like a fish out of water, floundering and lost, but I couldn't give up. If I left this marriage, I'd be leaving with my eyes wide open, prepared and ready for anything that he might shoot my way.

Wes wouldn't lie down and play dead.

He'd fight. Hard.

So I started out slowly telling myself three important things.

I have to be careful.

I have to outwit him.

I have to survive.

And now it was time for step one.

Barefoot, I padded toward Wes's office and stared down at the keypad directly above the doorknob. When we moved in Wes was adamant about installing cameras and a security system. The cameras were angled toward the backyard and the front door, with another leading toward the garage. Every time the front doors opened or closed, a beep would ring out once. When the doors were unlocked, you had twenty seconds to put in the key code or else the alarm would go off.

I punched in the code for the front and back doors: 049319.

It didn't work.

I tried the same code two more times. After the third failed attempt, the screen went blank. Then four black dots flashed across it and the alarm went off. It was so loud my ears started to ring.

The only time I'd heard the alarm was when the security system was installed. The man who set it up explained that the second it went off, the security company would call either Wes or me. Right now, Wes was in court. His phone was off and all calls were being forwarded to his secretary.

I waited. Twenty seconds went by. Then a minute. Soon I started to doubt whether the company would even call, then finally my phone lit up. I answered on the third ring.

"Hello?"

A cheerful woman named Terri told me they had a security alert on 4376 Bellamy Road. Was everything okay?

"Yes, that was me. Everything's fine, everything's fine. I'm

Mrs. Donovan. My husband is at work and he needed me to pick up some papers in his office. I thought I knew the security code, but clearly I got it wrong. I'm so sorry," I said in my most sincere voice.

"It's no problem; this happens all the time."

Thankfully, the alarm was turned off.

She went through the standard security questions: the name of your first dog. Mother's maiden name. The color of your first car. I got them all right.

"He keeps meaning to have the passcode changed, but you know men," I said with a laugh. "My husband would lose his head if it wasn't attached to him."

The woman chuckled. "Oh, don't I know it."

I smiled. The tension in my shoulders faded. I was so close to getting the passcode. I could feel it.

"The passcode I have right now for alarms one and two is: 049319. Is that correct?"

"Yes."

"And the passcode for alarm three is: 78910424."

Bingo.

That was the one I needed.

Quickly I scribbled down the numbers. It was my birth date backward. "Now, is that the main security code?"

"Let me double-check." The line went quiet as Terri hurriedly typed.

My pulse quickened; I knew I was so close to getting what I wanted. It was almost too good to be true.

Terri came back on the line. "Yes. Those are all the codes."

"Thank you so much, Terri. You have no idea how much you've helped me."

"You're very welcome. Besides, where would a husband be without his wife?"

"Isn't that the truth," I replied, with the biggest smile on my face.

I hung up and stared down at my screen, still smiling.

Where would a husband be without his wife, indeed?

Find out the code to Wes's home office.

I crossed it off the list and hurried to his office.

Even though we'd lived in our house for more than a year, I'd been in his office only about four times. Other than Wes, the maid was the only person allowed in there and even then he watched everything like a hawk.

I punched in the code the woman gave me. It was my birthday backward, but I still double-checked the numbers before I pressed enter.

The screen went blank. Fear paralyzed me. Did I get it wrong? But then a green light flashed and the lock clicked. The door opened slowly. I held my breath as I stepped through the door, waiting for some alarm or booby trap to go off. I wouldn't have put it past Wes.

But there was not a sound.

Quickly, I took stock of the room. The dark blue curtains were opened, letting light in. It slanted across his desk and onto the floor. Behind the massive desk, his diplomas hung on the wall. Not a single frame was crooked.

The clock on the fireplace mantel ticked softly. On the large desk, in the left-hand corner of it, were two pictures: one with the two of us on our wedding day and the other of just me. I halted my search to pick up the picture. I remembered that moment. We had been dating for a mere three months and were spending the weekend with my mother for the Fourth of July. It was brutally hot. In the picture, my legs are dipped in the water and my palms lie flat against the towel behind me. Wes came up suddenly, called out my name, and took the photo. Even with my sunglasses you can see how crazy in love I was and how I thought that what we had would last forever.

But look at me now. I'm hiding bruises and sneaking around behind my husband's back.

I glanced at the built-in mahogany bookshelves across from me. There wasn't a speck of dust on them. Not that I expected there to be; Wes was meticulous, almost verging on OCD. Everything had a place and when it wasn't in said place, he got irritated. I added dust to the ever-growing list of things that seemed to set him off.

All the shelves were lined with books. My fingers grazed across their spines. I was doubtful as to whether he had read most of these books. Since I'd known him he'd never been a voracious reader. A part of me wouldn't have been surprised if they had been there for display. I stared at the titles carefully. The spines that hadn't been cracked, I pulled out. The pages of each were pristine, never dog-eared. The last book I selected was a book on how to keep a marriage alive. The irony wasn't lost on me. I made sure everything was back in its place, shut the door behind me and reset the alarm.

Not once did I ever think I'd be going behind my husband's back. But I truly felt my options were limited. Our relationship was down to the bare bones. There was nothing left and I needed to be ready for whatever came next. I needed to upstage him, to out-think him every time.

I knew it wasn't much. I knew it was nothing to celebrate, but I could feel it. The tides were changing. Very slowly, I was taking my life back.

27

August 2014

Sunny or cloudy.

Indoors or outdoors.

It didn't matter. I kept my sunglasses on wherever I went.

The harsh reality of my marriage revealed itself in my eyes. I saw it every time I looked in the mirror. Sometimes I wanted to drape towels over every mirror in the house so I couldn't see the truth. And if I could barely look at myself, why would I want anyone else to see me like this?

But today I had an actual reason to wear them. There was not a cloud in sight. It was the kind of day where the sky looks so perfect, you want to touch it.

I brushed the sweat from the back of my neck and hurried into the library.

I couldn't remember the last time I was there. Maybe when I was nine or ten? My mother and I would roam aisles and aisles of books. I would pick out a stack of them and go to the small reading corner for kids and lose myself in the stories. I loved the peace that it always brought. That same peace instantly returned. My shoulders relaxed. In here I felt safe from the pain that seemed to follow me wherever I went.

The librarian, an older man, said hi. I gave him a smile. When I didn't take off my glasses he gave me a strange look and I quickened my steps to escape his stare, reminding myself that a stare is better than pity. I walked through the rows, looking for the gardening book Renee suggested. I finally found the right aisle. The lighting was poor and I had no choice but to take off my glasses.

Kneeling down, I pulled the book off the shelf.

Very swiftly, my hobby for gardening was becoming a passion. I hated being idle. I hated going to bed knowing I'd done nothing productive, but in my garden I felt useful. In my garden I could chat with Renee and relax. I crouched down and flipped through the pages.

"Victoria?"

My body locked up. Lately, anytime I heard my name I braced myself for something bad. I continued to peruse the books, hoping the person would just give up and walk away.

"Victoria?" the female voice repeated.

I closed my eyes and took a deep breath before I stood up and turned around.

"Taylor?" I asked in disbelief.

I couldn't believe it was her. She lived in the same town as me, but she might as well have been living on the other side of the world. She'd changed so much. Her blond hair was cut into a short bob. The energy that she used to possess had slightly dimmed. She looked tired and a little frazzled, but she looked happy, and that was all that mattered. Both hands were curled around a stroller that held a sleeping baby girl. A diamond ring glinted from her left hand. Taylor had a family and I didn't even know.

She smiled and gave me a hug and all I could think about is how I could put my glasses back on without her noticing.

"It's so good to see you after so long," she said as we pulled back to look at each other.

"Clearly you've been busy," I said, gesturing toward the stroller with a smile. "I didn't know you were even seeing anyone."

"I started seeing this guy after you left the hospital. It was a whirlwind romance. We got engaged and, well"—she stared down lovingly at her baby—"we had a little surprise."

My smile was starting to hurt, but I didn't let it fall, for fear that it wouldn't come back. "What's her name?"

"Hayley."

"She's adorable," I whispered.

"What about you? Are you still trying for a baby?"

I should've expected her question. I should've had an answer ready and waiting, but instead I was caught off guard, frantically thinking of a reply. "Oh, well . . . we're still trying," I lied. "We figured if it happens it happens and if it doesn't we'll enjoy the practice."

I laughed lightly and Taylor joined me. For a second, I felt normal. Like the former version of myself.

My shame was strong, staking its claim on my pride and

dignity. It didn't stop there though. No, it oozed from my pores and wrapped itself around me like a coiled snake.

It controlled me.

"Well, enjoy the quiet now while it's still there."

"Oh, we are." I tucked a piece of hair behind my ear and shifted from foot to foot, anxious to wrap up this conversation as soon as possible.

"How are you and Wes?"

"We're good . . . we're good." I gave her another bright smile.

Taylor frowned slightly as the most uncomfortable silence circled us. She gave me that nurse stare. The one that I had used so many times before. For a second, I thought she could sense that I was trying to hide something.

I was terrified that she was going to ask more questions, but I was saved by her baby. Hayley stirred and Taylor swooped into action, giving her daughter a pacifier and me an apologetic smile. "I should probably be going. In a few minutes Hayley will be wailing if she doesn't get a bottle."

I nodded as if I completely understood. "It was good seeing you," I said.

She backed the stroller out of the small aisle and gave me a small smile. "You too."

When she walked away I waited a few seconds, just in case she turned around, but she didn't. I slumped against the bookshelf and took a deep breath.

Seeing her again lit a small fire in me. It was nothing. Barely noticeable. It could die out at any minute. But at least it was something. I hurried over to the computers before I lost my nerve.

You can do this, my mind chanted. *You were once like Taylor—strong and confident—and you can become that again.*

It was extremely quiet in the computer section. Some guy in his midtwenties occupied one of the machines. I made sure to keep a good amount of distance from him. Not that he would even notice. He had earbuds in, nodding his head along to the beat of some song.

I gave him one last look and then got to work.

The days of using my laptop at home were long gone. I didn't trust Wes not to go through it and look for anything he could use against me.

So I went here to look up anything important. I pulled a small notebook out of my purse and grabbed a pen and flipped through the pages. I had the numbers and addresses of some of the best lawyers in the surrounding areas.

I would glean information from multiple message boards on how to leave an abusive spouse. Some pages would give you warning signs of an abusive relationship, but I was far past that.

If I was going to leave Wes, I wanted to have all my bases covered so no matter what he did, I was ready.

28

September 2014

Since the morning my mother came over, things had been strained.

I didn't want to have another conversation revolving around my relationship with Wes and I sensed she didn't want to know any more than she did. Doing so would mean confronting something that was outside the lines of what she saw as a perfect marriage.

But tonight she asked to have dinner with me and I relented. My secret was safe with Renee, but I thought there was always going to be a side of me that wanted to tell my mother everything and have her unfailing support.

That was never going to happen, though.

The whole dinner at the restaurant, she talked about her friends and the tedious problems in their lives. It all went in one ear and out the other because, deep within my purse, my phone kept buzzing. I didn't want to reach down and press IGNORE, much less answer it.

Without checking, I knew all the calls were from Wes.

"You've been so quiet tonight. How are you?"

I chewed my food as slowly as possible, trying to stall for time. "I'm great," I finally said.

"How is everything with you and Wes?" My mother presented the question so innocently, but I knew that was the only reason why she wanted to have dinner with me.

For her sake, I wanted to lie and say everything was fine. That we'd never been better or more in love. It would sound right. It would sound perfect, so I said just that.

She beamed. "I knew things would get better. I knew it." She patted my hand. "I told you couples go through rough patches."

All I could do was nod.

Months had passed since Wes's last outburst, but that had done nothing to change the apprehension and fear that was living inside of me. Like a pair of squatters, they made themselves comfortable, showing no signs of leaving anytime soon.

Soon our plates were cleared and an awkward silence hung between us. It's the kind with unsaid words lingering on the tip of your tongue and refusing to come out. My mother could feel it. She sighed loudly and smiled brightly. "It's getting pretty late. I should be going."

I wasn't going to point out that it was only nine thirty, because I was anxious myself to end this uncomfortable dinner.

We walked out of the restaurant together and outside. The black sky was clear, with a smattering of stars gleaming down at us. A couple walked past, arm in arm and clearly in love. I was tempted to stop them and tell them they should appreciate the happy times, which might not last forever. Underneath the portico, my mother turned and gave me a hug. "I am so happy that things are getting better between you and Wes."

Oh, if only she knew the truth. If only she knew that my heart was drifting further from Wes each day and in the direction of Sinclair. Our kiss was seared into my memory. Sometimes all I could think about was the protection I felt with his arms around me.

I was starting to believe that I would only ever feel that way with Sinclair.

My mom and I parted ways with promises to call each other, even though I had no intention of doing that. As I walked across the parking lot, my body started to shake. I gripped my car keys so tightly they made indentations in my palm. The night after the party haunted me. I could never shake the feeling that someone was always watching me. It didn't matter that things were fine at the moment, because I was not.

I hurried to my car and when I slid into the driver's seat, I instinctively locked the door and took a deep breath. It was then that I pulled out my phone. I had sixty missed calls.

Twenty-one texts. And six voicemails. Every single one was from Wes.

I took a deep breath and quickly texted him: *Be home soon*.

His reply was instant: *Okay*.

The drive home felt like torture; all I could think about was what was in store for me when I got there. Maybe I'd luck out. Maybe he wasn't home. And if I was really reaching for the sky, he might be out all night.

I drove as slowly as possible and even took the scenic route. I didn't turn on my phone. I didn't want to see how many more times he'd call.

When I pulled up into our driveway, I stayed perfectly still, listening to the engine tick. Our street was quiet. Cars were parked in their garages. Lights were on and blinds were shut. I felt the peace seeping from those massive houses.

No so long ago, I looked at our own house with awe and happiness. I saw it as a blank slate. A chance to start over and create a happy life, with a happy little family. The American dream.

And now I could barely glance at it. My feet dragged toward the back porch. I didn't want to go inside. I didn't know what awaited me.

As I opened the back door, I told myself that if it was bad, I didn't have to stay there. I could leave.

I can leave.

I can leave.

I can leave.

Every light on the first floor was off, instantly putting me on guard. Instinctively, I reached out, my fingers crawling over the wall until I flipped on the light switch.

"Wes?" I called tentatively.

"Upstairs!" he shouted. His tone was light, even friendly. I took a deep breath and tossed my keys on the counter. They slid across the smooth surface and hit the mail. It was a small stack, filled mostly with bills. I flipped through them and stopped when I got to an envelope with my name on it. The handwriting was feminine. My name was written with a flourish, as though someone had written it many times before. There was no return address. I flipped the envelope around and broke the seal. There was no note, but there were dozens of Polaroids of a brunette. If I had a doppelganger in this world, I was staring at her right now. Brown hair. Same build. Everything.

She was in an array of poses, wearing barely there lingerie or completely nude. In most pictures her eyes were closed. In some her eyes were open but there was a glassy look there, as though she had been drugged.

I peered closely at the rug in the foreground of the picture, trying to figure out where I recognized it from. When it finally clicked into place, I couldn't breathe. I let the pictures fall from my fingers.

These were taken at Wes's office at work.

There was nothing, absolutely nothing, that could have prepared me for this. It felt like I had just been punched in the gut.

Slowly, I gathered the photos into a stack. I felt dirty touching them, as if I were tampering with evidence. I was past the point of being angry. My steps were whisper quiet as I walked up the stairs, the pictures practically burning in my hands.

As I walked down the hall, slowly inching toward the master bedroom, I tried to think of what I should say to Wes, because right then I was speechless. I had no idea where to start. I didn't know how he'd react. Wes reminded me of a ticking time bomb, ready to go off at any second. There was no way to predict when, why, or how he would blow up. I just had to be ready.

When I entered the bedroom, I found Wes sitting in the tan overstuffed chair angled toward the TV. The end table beside him was littered with paper files. A few were even spread out across the floor, like missing puzzle pieces. Wes took off his glasses and smiled that charming smile that could allow him to get away with murder.

"How was your dinner?" he asked.

My blood ran cold. I couldn't have smiled even if I tried. I felt so much hatred it threatened to choke me.

Wes's smile faded. He shut his laptop and gave me a concerned look. "What's wrong?"

I shoved the pictures between us as if they were a live grenade. "I got this in the mail."

He frowned and stood up and grabbed the pictures. He scanned only the first few. His face paled.

"Do you know her?" I asked carefully, when all I really wanted to do was claw his eyes out.

His jaw clenched. I could see the gears moving in his mind. He tried to hand them back to me. I didn't take them. "Who sent these to you?" he asked.

"Answer my question first: Do you know her?"

"She's a client of mine."

My eyes widened. Wes swallowed the distance between us, but I held my hands out.

"Victoria, she's my client but I would never . . ." He waved the pictures between us. "I would never do this."

I didn't believe a single word he was saying. For the first time my fear took a backseat to my anger. I wasn't going to back down. "Why were they sent to me?"

Wes looked genuinely hurt by my question. "I don't know!"

I dropped my face into my hands. If I needed any proof that this marriage was over, it was this. But that didn't make the pain any easier; there's a big difference between knowing the truth and accepting it.

"Victoria, you have to believe me." Wes's hands landed on my shoulders. With my eyes shut I could picture the old Wes I fell in love with. Old Wes was the very reason why my heart felt like it was slowly splitting apart. Old Wes was the person my heart latched itself on to.

I ducked beneath his arms. I couldn't be here right now. I hurried down the stairs. My only thought was to get the hell out of that house. To where, I really didn't know. I just needed to process everything.

"Victoria!" he shouted behind me. "Stop running!"

I didn't stop. I grabbed my purse and keys on the counter and continued to the back door. My hand curled around the doorknob. The door opened an inch and then Wes slammed it. He grabbed my arm and whirled me around. My back hit the door.

He didn't look crazy or wild. But he was angry.

"Let me go." Inside, my heart was beating like a drum, but I kept my voice even, trying to conceal my fear.

"Let me explain. You're not even giving me a moment to talk."

"Because there's nothing to explain. The pictures kind of said it all, didn't they?"

For a second, his eyes flared. His grip tightened. But his hands dropped. He took a step back from me. Within seconds, my hand curled around the knob. "I can't be around you."

"Where are you going?"

"I don't know . . . my mom's probably."

He followed me out the door, hot on my heels. I hated having my back turned to him. I felt wide open for him to attack me.

"Victoria." I rolled down the window and stared at him blankly. "I love you," he said.

"You have the strangest way of showing it," I whispered.

29

My hands were shaking as I turned off the engine. I stared straight ahead at the empty street. Bikes were on front lawns. Cars were parked. A few porch lights were on. Lamps glowed inside. A few people had their curtains and blinds open, welcoming everyone to look into their lives, but most were closed.

Somewhere down the street someone was dribbling a basketball. This street was cozy. Like you could pull up and move in to your forever home.

I loved it.

I had no business here, but I couldn't have driven away even if I tried. My body felt weary and depleted of energy.

But being this close to his house already made my tension dissolve.

With a deep breath I opened my door and stared at his house. It was surprisingly modest. I'd always pictured something grand. Like the houses he builds. But his was a simple two-story bungalow. The front porch was small, with no furniture. I locked my door and fought the urge to run up the path. I wanted to blend in. Make it look like I belonged there and had in fact been there my entire life.

My heels echoed loudly on the tongue-and-groove porch floor. To me it sounded like bullets leaving a chamber. A warning that I needed to leave right this second.

I rang the doorbell. And then, for good measure, I knocked loudly on the door. A few seconds later the door opened, revealing Sinclair.

He opened up the screen door and I quickly stepped inside before I could lose my courage. It was less of a bachelor pad than I expected. The walls were painted a tasteful brown. Two tan couches faced a big flat-screen television. To the right I could see the stairs. Up ahead the hallway extended back toward what I assumed were extra rooms.

"What's going on? Are you okay?" Sinclair shut the door and turned to face me. My mouth opened yet not a single word came out.

"Seriously, what's wrong?"

He took a step closer and I snapped out of my haze. I didn't say hi. I didn't say anything. I just wrapped my arms around his neck and molded my body against his.

I'd done my best not to give in to my feelings. I'd spent

countless hours reminding myself that Sinclair Montgomery was something that would never happen, telling myself that it was wrong to feel this way about someone who wasn't my husband.

But I just didn't give a damn anymore. Something had been set free in me. What that was, I didn't know, but I liked it.

I sealed my lips across his. He was momentarily stunned, stumbling back a few steps until his back hit the wall. But within seconds he was responding, moaning into my mouth, his tongue gliding against mine. It was all happening so fast, but not fast enough.

It was madness, this kiss. Just when I thought I'd had enough and had sated my desires, I got a second wind. If I didn't stop now, our kisses wouldn't be enough for me. But there was no stopping me now. My hands were frantic, maybe even a bit desperate. They moved over his broad shoulders, down his arms, across his stomach.

And then, out of nowhere, Sinclair put a stop to it. He pushed himself away and dragged his hands through his hair. His internal struggle was apparent in the way his eyes darted between me and the door. There was a torturous second when I was afraid it was over.

Then he charged toward me and cradled my face in his hands. "Tell me no and this stops right now."

My hands dropped to his narrow waist. They lingered before they drifted up his chest. "I can't," I whispered.

"Then you're mine tonight."

In one fell swoop he was kissing and touching me. He held my body tight, one hand banded around my waist, the other curling around the back of my head. I liked how tightly he was holding me. It was an affirmation that he needed me, needed *this* just as much as I did.

We moved out of the kitchen. My blood was roaring through my veins and I couldn't stop myself from shaking in anticipation. As we moved along the wall, I grasped at the hem of his shirt, slipping my hands underneath. Greedily, my fingers rakcd down his stomach, making the muscles beneath his skin tense. My hands drifted lower and lower and when they skimmed his belt buckle, Sinclair swore underneath his breath.

We entered what I vaguely realized was his room. But the setting didn't matter; there was this charge between us. It was so powerful, controlling each of our actions, making us frantic. Sinclair backed me farther into the room.

"You drive me crazy," Sinclair groaned.

"Yeah?" I breathed.

I felt him nod. His fingers curved around the back of my neck, holding me in place. "Every single day. Every fucking hour. Every second you're on my mind." His tongue skimmed the curve of my neck. I tilted my head back. Instinctively, my eyes closed. "You don't know how much I want this," he whispered.

I pushed back. Even in the dark I could feel his heated gaze on me. "So show me," I said.

A moan tore from his throat and in one swift move he hooked his hands around my thighs and lifted me up. My legs wrapped around his waist and the two of us fell back, landing on the soft mattress. With his body molded against mine I could feel the rapid beating of his heart, the warmth of his skin. He shifted slightly, his dick brushing against my lower stomach. Instinctively, my body arched up.

He lifted himself, resting his weight on his elbows. "Clothes off," he demanded.

I shook as he undressed me. Sinclair's eyes were riveted on my body and I ached for him in a way that I never thought possible.

On the inside and out I was on fire.

He unbuttoned his shirt with deft fingers and shed it quickly. Before it touched the ground, my hands were all over him, exploring every part of him—arms, chest, abs. My lips followed after. I had a one-track mind and my attention was all on Sinclair. My nails dug around the strong V above his boxers. I knelt, my tongue gliding down the center of his six-pack. Looking up at Sinclair from beneath my lashes I saw that his head had tilted back. Eyes closed. Mouth open in ecstasy.

It was the most erotic thing I'd ever seen.

With my eyes closed, I undid the fly of his pants. The tell-tale sound of the zipper sliding down made my heart race; I was that much closer to touching him.

His pants fell midway down his legs and I grabbed ahold of his black boxers and pulled down.

He caught my hands, making me look up at him. "You don't have to do this."

As I stared at him, I hooked my fingers around the material and tugged. Sinclair sucked in a sharp gasp. I curled my hand around the length of him, giving him a half smirk. "I *need* to do this."

With that said, I took him into my mouth.

Sinclair's hands glided up from my shoulders and sank into my hair, holding me tight against him. The action made me suck even harder.

An anguished groan escaped him.

When he reacted like that, it made something inside me go up in flames. I gave, he took. Vice versa. And I loved every part of the exchange.

My left hand curled around his cock and slowly slid up and down at the same time as my tongue brushed against the very tip of him.

"Fuck!" he shouted.

I continued the torture for the next few minutes. Until I'd driven him crazy. Until he was guiding my head up and down. Until I knew Sinclair was about to come.

"Stop," he panted. I stopped midsuck and glanced at him. "Come here."

He jerked me up. I wiped my mouth but I had no time to take a breath before he jerked my underwear down around my ankles.

Sinclair moved me up the mattress. I expected him to grab me, but instead he took me in with his eyes, looking me up and down in such a way that my body started to tingle.

I reached my arms around his shoulders and pulled him to me. Sinclair's perfectly defined body pressed into mine. His skin was warm, like fire against my own. I glided my tongue across the seam of his lips. He groaned against my mouth and deepened the kiss. When Sinclair was all in, he was all in. He didn't do anything by half measure. My mouth opened and his tongue flicked against mine.

He laced my hands through his, guided them up, and held

them captive against the headboard. My body arched. My nipples tightened. Instinctively, I wanted to get closer. There was this animalistic hunger that I had with Sinclair that I'd never experienced with any man. His fingers trailed across my skin as if my body was Braille and it would show him the way I wanted to be kissed, touched, fucked.

He lowered himself and I felt his dick brush against me. My entire body jolted.

Sinclair propped himself on his elbows. His eyes never left mine as he slipped into me. All the way. Fully. Completely.

I sucked in a sharp breath and closed my eyes, head tilted back, brushing against the headboard.

Sinclair started out slowly, deliberately moving in and out of me as if he had all the time in the world. Every time he surged back into me, I swore he was deeper than the last.

We found a rhythm that made every part of my body come alive. He moved his hips in a circle. Sweat dripped from his forehead and fell onto my chest. The sheets drifted down the bed and fell to the floor. The bed creaked loudly, yet we continued to move.

Without warning, Sinclair moved my legs around his waist. The action made him sink even farther into me. I felt myself stretching, slowly but surely making room, and soon all I could feel was him.

For a second, Sinclair paused. He was panting just as much as me. His hands covered my breasts and squeezed hard enough to make my body arch.

"I swear your body was made for me." Those intense green eyes were focused on my face and nothing else. I didn't look away even though I wanted to.

"Ask me to stop," he demanded. His lips brushed against my ear.

Hissing in a sharp breath, I raked my hands through his hair.

"Go ahead, Victoria. Ask me to stop."

"I can't."

A corner of his mouth curved up. "Exactly." He rocked into me. His forehead touched mine. "What we have is uncontrollable."

Sinclair smiled, his lips damp. He glided out of me slowly, with just the tip resting inside before sliding back into me. Torture. Agony. Perfection.

From this vantage point, I could see only his lashes against his cheeks, since his eyes were closed. His hair looked coal black even with the moonlight shining down on it. And that smooth skin of his was dusky, making the definition of his sinewed muscles even more apparent. I could see the tendons in his arms straining. He had a potency about him that most men wish they could have.

He's mine. All mine, I thought to myself.

I moaned so loudly, he covered my mouth. "You know what those noises do to me?"

I opened my eyes long enough to look up at him. I saw him staring at me, his eyes blazing.

"Makes me want to fuck a little harder, go even deeper, so you scream my name so loudly everyone will hear."

My hands, wrapped around his neck, were suddenly ripped away. He grabbed them and held them against the headboard, swallowing my wrists with his large hands. He was buried in me so deep I could hardly breathe.

All my control broke.

My fingers stretched into the air as I gasped for breath.

My muscles locked, my body bucked. I felt myself come and it was complete bliss. Unlike anything I'd ever felt before.

My eyes wanted to close, but they never wavered from Sinclair's. I felt the slightest tremor of panic because the emotions running through me were almost too much.

This was soul sex. Where it's less about the act and more about the feelings rushing through you. Every breath you take becomes amplified.

Our eyes remained locked as I cried out, his name spilling from my lips.

As Sinclair collapsed on top of me, I realized that my heart had been made up about him long before I knew it.

I would die for him. Kill for him.

I loved him more than life.

I couldn't let him go. I'd found a man who could undress me with just one look. He spoke and I was undone.

His actions unraveled me.

30

It's been two days since my outburst.

Everyone, including the other patients, has given me a wide berth, staring at me as if I'm poisonous. You know you're in bad shape when even your fellow patients are scared of you.

During breakfast and lunch, I keep to myself, very much aware that every move I make is being monitored by nurses. I can feel Alice's cold eyes on my back, burning two holes through my clothes. During group therapy I sit still, my arms encircling Evelyn. She sits in my lap totally silent. She seems to pick up on my change in personality like a bloodhound.

Now it's art therapy time. Each table in the dayroom has been transformed into an art station. Blunt-tipped scissors, crayons, markers, glue, colored pencils are scattered on each table. A lot of the patients immerse themselves in their art. I've never been one to get lost in coloring and creating. But I make an effort today. I end up making a rainbow that looks like it was crafted by someone on an acid trip.

There's a girl at a table across from me who swipes a stapler from a fellow patient. She steals one of the staples and tries to inscribe words on her skin. Immediately the nurses surround her, extracting the staple from her hand. The girl is dragged away, but not before I see the hurried attempt at self-infliction. The letters *H* and *E* are clear as day, dark red blood pooling out of the letters.

What's the rest of her message? I'll never know. I don't want to know.

Reagan is sitting at another table. She'd winked at me when I walked into the room before Susan steered me away from her.

"Very nice, Victoria. Very nice," the art teacher says. I'm pretty sure this lady who comes every Tuesday is the art teacher at the local high school.

I nod bluntly.

"Now what does this represent?"

"It's a rainbow."

"But what does it represent for *Victoria*?" She taps her chest emphatically. "What's inside you that's nothing but light and color?"

Her words are cliché, like they've been stolen from an after-school special. I try to take her words to heart, though. I really do. I tilt my head and focus on my deranged art. No matter how many times I stare at my rainbow, I can't find the light that the art teacher keeps talking about.

The balance of my world is tipping. Thoughts and memories are sliding this way and that and I don't know what to think or believe.

Art therapy ends. The scraps of papers are picked up. Supplies are put away. The room clears out. Only a few people remain. I am one of them.

The television is on in the dayroom. There's some soap opera playing. Only the nurses who are sitting in there are watching. I stare at the screen with boredom.

A man is having a heated conversation with a woman who looks torn up and confused.

My chair screeches as I push away from the table and stand up. I have this restless energy that refuses to die. I pace the dayroom. I feel useless. I feel idle. I need to do something. If no one will help me, I need to help myself.

My head is throbbing. I should probably go lie down. I asked one of the nurses for some Advil more than an hour ago. I quickly washed them down with water. The pills aren't helping. The pain in my head seems to be getting worse.

Evelyn's in my arms. She's not screaming. Just fussing, constantly squirming, as if she can't make herself comfortable.

Just then, Reagan walks into the room, making a beeline in my direction. My body locks up. We haven't spoken since I attacked her. Just as I predict, she confronts me head on, her signature smirk on her face. "Hi, Victoria."

I stare at her dully. Because of her, I was locked in my room. She's the last person I want to see right now.

She drums her fingers on the table and looks around. Things are quickly going from tense to awkward. I know I should apologize for attacking her, but I can't get the words to roll off my tongue.

"Look, I've decided to forgive you for the whole"—she wraps her hands around her neck and rolls her eyes into the back of her head—"choking thing."

"I didn't mean—"

She holds her hand up. "Please. I know you did. And I know I deserved it. Plus, I like you so let's put it in the past, all right?" Reagan holds out a hand.

A truce with Reagan would feel like a truce with Satan. Maybe everything that's happened the past few days has worn me down, though, because I reach out and shake her hand.

"Great." She leans forward and in her best reporter voice says, "Now don't you feel better?"

"Why are you really talking to me? It can't be to make up."

"I kind of like you, Victoria. You're a calla lily in the midst of black roses. Obviously, you have your issues, but you don't belong here. Plus, we both have that persona non grata vibe going on here. We can bond over our craziness. You tried to kill me, and if that doesn't break up a friendship then I don't know what the hell will."

This may be one of the most honest—if not the kindest—things that Reagan will ever say to me. For a second, I just stare at her.

Before I can reply a nurse walks by and gives us a double take. "Hey," she says slowly. "Should you two be around each other?"

"Relax. We're best friends now," Reagan replies with a

sweet smile. "In fact I just got done brushing Victoria's hair and talking about the latest episode of *Scandal*."

The nurse rolls her eyes and keeps on walking.

Reagan looks over my shoulder and stands up. "Well, it looks like my visiting hour with you is over."

I twist around in my seat and see Sinclair coming my way. My relief at seeing him is palpable. I thought he wasn't going to come back. And if he didn't, I couldn't have blamed him. Even I was scared of the side that came out of me that day. It's humiliating that Sinclair saw me at my lowest point. If I could go back and redo that moment I would.

He walks toward me. He smiles, but it's strained, as if the incident has tortured him and drained him of energy. For a second, I fear that he's here just to tell me that he's giving up and never going to see me again. That can't happen.

Before he makes it to the table, I stand up and meet him halfway. I don't want to talk to him with multiple sets of eyes on me. I point to my right, where the magazine rack is. "Let's go over there."

He follows behind me closely enough that as I weave around the tables his arm brushes my back. The action sets my skin on fire. When we reach the corner, I lean against the wall. I have to stop myself from wrapping my arms around him and never letting go.

Saying "hello" or "how are you" seems lame. And pointless. The more I see of the past and the relationship I had with Sinclair, the more desperate I become for his presence.

Sinclair clears his throat. He shifts from foot to foot as though what he's about to say makes him uncomfortable. "I think we need to talk about what happened in the rec room a few days ago."

"I think we shouldn't."

"Victoria . . ."

"I can't talk about it."

"But I have to know what happened. I walk in and you had her pinned to the floor and you were choking her."

I grab a fistful of my hair and start to tug. Sometimes the riot of emotions inside me is too much to take. Like now. I just want to sort them, put them in their proper places. Maybe then I will breathe easier.

Sinclair's hands curl around my wrists. Very gently, he pulls my hands away from my head. I lift my head and see concern written all over his face.

"All I want to do is help you. That's all I've wanted these past six months, okay?" His voice comes out in a ragged whisper. "Talk to me and tell me what you're feeling. I love you and whatever pain you're feeling, I feel it too."

Hearing those words coming from him gives me relief. I want it to matter to him. To Sinclair Montgomery.

I take a deep breath. "S-she said I would be a bad mom." My anger starts to fade as I speak, and is replaced with sadness. It's ridiculous. Reagan and I have smoothed everything over. But this moment is just a perfect opportunity to show that you can forgive someone, but you can never forget their words.

"Victoria?" Sinclair says gently. "That's not true. You know that, right?"

I say nothing.

"She was trying to get a rise out of you."

I bark out a laugh and wipe the tears off my cheeks. "Yeah. Well, it worked." Suddenly I feel so stupid.

One of Sinclair's hands curves around my shoulder and gently pulls me to him. "You're not a bad mom and you never will be."

I lift my head. "Maybe she's right though. She's crazy, but some of the craziest people are the smartest—they say what everyone else is thinking!"

"No," he says quietly but fiercely. "Don't ever think that."

I keep talking as if Sinclair never spoke. "As Reagan said all this, I glanced down at my hands, and saw that Evelyn wasn't even with me. I gave her to the nurse."

"All moms need a break."

"But good moms don't. Good moms protect their child."

"That's not true," he laments.

We are silent. I don't have to crack open a piece of my soul for him to see just how much Reagan's words hurt. He's already inside me. He sees it all.

I tear my eyes away from the floor and glance at Sinclair beneath my lashes. "Are you going to give up on me now?"

Sinclair frowns. He looks defeated and his shoulders sag as if the weight of the world is upon them. "I told you once that I wouldn't leave you here alone and I meant that."

All I can do is smile.

Sinclair looks around and lowers his voice. "Are you remembering more?"

I nod. "I am. Dr. Calloway showed me some more pictures last night."

Interest lights up his eyes. "What did you remember?"

My head tilts forward. Mere inches separate us. I have to remind myself that we are not alone. "The time when we delivered those flowers for your sister?"

Sinclair turns and smirks. "Of course." He pauses for a second. "You remember that?"

"I do. I remember running into you at your sister's store. I remember going to your house. . . . You didn't expect to see me and I ended up staying the night." I pause. "Do you remember that?"

Sinclair lowers his glasses and meets my eyes. The force behind his gaze is still as powerful as I remembered. It still makes my brain short-circuit and my breath get stuck in my throat.

"I vividly remember that moment," he says gruffly.

A hot flush creeps up my neck and across my face. That night runs through my mind in concise flashes: nails digging into his skin. Lips trailing down my body. I shake away the memory before it completely consumes me.

Sinclair's gaze never wavers from my face and I know the moment is playing in his mind too. "Have you remembered anything else?"

"No." I exhale loudly. "I'm getting to the end. I can feel it. I'm about to find the truth and I'm scared to see what brought me here."

I clear my throat, anxious to change the subject. "Seeing what we were and where we are now. Would you . . ." I stop and start. "Would you do it again?"

"Absolutely. Every single second," he answers instantly.

"Are you being treated okay here?" Sinclair asks.

"What, in general? Or since the 'incident'?"

"Both."

I shrug. "Good, I guess. Everyone's been looking at me like I'm crazy, though."

"I don't think you're crazy. I'll never think that no matter what."

No one has ever said that to me. Ever. Hearing it deflates my anger.

I'm all too aware that Sinclair is mere inches away. A table blocks us but that means nothing. I can still feel him. Smell him.

I know he feels it too.

Just a day ago I felt like I was losing my mind. There's a good chance I still am but when Sinclair looks at me like that, crazy ebbs away from me and I almost feel human.

My heart starts to beat against my ribs like a drum. It's the most beautiful sound.

Ignoring everyone around him, Sinclair reaches out. He holds my face so tightly, it's as if he's afraid I'll disappear on him. He pulls me toward him, his eyes bright with need.

Our last kiss was voracious and strong enough to last me a lifetime. This one is slower, but there's an urgency to it—as if he's trying to reach inside me and find the person I once was.

I open my mouth farther and Sinclair groans.

Emotions rush through me, powerful enough to take hold of me, controlling each and every action I make.

I no longer feel broken.

I'm bold.

I'm brave.

I'm confident.

Just like my past, this man breathes life into me.

The hands that have been holding my face drift down; his thumbs brush against the base of my throat. Right where my pounding pulse beats. My tongue slides against his expertly, as though we do this every day.

I don't ever want to lose this feeling again. My hands curl into fists, my nails dig into my skin; I want to reach out. I want to hold him to me. I want to do a lot of things.

But for now, *this* is enough.

And when he's not here and his words fade, I have this.

"No kissing," a nurse bellows. For dramatic effect she claps her hands. My eyes flutter open just as the nurse advances on us. She points at Sinclair. "Out!"

Sinclair doesn't move. His eyes bore straight into mine. They're glazed over with lust and I know he didn't want to stop the kiss anymore than I did. My lungs expand and I greedily suck in all the air I can.

He looks like he has something to say, but that nasty nurse won't be deterred. "You need to leave now, Mr. Montgomery."

"Oh, come on!" Reagan bellows. "This is a psych ward, not a church youth group! This is the most action I've seen in weeks!"

Very slowly, he stands up. I'm not ready for him to leave so I mirror his movements.

He tucks his hands in his pockets and it looks like he's going to step away. Before I can think twice I reach out and stop him.

"How can you love someone like me? I'm in a prison for crazy people. I have no freedom and I can't remember pieces of my past. How can you love me?"

"You think you're not worthy of love and you expect me to believe the same thing, but I can't. You're a different work of art, Victoria. The seams of your soul are uneven, and fraying at the edges. But you were created that way and I think it's the most beautiful thing I'll ever see."

I stand there at a complete loss for words. Sinclair gives me a sad smile. "I'll see you soon, okay?"

And then he's gone, walking down the hall with the nurse reprimanding him the whole time.

I watch him walk away, and feel something break around my heart.

Hear the echo of my heartbeat?

I ache.

I ache.

I ache.

31

My feet drag toward Dr. Calloway's office.

Evelyn is with Susan and I don't care.

I don't care.

I really don't.

Does that make me a terrible mom? Absolutely.

My mind feels like a fighter in the ring being hit over and over with words and explanations. It is bruised and battered and very close to breaking.

I knock once before I enter Calloway's office. The door shuts softly behind me. I sit across from Calloway, my hands laced in front of me. The nervous energy is impossible to contain. It hovers around me like a swarm of bees, threatening to attack me at any second.

"You look tired, Victoria," says Dr. Calloway. "Are you not sleeping well?"

"I'm sleeping fine," I mumble. It's a complete lie, but how am I supposed to explain that the voices inside my head are getting louder, more aggressive, more demanding as time goes by?

It's simple: I can't.

"Where is your baby today?" Dr. Calloway asks. I see a trace of concern in her eyes.

"She's with Susan."

"That's good."

"How so?"

"You're getting a small break," she explains. "Some breathing room."

I snort. "If you say so."

"Everyone needs time to themselves," Dr. Calloway says. "There's nothing wrong with that."

"Everything is wrong with that." The words tumble out before I can process them. After that there's no controlling what I say; I have to get it off my chest. "Good moms love and protect their child. No matter how they're feeling."

I watch Dr. Calloway carefully, looking for any trace of judgment. But there's nothing.

"You don't feel like you're protecting your baby? I promise you that Susan will take good care of her."

"It's not that. It's just . . . it's . . ."

"It's what?"

In frustration, I close my eyes, rub my temples, and take a deep breath. I try to sort through my thoughts and feelings so I can adequately explain myself.

"It's just that lately, my daughter can't stand to be around me," I finally confess.

"What makes you think that?"

"All she does is cry." I tuck my hands one beneath the other to stop myself from picking at my nails. "No matter how hard I try she doesn't calm down. It's like . . . it's like she hates me."

Dr. Calloway sits back in her chair. "I'm sure she doesn't."

Abruptly, I stand up and start to pace the room. "But she does. Lately, whenever I stare into her eyes, I see no acknowledgment. It's like I'm a stranger to her."

"How does that make you feel?"

"Awful!" I explode.

"What I mean is, do you feel yourself becoming distant from her too?"

I stop walking and turn to face Calloway. "Yes."

"And it makes you feel like a bad mom," she says.

Anxiously, I nod my head. "Yes, absolutely."

"There's nothing to worry about." I give her a dirty look. All she does is smile. "I mean it. You're under a lot of pressure right now, experiencing pieces of your past that aren't always easy to experience a second time."

I drag my fingers through my hair. I want to scream. I want to cry. I want to laugh. I want to do anything and everything and nothing all at the same time.

It doesn't make sense, but nothing about me right now makes sense.

Dr. Calloway turns a paper and slides it toward me. The dates and words blend together. I can decipher nothing. What I know with a certainty is that this time line is insanity by numbers.

Why did I do this? Why did I open Pandora's box? Is my life here truly that bad that I willingly put myself through this torture?

There are so many questions and I can't give a single honest answer.

"I'm losing it. I'm really losing it," I say into my palms.

After a moment of silence, my hands drop to my sides. I lift my head.

Dr. Calloway doesn't say a word. Her eyes are blank. No judgment. No pity. But honestly, on some level she has to think I'm insane. Just like the other doctors.

"Do you think I'm crazy?"

"Absolutely not. No one's crazy. But the world is. Everything has a label and a place. But it's impossible to group everyone's feelings and reactions into boxes. Especially reactions. Everyone is different and everyone will react to situations differently. You're being incredibly hard on yourself. If anyone were to travel back through their past, forced to watch the good, the bad, the ugly, they would easily be feeling the same way."

She may be humoring me. She may be doing reverse psychology on me. Right now it doesn't matter. "You think so?" I ask.

Dr. Calloway nods. "Of course. To be honest, I think you're holding up pretty great."

I want to believe her so badly. But I'm scared.

"You can keep doing this," she says gently. "You've survived your past before. You can do it again."

I find myself nodding. I find hope that's been dying inside me slowly come back to life.

"More pictures?" she asks tentatively.

"More pictures."

The first one is of a positive pregnancy test. It seems ridiculous—bordering on silly—to take a picture of a thin stick. For a second, I'm pushed back into the moment. The test was balanced on my knees. My hands were shaking so badly I had to take multiple pictures before I got one that wasn't blurry.

The third is of my mother and me sitting at a table at what looks like some kind of event. My cheeks are rosy and even sitting down it's impossible to miss my burgeoning belly, straining against my dark purple dress.

The pace picks up. Dr. Calloway moves the pictures so rapidly that one picture falls out of the stack and flutters to the floor. I break my concentration and bend to pick it up. When I turn it over I scream.

At least I think I do.

My ears start to ring and my blood runs cold. My mind is begging for me to look away, but I can't. The dead body is all I can see. It's lying flat on an embankment, with water lapping at the grass. The body is badly decomposed. Any skin that's left is brown, looking as rough as tree bark. It's impossible to distinguish any features. It's like the lake and fish joined forces to eat the body down to the bare bones. Where the eyes should be are two black pools of nothing.

My hand shakes as I wave the picture in Dr. Calloway's face. "What is this?"

Dr. Calloway stands. She snatches the picture out of my hands. When she gets a good look, her face goes pale. "I don't know how this got in there."

I know that this is the photo that makes everyone assume Wes is dead. Can I blame them? The clothes are the same ones he always wears when he visits me, but in the picture his white shirt has tears in it. The sleeve of his jacket is torn, hanging off his arm. One of his shoes is off.

"Why would you have that?"

"Victoria, I've looked at this stack of pictures a handful of times. I've never seen this before."

"It's not him." Rapidly, I shake my head. "It's not Wes. That's not him."

Dr. Calloway nods and slowly walks around her desk. "Just take a few deep breaths."

"He's doing this to me. He set this up!"

"Who?"

"WES!" I scream out his name so loudly, my ears start to ring.

"Just take a few deep breaths," Dr. Calloway repeats.

Doesn't she see that I'm so far past the point of deep breaths? I hunch over, my hands resting on my knees, and gasp for air. I see the pictures in perfect order and the crazy part is that it makes sense. It fits. But there's not a single part of me that wants to admit that maybe everyone is right.

Maybe my husband has been dead all this time and I've been talking to the ghost of him.

Maybe I really do belong at Fairfax.

The pictures are a distant thought, but the wheels of the past are set into motion. I'm not eased slowly into the memories, as I usually am. This time they hit me so hard I fall to my knees and drop my face into my hands.

32

For the past month, I'd been living with my mother. It was a temporary living situation until everything with Wes and me was figured out. I'd been back to the house once and that was during the day, while Wes was at work, so I could pack up my clothes.

I saw Sinclair frequently, but we weren't living together; there was a big part of me that was terrified of what Wes would do to Sinclair if he had the chance.

I shuddered at the thought.

My heart was still this fragile thing, slowly trying to piece itself together, but I loved Sinclair. He knew the basic facts, but he didn't know why. It was bad enough that I had to face the truth of my relationship with Wes; why would I have wanted to share that with the world? I felt embarrassed, humiliated.

Every day Wes called me begging to talk. Every day I pressed IGNORE, because I couldn't do this anymore. I couldn't get sucked back down into his life, even if I couldn't completely ignore it.

As much as I wanted to hide beneath my covers and avoid everything, I had to face reality.

I stared down at the screen for a second longer and pressed CALL.

It rang twice before he picked up.

"Victoria? Victoria?" Wes sounded out of breath, as if he had run to get to the phone.

I took a deep breath. "We need to talk."

In my mind, I saw this conversation going south. All I saw was Wes getting angry.

In fact, I was counting on it. That's why I wanted to break up during dinner. In public. With witnesses. I picked out a restaurant that he took me to frequently when we were still in love. It had good memories. There had been so much darkness in our relationship since then that I just wanted to hang on to a small piece of good.

"Sorry I'm late," Wes rushed to say. He kissed the crown of my head, a gesture he used to make all the time in the beginning of our marriage, but rarely now.

"It's fine."

Wes didn't offer an explanation for being late and I didn't ask; I already knew the answer. Work.

He sat down across from me, scanning the menu with focused concentration. The waiter got our order and there were no more distractions.

We looked at each other. He gave me a wide smile and asked me about my day, seeming genuinely interested in what I had to say. It was disarming.

But that was his MO: a long stretch of kindness and short bursts of anger. If I kept that fact in the forefront of my mind, I could get through this.

"Victoria, are you okay? You look a little pale."

Before I replied I downed the rest of my wine. My hands were shaking. I laced my fingers together and waited.

The first course arrived.

Now or never, I told myself. *You have to tell him.*

"I can't live like this," I blurted out.

The truth can do one of three things: free you, break you, or complete you.

I hovered among the three, just waiting for Wes's reaction. He wiped his mouth with his napkin and frowned. Confusion was written across his face. "Like what?"

"This. Right now." I gestured at the space between us. "I can't do this anymore."

I braced myself for an outburst. Violence. But instead I was met with silence. It was unnerving and threw me off guard. Maybe I was making a mistake. Maybe things could go back to normal. Maybe . . .

No, my mind whispered fiercely. *You have to do this.*

Swallowing my nerves, I said very quietly, "I want a divorce."

The words were just as painful to say as I thought they would be.

Wes dropped his fork. His hand moved across the table for my hand. I tensed, but at the last second he pulled away, looking like a man at war with himself. "I can't believe this," he muttered gruffly.

I didn't reply, just carefully tracked every move he made.

"Where did this even come from?" he asked.

His shoulders drooped in defeat and he hung his head, staring blindly at his food. He said nothing and the conversations at other tables drifted around me. On some level, I think he knew this was bound to happen.

Ignoring the others around us, he reached out for my hand. I pulled back at the same time. Only our fingertips touched.

"I love you. I thought everything was perfect between us."

At that, I frowned. "Perfect?"

"Everything was stressful because of work and you not being able to get pregnant—"

"This has nothing to do with work or pregnancy," I quickly cut in. "At the beginning I might have thought that. But, no, *this* has everything to do with how you treat me."

"I treat you fine. I give you everything, Victoria. A few fights and you're ready to walk away? Come on now. I love you." He said it sadly, looking like a man devastated.

This is what he does. Don't buy it. Not for a second.

He was going to tell me how sorry he was, how much he loved me, but I knew a tiger couldn't change its stripes.

"Are you trying to make me believe that you have no love inside you to fight for us?" he challenged.

Only a small hint of frustration seeped into his words. Considering the magnitude of our conversation, he wasn't even close to reacting the way I had expected him to.

"Of course I have love for you. But it's not enough anymore."

My reply threw him off. He sat back in his seat, staring at me with his "lawyer gaze," the one where he shrewdly picks apart a person and tries to call their bluff. He could keep looking, he could dig deep into me until he reached my marrow, but he'd find nothing but the truth.

Very carefully, I thought over my words. "Neither one of us is happy anymore."

"What are you talking about? Everything is perfect between us."

I stared at him, dumbfounded. I was starting to feel like I was in the Twilight Zone. Was he delusional? I leaned in slowly and lowered my voice. "Nothing about us is perfect."

"Then that's the problem, because I see a relationship that's strained. But I love my wife enough to stick it out."

"Stick it out?" My voice went up an octave, earning the gazes of people around us. "That's all I've been doing for a year!"

"A year?" Wes snorted. "And now you're magically asking me to buy in to this idea that you're unhappy?"

"Yes, that's exactly what I'm asking you to do."

"Un-fucking-believable."

"I didn't reach this point suddenly. It's impossible to forget the years we've been together and the memories we have."

"If it's impossible, then stay with me."

His hand reached out and this time I hesitated, because it would have been so easy for me to give in—to shrug my shoulders and agreeably say okay.

I dropped my hand into my lap. "I can't, Wes. If I stay with you, then I stay with pain. I stay with abuse."

"There's no abuse. Just moments where I lose my temper."

"And that right there is exactly why I can't be with you anymore."

The imploring expression disappeared, replaced by a coldness that I'd expected. To me it seemed like the reality of the situation was finally sinking in for him. There was no amount of "sorrys" to bring us back to where we once were.

"Is there someone else?" he asked, a biting tone in his words.

For so long I had agonized over whether I should tell the truth, but I was also extremely aware that Wes would use that against me and it would put me in a bad light. Never him.

I sat up straight and looked him in the eye. "That doesn't matter."

"Of course it matters. Why can't you answer the question? 'Yes, I'm with someone else.' 'No, I'm not with someone else.' Two easy responses."

"You're going to sit there and give me the third degree, yet you've been seeing someone on the side."

Wes slammed his hands on the table. "I told you that I'm not seeing her!"

Conversations around us died. I could feel the stares. Wes looked around and instantly lowered his voice. "If you want to divorce, get a divorce. I can't stop you. . . ."

I waited; he was getting ready to deliver a blow. "But I'm not going to make this easy." His brusque tone was what I expected yet it still managed to give me chills.

As Wes asked for the check, I stayed in my seat. Not because I had to. Not because I was scared. Not because I was sad. I stayed because I knew this would be the very last meal we would ever share as Mr. and Mrs. Donovan.

We walked out of the restaurant together, saying nothing. The silence was unbearable, masking unsaid words that the two of us were just dying to hurl at each other.

We left in separate cars. I watched him take a right and peel out of the parking lot, toward the direction of our house.

I took a left.

I drove toward Sinclair.

33

October 2014

No one in good conscience wants to get a divorce.

You don't plan your wedding and go through all the work, thinking to yourself, *Oh, I can't wait for the divorce. That'll be even better!* That's like building your hopes and dreams with glass and letting them fall in the middle of a rock quarry.

But I knew what I had to do. My heart was a completely different story. It was attached to the former version of Wes—the one that promised me everything and molded my dreams of the happily ever after.

"Why are you scared? You're much braver than you think," Sinclair had whispered in my ear that morning.

I needed to remember his words. I needed to capture them all and bottle them up to use in moments like this.

"Are you ready to do this?" Renee asked.

It had been a week since I told Wes I wanted a divorce and now I was in Richmond, about a two-hour drive away. I did that on purpose. I wanted my lawyer to have no clue who my husband was. If I chose a lawyer from McLean or Falls Church, I could just see them balking and running away.

Sighing loudly, I unbuckled my seatbelt and nodded at Renee. "I'm ready."

This was a fairly busy area, with a parade of large buildings lining the road. Most parking spots were filled. People walking down the streets kept their heads down, eyes glued to their cellphones. No one noticed me. No one cared and I slowly felt the tension leaving my body. Lately I felt like there was a huge sign over my head, along with a flash blinker that said: *Look at me! I failed my marriage!*

Across the street, directly in front of us, was a four-story brick building. On the second floor was Randall & Fernberg, P.C.

Randall & Fernberg was a top-rated law firm. Their office was on the third floor. In the elevator, Renee and I were silent. I could feel her eyes flick toward me every few seconds. I felt sick to my stomach.

As we stepped out of the elevator Renee held me back for a moment. Her hands settled on my shoulders and gently squeezed. "Everything will be fine."

I gave her a blunt nod and then we walked into the office. Decorated with dark furniture, white walls, and framed pic-

tures of natural scenes, it was a typical office. The receptionist greeted us with a smile.

"I have a one o'clock appointment with Mr. Randall," I
said quietly, as though Wes were hiding around the corner,
ready to change my mind.

The receptionist told me to sign in. I couldn't get a firm
grip on the pen, which made my signature look like wavy
lines. "He'll be with you shortly. You can take a scat."

The magazines stacked on the end tables were aging. In
the corner, right in front of a window, were Styrofoam cups
and a full pot of coffee. I couldn't imagine anyone stepping
into this office finding comfort in a good cup of coffee. I
could barely concentrate on the magazine on my lap.

I nudged Renee and pointed to the ceiling. "There's a
small water stain."

"Yeah, and your point is?"

I leaned in. "My point is, why hasn't it been fixed? Maybe
this law firm is going down the drain. Maybe I should look
for a new lawyer," I hissed.

"Okay. Relax. You're getting way ahead of yourself. That
means nothing. You picked a good lawyer."

"How do you know?"

Renee shrugged and went back to flipping through her
magazine. "I did my research too."

I had never consulted a lawyer and the only time I'd ever
been to a law office was to visit Wes. Even then I didn't pay
attention to the people in the waiting room. Wes brought
home cases but he never discussed them with me and I didn't
pry. I wished I had. How many people had Wes represented
who were trying to leave an abusive relationship? This was

Wes's stomping ground. He knew the ins and outs of the law. How to win cases and where to really hit a person.

I thought I had done everything I could to cover my bases, but in the back of my head I kept feeling like I was missing something. I wrung my hands together and stared at the clock on the wall. Time felt like it was frozen.

It felt stuffy in there. Even though it was October, it was unusually hot out. Why didn't they have the air conditioning on? I felt like I was choking.

I had gone to stand up when a short, stout man stopped next to the receptionist's desk. He looked like he could be my grandfather, with gray hair and a face lined with wrinkles. He didn't look like any cutthroat lawyer. He looked like he belonged in a Norman Rockwell painting.

"Mrs. Donovan?" His eyes veered between Renee and me, unsure of which of us was her. I turned my head and nodded, smiling weakly. "Come with me," he said. "I'm Mr. Randall."

Before I walked away, I turned back to Renee. She was still flipping through the glossy pages. She looked up at me. "What?"

"Come on."

She lowered the magazine. "You want me to go with you?"

"You didn't come all the way here just to sit in the waiting room, did you?"

She shrugged and grabbed her purse from the floor. Mr. Randall merely raised a brow as we walked through his doors.

Whether it's a therapist, lawyer, doctor, or businessman, they all have one thing in common: their offices. Those large, imposing desks. Degrees mounted on the wall. A couple of bookshelves. It is always the same.

Mr. Randall's office was no exception.

He held out a hand. "Doug."

I shook his hand. "Victoria. This is my friend Renee."

"It's great to meet you both. Please have a seat."

I sat down across from him. Renee took another chair, slightly to the side. Shafts of sunlight peeked through the blinds and made precise lines on the floor. I wanted nothing more than to be outside and miles away from this place. But I came this far. I had to finish this.

"What can I do for you?"

"I want a divorce," I rushed out. I expected to feel better, but the words had a bad taste. I wanted to vomit.

He nodded his head, looking completely nonplussed. "All right. First, let's get down the basic information."

I nodded hesitantly. I shot a glance at Renee but she was in the dark as much as me.

"Full name?"

"Victoria Isabel Donovan."

"Maiden name?"

"Aldridge."

"Date of birth?"

And so the questions continued. I answered each one, expecting my nerves to calm down, but that didn't happen.

"And what's the name of your husband?"

"Wesley Donovan."

Mr. Randall glanced up from his legal pad. He took off his glasses and sighed. "Well, this changes things."

"How so?" Renee asked, anger creeping into her words.

Mr. Randall answered Renee's question but kept his eyes on me. My hands curled around the edge of the chair. I already knew what he was going to say. "I know of your husband, Mrs. Donovan. He's very . . . cutthroat in the courtroom."

Renee snorted underneath her breath.

Mr. Randall shifted uncomfortably in his seat. "How many years have you been married?"

"Two and a half."

"And is there any way that counseling will help you?"

"No."

"Do the two of you have any children together?"

"No."

"Assets?"

"Yes."

"What's with the twenty questions?" Renee blurted out.

I knew that this was part of the process, but Renee didn't. She looked shocked and pissed-off.

"These questions are standard. I need to go in knowing as much information as I can."

Renee sat back and gave him a brief nod.

Mr. Randall glanced at me with his sad blue eyes. "If you are to petition for divorce, seeking damages, spousal support, etc., there's a good chance that he will fight back. He's cunning enough to make sure you walk away with nothing."

"I know that."

"Again, I'm not trying to discourage you. I think it's fair that I be up front in the very beginning about this process. It's not easy. In a perfect scenario you file. It's an uncontested divorce. You go to mediation. You sort everything out and the paperwork is filed. Now, that's most cases. But some-times it can get ugly. Very ugly. You need to be prepared."

I nodded.

The look on his face showed that he was doubtful. He cleared his throat. "What are the grounds for divorce?"

"I want it to be uncontested."

There was my journal and the pictures of that mystery woman that could back me up if I decided to fight, but all I wanted was to leave this marriage and move on.

"Have there been domestic disputes?"

I hesitated and he pounced on my silence like a lion. "Please be honest."

Both he and Renee stared at me and I felt myself caving in. "Yes."

"Is there proof? Have you ever called the police? Filed a report?"

"There's proof, but I don't want to make this difficult. I just want to cut ties with him once and for all."

"I understand that," Mr. Randall replied patiently. "But it might not go as you've planned."

I took a deep breath and stared out the window. A long silence followed.

"Do you still want to move forward?" he asked gently.

I swallowed loudly, staring at the kind man in front of me. "Yes."

Mr. Randall looked surprised by my answer. He dropped his pen and stood up from his desk. "Very well."

The next hour was filled with nothing but heavy ques-tions and filling out an insane amount of paperwork. What documents would be filed and what was required of me. By the time I stood up to leave my head was reeling. But I had jumped one hurdle and for right now, that was enough.

When it was time to go, he stood up and shook my hand. I swore I saw the smallest amount of respect in his eyes.

"What happens now?" I asked.

"Well, Wes will have to be notified that you've filed for divorce. You can't serve him the papers. In most circumstances anyone else can serve him the papers."

"I'll do it," Renee chimed in.

I shot Renee a look. "Is there any other option to serve the papers?" I asked him.

"Of course. It can be through mail. Service by picking it up. But I think the best option is personal service, where the spouse is personally delivered the papers. This also means that the court can have personal jurisdiction over the spouse."

Hesitantly, I nodded. "Let's do that."

"All right. The second he is served, you'll be notified."

"What happens after that?"

"After that we'll go through any assets or outstanding debts that you have together. What belongings in your household that you want or don't want. A court date will be set. You'll go before a judge. And if all goes well, then the paperwork will be finalized."

"And if it doesn't go well?"

He shrugged, the look on his face grim. "Then this divorce could take years."

My body was shaking as we walked toward the car. Renee and I were quiet as we drove back home. I stared out the window, bouncing back and forth between relief that I did the right thing and fear that it would all blow up in my face.

I would spend the next few days a nervous wreck, waiting to hear when the papers were served.

This was one more hurdle that had been jumped and I knew I should be relieved and a small part of me was. Aside from actually telling Wes that I wanted a divorce, I knew filing would be one of the hardest parts of this whole situation. It hurt just as bad as I thought it would.

"I'm proud of you," Renee said.

I didn't reply.

"I know I sound all mushy and dramatic," she continued. "But I really mean it."

Renee sighed and gave my hand a pat. I continued to look out the window, staring into the traffic, feeling the weight of this situation pressing harder on my shoulders.

I'd seen the ugly side of my husband enough to know that it could get uglier, and my gut told me that it was about to get *much* uglier.

34

I took a pregnancy test in the bathroom at Wal-Mart.

Waiting ten minutes until I got home to pee on that damn stick seemed like it would be an impossible feat. I had to find out and it had to be right now.

My hands shook as I yanked the test kit out of the box. So many times had I taken the test, hoping with all my might for a positive result, only to be disappointed.

Right now I didn't know where I stood. Out of all the times in my life a pregnancy should arise, now was the worst. Still, the thought that I could be pregnant, that one of my dreams could actually be coming true, plowed over all the cons.

I stared blindly at the graffitied door in front of me as I peed on the stick. As I waited for the results I read how Britney was a whore. Annie and Devin were meant to be 4eva. And Savannah, Kaylee, and Lucy were BFFs.

Dear God, I hadn't thought this through. Did I really want to find out life-changing news while the lady in the stall next to me told her son not to pee on the walls?

Faucets were turning on and off and someone coughed loudly. I didn't really care; my focus was on that thin white stick. It said to wait three minutes. Such a short amount of time but it stretched out in front of me, feeling more like three years.

Nervously, my legs bobbed up and down. I told myself to breathe, that everything would be okay. No matter the results it would. Be. Okay.

My nerves were shot. I finally peered down at the test and saw the positive line. I blinked a few times, waiting for the horizontal line to fade away and reveal the truth. But it stayed the same.

My life did not.

Funny how such a small test can change the course of your life.

I grabbed my purse and with my left hand gripping the test stick, hurried out of the bathroom.

Renee was slouched over the cart, slowly scrolling through her phone. When she saw me she stood up, her eyes overflowing with curiosity. "Did you take it?"

My words were trapped in my throat. All I could do was nod and hand her the stick. Her eyes widened in disbelief as she looked between me and the test. "Are we happy?" she asked cautiously.

I should have felt elated. This should have been an exciting time, but I was scared.

Frantically I tried to do the math in my head. How late was my period? I'd never kept track of my periods. Like most women, I relied on my body to remain consistent. I think I was a week late. I think.

I grabbed the test and stared at the results. "We're happy," I replied.

After that it was nothing but an exchange of hugs and tears. "But don't tell your brother."

"When are you going to tell him?"

I tucked the test into my purse. "Soon. As in a few hours soon. But I need to wrap my head around this."

Before we left the store I ended up buying ten more test kits. As if the first one wasn't clear enough.

All I could think about was how Sinclair would take the news. Things were amazing between us, better than I could ever hope for. I couldn't say the same for Wes and me. True to his word, he wasn't making anything easy. He moved out of the house a week ago and soon after announced he wanted to put the house up for sale. Fine by me; the house deserved to have a happy family living in it. But Wes wasn't done. Any credit card debt? He felt I had to pay it off, arguing it was me who had spent the money. The items in the house, maybe the simplest things to deal with, were taking forever. He wanted to keep random things: pictures, a rug, our king-size bed. The chair in the living room. Can't forget the flat-screen TV.

The only things that we'd both agreed on him taking were the belongings in his office.

He was grasping at anything he could get his hands on. Sinclair saw the frustration and hurt I was going through.

My patience was unraveling. The days were going by so slowly. If it weren't for Sinclair, I think I'd have gone crazy.

The icing on the cake was my relationship with Wes's mother. Well, our former relationship. Lee Donovan was painted a different picture by her son. She was indignant: shocked, hurt, and more than angry that I would ever leave Wes. After two conversations in which she told me I didn't try hard enough and that maybe I was the problem, I stopped answering her calls.

There was no doubt in my mind that by now half of Falls Church knew that Wes and I were separated. I had an even stronger suspicion that Lee had portrayed me in the worst possible light.

I continually reminded myself that if that was the worst things would get, then I was lucky. And it was actually working.

Until now.

I sat on the floor of my room, my back against my bed. All ten tests were spread out around me like scattered puzzle pieces. I wished it were that simple. I'd move a few pieces around and then, before I knew it, the puzzle would be complete and I would have my answer.

I stared down at my BlackBerry and scrolled through my contacts. Sinclair's name and number flashed on my screen, daring me to call him. I had no idea how he would take the news. Bringing another life into our relationship could make or break us. I was afraid it would be the latter. I genuinely wanted to believe that he'd accept the news with open arms, but I was jaded by the past. I was used to the bad, not the good.

My mother and Renee called. I let both calls go straight to voicemail, and quickly made a call of my own before I lost all nerve.

It rang twice before he answered.

"Hi."

"Hi," I said, my voice catching.

He picked up on my fear immediately. "What's wrong?"

I took a deep breath and held it. My gaze remained rooted on the test. I knew that once these words were out, I could never take them back. "I'm pregnant."

Silence.

I frowned. "Are you there?"

"I'm here." Another pause. "Hold on, let me go somewhere private."

My left leg started to bob up and down. I couldn't calm down. I brushed my hands across the beige carpet while telling myself that everything was going to be okay.

It was.

It was.

I heard a door shut, and seconds later Sinclair said: "Are you sure?"

"Yes. I took the first one at Wal-Mart and then ten more when I got home."

"You took the first test at Wal-Mart?"

"Can we focus on one thing?" I snapped.

"Of course." Sinclair paused. "You are pregnant."

I could feel his smile through the phone. "What are you thinking?"

"I'm thinking that you having our baby is the best news I could ever hear."

I laughed nervously. Instinctively, my hand dropped to my waist. His words gave me hope and courage for the future. They made me believe that everything was going to be okay.

With a smile on my face, I picked up one of the many tests. "I still can't believe it."

"Neither can I."

The line was quiet. Both of us were lost in our own thoughts and then he said: "A baby . . . a baby!"

His happiness made my own grow a thousandfold.

"Thank you for taking this news so well," I said.

"Did you expect me to be upset?"

"Yes," I replied truthfully.

"I can't be upset about this, Victoria. It's the best news I can imagine. Our lives can really begin."

"I love you," I whispered.

"I love you. Everything is going to be okay. We'll get through this."

I believed him because it was the only thing I had left.

35

January 2015

Thousands of snowflakes danced in the air, softly falling all around me. Very carefully I walked up the pathway, the snow crunching beneath my feet. When I was finally on the porch I took a deep breath and stomped the snow off my shoes. I leaned heavily against the door as I searched for the house key.

Then the door opened and I was yanked inside and pulled flush against Sinclair. I felt every ridge of muscle. The smell of his cologne was all around me. His warm breath caressed my neck.

His lips slammed against mine. The tension eased from my body, and my hands hung limply at my sides. There was an exigency to this kiss. It was frantic and scared. Every slant of his lips, intake of breath, the way his tongue glided against mine revealed that he didn't want to take a single moment for granted.

Every move he made, I mirrored. We were in perfect harmony.

My fingers gripped him tighter, pulling him closer. Kissing him should be enough. Being in his arms should be enough. But for me it wasn't and I didn't know if it ever would be.

So I held him tighter and he kissed me deeper. His hands moved up my body, skimming my ribs, brushing against my bra before they stopped at my neck.

Sinclair pulled away.

"Hi." His voice was deep and sensuous. It pulled at me, drew me closer, as if an invisible noose were around my neck.

"I need you," I said against his lips.

He hesitated for just a second. His forehead rested against mine. Neither one of us moved. My breathing increased. I forgot what desire could do to you. It felt like a fire was lit inside me. Flames licked beneath my skin, making me tingle everywhere.

He chuckled and the sound scraped against my skin. It spurred me on and made my body tremble.

"Did you miss me?" he asked.

"Yes."

Behind me was the hallway leading to his bedroom, but it was too far away for me. I think Sinclair felt the same; he guided us toward the couch, sitting down first and pulling me down so I was straddling his lap.

He was under me. This strong man was under me and all mine. It sent a thrill down my spine; it was almost more than I could take.

I tried to make quick work of his clothes but my hands wouldn't stop shaking.

Sinclair reached out and turned off the lamp. Instantly, we were bathed in darkness. I liked it this way; it made us rely solely on touch and words. Those two things make you work harder but the end result, the way it makes your body come alive, is worth it.

My coat dropped to the floor and my clothes quickly followed. I kicked off my shoes. They hit the floor with a loud thump.

His fingers curved around my hips. My palms slid over his shoulders, down over his back. I memorized every muscle, the feel of his warm, smooth skin. I kissed the side of his neck and gently bit down.

"Slow down," he whispered gruffly into my ear.

"I'm trying," I panted.

I really was. But my body ignored my pleas and took control until there was nothing but frantic touches and kisses. It should be dangerous to feel this way, but it wasn't. It was intoxicating. There was power in shutting down your mind and letting your body take control.

Sinclair's hips lifted from the couch long enough for me to tug his pants down. With a whisper-soft touch, my fingers drifted down his body. Muscle after well-defined muscle. Sinclair groaned when I reach his boxers. I glanced at him from beneath my lashes and smirked. My fingers hooked around the edges. He took in a sharp breath. I was so close to where I wanted to be. I could reach down just a few inches and wrap my hand around him. I resisted the urge.

I could feel his gaze. The intensity coming from him was enough to make me squirm on his lap.

"Don't do that," he warned. His hands were splayed against my skin, gripping me possessively. He exhaled harshly. "You're not making this easy."

"When has anything ever been easy between us?" I whispered.

His fingers dragged through my hair. He held my face immobile. "I want to make this last as long as possible." His hands loosened and drifted down my neck. His touch was like a feather skimming very gently over my body. "I want this just as bad as you," he rasped.

His hands reached behind me and deftly unhooked my bra. The two flimsy straps that held it up slid down my arms. The material was dangerously low, almost exposing my breasts. At the thought of that my back arched. My bra dropped between us. I made quick work of shedding my underwear.

He dipped his head. I smiled wickedly as he kissed the skin above my belly button, moving up, up, up until he reached the path between my breasts.

"I love these freckles," he whispered against my chest.

"Yeah?" I whispered back.

When he nodded, his lips brushed against my skin and I had to stop myself from groaning.

I couldn't breathe. I couldn't move because his touch set me aflame.

He knew my body like the back of his hand.

He cupped my breasts. They filled his hands and it was as though I was made for him. And maybe I was. Maybe everyone has someone in the world who fits them perfectly, like a puzzle piece sliding into place.

I felt his lips wrap around my nipple. When his tongue flicked against the very tip, I groaned. Gently he caressed it as he kissed me. Every second was torture and complete bliss—the best kind of buildup.

Our bodies intimately touched and instantly I became wet. Sinclair wanted to make this last. I couldn't though.

"Now," I whispered. "Right now."

I leaned down and kissed him with all the passion and lust I had for him. Sinclair's arms banded around my waist. He sat up and my body was intimately pressed against him. The very tip of him rubbed against the most sensitive part of me. I gasped into his mouth and moved against him. He caught my hips. This was torture.

"I'm not ready," Sinclair all but growled.

"I am."

Sinclair smirked.

He didn't force.

He didn't hurt.

He never dominated.

He let me take control, all the while knowing that just one brush of his hands and I was his. Sinclair lifted me up until I was on my knees and positioned me above him.

There was a single pause where it was just the sound of our heavy breathing.

When he slid into me it was with confidence and power.

He was as deep as he could get. I felt nothing but him, pulsating inside me. He held my body captive. He growled into my ear, causing thousands of goosebumps across my skin. He knew how to move. How to move his hips. When to speed up and slow down.

Every single turn and lift of my body brought more pleasure. Beneath me, Sinclair was barely in control. I loved him naked, bared before me, and all mine. My hands glided up his stomach. His muscles jumped in reaction and I smiled. I watched in fascination as his hips bucked upward, every time I moved.

"Fuck, Victoria," Sinclair said through clenched teeth.

Sex with him was just like his kisses. The faster he moved the faster my sanity vanished, until all I could think about was him.

My head tilted back. My eyes closed. Every muscle in my body strained. My hands gripped the back of the couch as we moved in unison.

"I love you," I said, my voice barely above a whisper.

This was the kind of love that I could stretch my arms wide and never feel constricted in. I could take a deep breath and the air would never be stale.

I could live in this love.

Then I let go and screamed so loudly, my throat ached.

Sinclair's forehead rested against my breast as he surged into me one final time. A groan tore from his throat. I really didn't think there was anything better than watching a man lose control and knowing that you caused him to reach that point.

Sinclair sucked in a deep breath and opened one eye, then gave me a smirk. Sweat dripped down our bodies, mingling together to create a scent that only we could know.

After a few seconds of nothing but panting he told me I was the only woman who could bring him to his knees, but to me it was the other way around.

Touched.

Burned.

Branded.

This man owned me.

As if he could sense my thoughts, Sinclair lifted his head and looked me straight in the eyes. He cupped my face with his rough hands.

"I'd risk anything for you," he said.

I believed him.

Later on, after we had showered and changed and were lying in bed, Sinclair and I went through baby names. I was only four months along. It was too soon to tell what I was having, but I was almost certain it was a girl. It was a feeling in my gut. Sinclair was convinced it was a boy.

The TV was on, emitting its glow across our faces. Time didn't exist when we were together. It loomed outside the door, waiting to latch back on to us. But here we were free from it and everything else that haunted us in our real life.

These moments were the only thing keeping me sane. The divorce was moving along at a snail's pace, so slow that sometimes I wished I had just run away with Sinclair and started over somewhere else. I was convinced it would've been easier.

I turned the page of the book and scanned the baby girl names starting with *E*. "I like Evelyn," I said.

Sinclair lifted a brow.

"You don't like it?"

"I gotta think about it."

I rubbed my belly. "We could call her Evie."

"You could," Sinclair said agreeably. He rolled onto his back. With his hands laced behind his head he stared up at the ceiling, looking deep in thought.

For the past few days we'd been going over names. Back and forth we would fire off names, like it was a game. I hadn't settled on anything yet. Nothing had really stood out to me. I figured I'd know when I heard the right name. Everything would just click.

I had gone back to looking through names when out of nowhere Sinclair shouted, "Evelyn Montgomery!"

My baby book flew in the air and I just about fell out of the bed. "What the hell was that?"

"I was testing out the name."

"For what?"

"At one point, we're going to shout out our child's name. So we need to find one that works that way."

I blinked and stared at him as if he had grown three heads.

"Do it," he urged.

"You're kidding."

"Completely serious. Try it."

I lay back and stared up at the ceiling. I pointedly ignored Sinclair but I felt his eyes on me. "Stop smiling," I said. "You're making me feel ridiculous."

He covered his eyes. "Fine. I won't look at you."

I smiled and took a deep breath and shouted out her name.

Sinclair dropped his hands. He quirked a brow and gave me a look that said: *Well? What do you think?*

"I like it. Fits perfectly. But we'll never yell at her."

"Something tells me that there are millions of parents before us who have made the same declaration," he said.

"What makes you so sure it's a girl?" Sinclair asked a moment later.

"I can just tell. The kicks she gives me are powerful. She's a female who wants to make her presence known."

"But if it's a boy . . ."

"It's not."

"Humor me for a second, V. *If* it's a boy, what names do you like?"

Sinclair didn't want to know the sex of the baby. He said he wanted to be surprised. I, on the other hand, wanted to know. I had to know. During the last sonogram, the doctor had said that they couldn't get a clear view to see if it was a boy or girl, but she predicted girl.

"Well?" he prodded.

I sat up and closed my baby book. "I like Peter."

"Peter?"

I nodded. "Please don't shout out the name."

"We've had enough name shouting for tonight. I'll wait for another time."

"Good." I traced the letters on the front cover. "So . . . do you like Peter?"

Sinclair was quiet for a moment. "I do. It fits." He reached out and wrapped a hand around my arm and yanked me to him. He nipped at my finger, making me jump slightly. "I love you. Your name is written on my heart, you know that?" he said into my hair.

"Yeah?"

He nodded.

I reached out and traced a *V* against his chest. He stayed perfectly still. His hands braced against my head. I slowly wrote my name out. I crossed the *t* and dotted every *i* with precision.

I could see my name. It was perfect and it had never looked better. I leaned in and sealed it with a kiss. His eyes became half-masked.

"Sometimes you scare me," he said.

"Why's that?"

"Too much power. You're a dangerous woman."

"There's nothing dangerous about me."

"Of course there is. You made me fall deeply in love with you. All the power is yours."

"I love you," I whispered.

And I meant it. Every single word.

I kissed him. Not sweetly, but deep. It was so intense that I could feel a piece of myself being given to him. Millions of heartbeats in this world and I knew someone could hear mine. I knew that I was heard.

I had finally found a love that involved no pain and there was nothing in the world that would take this from me.

I settled back against him, my head against his chest so I could hear the steady beat of his heart. In these quiet times came peace, but sometimes I felt a fear. Fear that we came together at the most unexpected time. For all we knew we could be cursed from the beginning and never even know it.

I didn't want to imagine a life without Sinclair.

"Do you think we'll survive this?" I asked.

"Of course we will." He rubbed my arm. "Never, ever question us."

How could I explain to Sinclair that it wasn't him I feared? It was what Wes was capable of.

Minutes later Sinclair turned off the TV and the lights. We settled in for the night. I was close to falling asleep when Sinclair whispered into my ear, "If you ever worry about us you just have to press your palm to your chest and feel your heartbeat. For as long as you still have a beating heart, you have my love."

I laid my palm against my heart. He placed his hand over mine.

"Heartbeat?" he asked.

"Heartbeat," I whispered back.

36

March 2015

"I feel like an elephant compared to these ladies," I muttered to my mother.

We were attending the Ladies Luncheon of Falls Church. It was an annual brunch that took place at a nearby country club. These "luncheons" were all under the guise of raising money for numerous charities, but it was really just the richest women in Falls Church getting together to gossip.

Even so, I went for one reason: my mother. I had attended the event with her almost every year since I was sixteen. I would sit next to her as everyone sipped their champagne and drink my water. Every so often a friend of my mother would compliment me while my mother sat there beaming.

But this year it was different. Walking toward our table, I saw how the eyes locked on my stomach, drifted up to my face and then back down. Quickly the ladies would look away and talk to the person next to them.

I was branded as this terrible wife to a wonderful husband. I was a whore. In their eyes I was a modern-day Hester Prynne. Give these ladies a few minutes and I was sure they'd try to slap a scarlet Λ on my dress.

"I shouldn't be here," I said out of the corner of my mouth.

My mother kept her head held high and smiled to this woman and that. "You're staying. Let them talk."

We were escorted to our table. It was beautifully decorated with a pale pink tablecloth. A stunning bouquet of flowers in a glass vase was in the middle. The crystal champagne glasses sparkled. And on top of every plate was a place card. When I found my name card, I grabbed the edges of my seat and sank into the chair with a deep sigh. I rubbed a hand over my baby bump. It seemed like I was pregnant with no visible proof and then POP!

It felt like the baby was using my bladder as a squeeze toy. If this was just six months along, what would I be like at the very end of the pregnancy? Still, deep down I knew I was going to miss these moments. A niggling voice in my head told me to cherish every kick. Every muscle spasm. Every bathroom run. Because I would never have them back.

Ever.

Two tables to my left was Wes's mother. Every few seconds I could feel her eyes on me. I didn't look at her once.

Unsurprisingly, our relationship had turned sour quickly. Whose side was she going to take in the separation game: that of her daughter-in-law of two and a half years, or her perfect son's?

I didn't stand a chance.

But what was shocking is how fast she spread the word. She didn't live in Falls Church, but that clearly didn't matter. She was hell-bent on telling the story her way, so that perfect son of hers always had a light shining directly above his head, making his halo sparkle. People ate up her words like vultures, which just goes to show that nothing bands a group of ladies together more than good gossip.

My mother didn't agree with my decision to get a divorce. Over and over she lamented how I needed to work things out. But she'd be damned if any person outside our family was going to speak ill of her daughter. She told her version to anyone who was willing to listen and she'd always end the conversation with a firm statement: "You shouldn't believe everything you hear." Which left most ladies standing there, beet red, embarrassment curling around them.

No, my mother and I would probably never see eye to eye on most things, but this was the closest thing to respect I'd get out of her. Greedily, I took it.

A perfectly polished blond woman stepped up to the podium to speak. We all clapped lightly. She began her speech but I tuned her out. I sipped my water and looked around the room. There was no one there that I really wanted to talk to. Today was a waste. I could leave right then and no one would know I was even gone.

A few minutes later the speech ended. Automatically, I clapped along with everyone else.

Lunch was served directly after. It was nothing but small portions of garden salad, grilled salmon, and asparagus.

The ladies around me cut their salmon in delicate, slow motions. I had to hold myself back from inhaling it all. I finished within minutes and pushed my plate away. Idly, I looked around at the dining room. It was the same old same old.

In the doorway there was a flash of red. I sat up in my seat and craned my neck. It was then that I saw her. We made eye contact. Her eyes widened in shock and then she was gone.

I started in my seat, jarring the table with my knees. My mother said something but I ignored her.

My heart sped up.

It couldn't be.

Abruptly I stood up.

"Victoria," my mother said. "What are you—"

"I'll be right back," I said distractedly.

As quick as I could, I made my way to the back of the room, my eyes never leaving the brunette. She looked over her shoulder once and when she saw me walking toward her, her eyes widened. She quickened her pace.

I bumped into a woman and then a waiter carrying a tray of champagne, but I never removed my gaze on the woman.

When I exited the dining room, I half-jogged.

"Hey!" I shouted at her retreating figure. "Hey, wait!"

She ran across the front lobby and took a sharp right toward the bathrooms. People turned and stared at the two of us. I didn't care. I had to speak with her. Before she slipped out the door, I grabbed her arm.

She stopped in her tracks and slowly turned around. The woman locked eyes with me. And here she was: the woman from the pictures.

All the air escaped my lungs.

I couldn't move.

I couldn't think.

I couldn't breathe.

Seeing her in the flesh, our likeness was even more apparent. Her dark hair was swept behind her shoulders. Even her eyes were a bright blue like mine.

"Who are you?" I whispered.

The woman flinched and fidgeted with the strap of her purse. "Melanie." She lifted her gaze and stared at me with torment in her eyes. She winced as if the sound of her name brought her physical pain and slowly nodded. "And you're Victoria," she said finally.

I nodded and absentmindedly patted my belly. Melanie watched the action with rapt attention. "I've wanted to meet you for a while," I confessed.

"How did you know me?" she whispered.

The pictures were the last thing I wanted to mention, yet it was unavoidable. "Pictures of you were . . . were sent to me."

Her face fell. She made no effort to hide her guilt. In another time or place, anger would have controlled me. But right then I just felt so much sadness that we had been broken down by the same man.

"Why did you come here?"

She seemed taken aback by my calm tone and words. "I

wanted to tell you I'm sorry." She swallowed loudly and blinked back tears. "At first I didn't know he was married."

"How long were you with him?"

Melanie looked a little lost, unsure if she should answer me truthfully or lie. "Almost a year."

It's one thing to accept that your marriage is broken and that love has been lost for a while, but it's a whole other thing to hear it.

"But I broke it off months ago!" she quickly added.

"It doesn't matter anymore. Wes and I aren't together." Her eyes widened with guilt. "It wasn't because of you . . . although it certainly didn't help."

"I'm so sorry." Her eyes welled up with tears.

I didn't hate Melanie. I didn't see her as the other woman, or the villain. That title didn't belong to her. Who knew what Wes said to her? I knew it had to be something big because she looked more devastated than I did.

"Where did you meet him?"

There was a brief silence that made me think she was going to completely ignore my question but she finally spoke up. "That's quite the loaded question." Her voice was quiet and I found myself leaning in to hear her better. "I met him on the street. We ran into each other and he more or less swept me off my feet." She smiled somewhat bitterly. "He was always so confident. I loved that about him."

That admission knocked the air out of me. It shouldn't have hurt, but it did. I nodded. I understood her all too well.

"He said he loved me," she said as she stared blankly at the floor. "And I believed him."

"I believed him too."

There may be a small part of my heart that was wounded by Wes's betrayal but it was clear that for Melanie this was still a fresh wound. She still loved him.

"Is the child his?" she asked.

I placed a protective hand over my stomach. "No," I replied quickly. "No, it isn't."

"Oh." She looked relieved.

"You're going back to him, aren't you?"

She shifted from foot to foot. "No. Definitely not." Her words were frail, unable to stand for a second before they collapsed.

"Has he hurt you?" I asked bluntly.

"N-n-no," she stuttered.

Her answer was all the confirmation to know that he had. "You have to get away from him," I said urgently. "He's not a good person."

"What do you mean?"

"He will kill you here." Gently, I tapped her chest, right where her heartbeat was. She flinched. "And then when there's nothing left of you he'll suffocate you so your last breath is his."

Somewhere down the hall someone laughed. The sound made Melanie practically jump out of her skin. She glanced around before she took a step back from me. "I have to go," she whispered.

I grabbed Melanie's arm so tight she winced. I had so much to ask her. She couldn't leave now. I was so close to untangling Wes's past. She pulled out a set of keys and I could see that her hands were shaking. Before she turned and walked away, she gave me one last look. "I'm sorry." Her throat tightened. "I'm so sorry."

Melanie backed away from me slowly and then practically ran down the hall. I walked behind her, saying nothing but refusing to let her leave my sight.

I watched as she walked out of the lobby. She brushed off the valet and hurried toward an old Corolla. She pulled out of the parking lot like the devil was nipping at her heels. Not once did she look back at the front entrance to see if I was watching her go. But I think she knew I was there.

37

After dinner, I slowly walk back to my room.

The memory of telling Sinclair I was pregnant is seared into my mind. We were so happy. So hopeful. I glance down at my daughter. Evelyn was his. All this time she's been his. So why wasn't Sinclair happy to see her? Why didn't he ask to hold her? Love on her?

Just when I take two steps forward toward uncovering my past, I end up having to take twenty steps back. So many times I've reminded myself that the bad has to happen in order for me to reach the good, that there's light at the end of the tunnel if I look close enough.

Yet I can't see that light anymore and I don't think I ever will.

I've had enough of the memories. And of Fairfax.

Yet all my thoughts come to a screeching halt the minute I turn the corner. I'm a few steps away from my room, but I know something's up. The nurses who normally linger in front of the nurses' station are gone. A few patients are standing outside their rooms. A few form a little circle. Yet all of their eyes turn my way. A new girl turns away and starts to giggle when I look back at her.

Ignoring them and the warning bells ringing through my head, I hurry to my room. The door is open. Nurses are talking quietly among themselves. When they see me standing there, they step to the side and reveal Alice.

She smiles at me viciously and holds out a pile of pills. "Well, this is interesting."

She steps closer. I take a step out into the hallway. Yet that's not good enough; I feel like the walls are closing in around me, shrinking my chances of ever escaping this place. "This is at least six, almost seven weeks' worth of pills."

There's no use in denying they're mine. I stare at her solemnly, bracing myself for what she's about to say next.

The rest of the nurses filter out of my room. Kate's one of them. She doesn't make eye contact with me.

Coward.

"Something like this doesn't go unpunished."

"My doctor isn't here. You can't do anything," I point out.

"She may not be here but going against the rules has consequences." Alice looks so sure. The hairs on the back of my neck stand up.

"You can't do anything," I repeat.

Alice shakes her head and smiles. There's nothing kind about that smile. "No, I can't. But the doctor on shift can." She holds her hands out. "Give me the baby, Victoria."

Instinctively, I hold Evelyn closer. "No."

"Give her to me."

"No."

Alice grabs on to Evelyn's stomach and tugs. I hold on, slapping Alice's hands away. But her grip is stronger than mine. She rips her away and holds my daughter close to her chest, as though it's her baby. Not mine. The action wakes Evelyn up. She wails loudly in fear. Alice smiles.

The anger that overcomes me is unstoppable. I'm a force to be reckoned with. I can't calm down even if I try. I lunge for Alice. For once she looks scared. Good. Even she should know that you never take a child away from her mother. It's like poking a sleeping bear. You won't like the results.

I hear raised voices around me. Someone grabs me around the waist, trying to pull me back. My hands are extended, fingers stretched, clawing at thin air.

Alice continues to hold my daughter.

My daughter.

I don't know if I've ever felt this much rage before. It scares even me. "Give her back!" I scream.

More people are starting to come out of their rooms. I don't care; I continue to yell at Alice, calling her every name in the book. It's a small consolation that her smug grin slightly fades.

Someone's hand covers my mouth. I bite down on her flesh. Someone cries out and instantly the hand is gone. Then they start dragging me down the hall. I resist. I fight with everything I have.

Alice follows behind me, like this is a funeral procession and she's getting ready to give me my last rites.

"You can't take her away from me!" I say. "You can't do this!"

Yet even as I say those words, I'm doubtful. It's nine o'clock. After hours. Dr. Calloway isn't here. She can't help me.

We turn the corner. Patient rooms are becoming sparse. I've been down this hallway before. It's not a place you want to be at Fairfax. At the very end of the hall is the white room.

The on-call doctor runs up toward us. He's so young he reminds me of Doogie Howser. He has no idea who I am and what my situation is. None of that works in my favor. But he does look frightened by me as his eyes jump from Alice to Kate.

I jump at my chance.

"Don't let them take my daughter away," I plead. "Please, just let me go back to my room. Please."

He looks shocked.

"She's been hiding her pills in the wall for weeks now," Alice tells him.

"Shut up! Shut up! This doesn't involve you," I snap.

Doogie opens the door to the white room. I've never felt such blinding fear. It's powerful enough to make me double over in pain.

I make one last plea. "Don't do it. Don't do it." My voice goes down and even to my own ears I sound like a child begging for its parent not to hurt them. "Please don't do it."

Alice encourages him, tells him that I'm out of control. He gives me an apologetic look before he sticks the needle into my vein.

The drugs don't kick in instantly. But it's pretty damn close. Already I can feel my body become weightless. I know I should move my legs and try to resist, but I can't think.

I feel light as a feather. In my mind, I see myself floating in the sky, slowly drifting toward the ground. The air dances across my skin. I stare up at the white ceiling. I smile and then I close my eyes.

The last thing I hear: *"Fairfax is no place for a baby. . . ."*

38

I'm a good person.

I know I am.

I don't deserve to be in here.

How much time has gone by: a few minutes? Hours? Days? I don't know. And that's the scary part. In a room where all noise is absent, time stands still. Your breaths become punctuated. And your conscience becomes this malignant creature, festering inside you, just waiting to turn your words around on you and watch you suffer.

In the white room you become your own worst enemy.

The second I woke, I stared down at my body. My sweats were gone, replaced with a hospital gown. On my right wrist is a blue wristband. And a green one. I don't know what they mean or why they're even there. Both of them say the following:

DONOVAN, VICTORIA
5-19-2015
#5213627

There's no reason for this. Why put this on me? I know my name.

This is ridiculous.

But maybe this is on purpose. Maybe they know I'm losing it, and I'll forget my name. Maybe they're helping me out.

Or maybe not.

Maybe they're planning something much bigger than me. To give me a drug so strong my memory will be wiped clean and I won't know who I am or what I've done or who I've loved.

Or maybe they simply want to rob me of my sanity.

The very thought makes me start pounding on the door, screaming to be let out. Now my hands ache. There will be bruises. My throat is raw.

All four walls are padded in white squares. I've counted them multiple times. The number is never the same. The ceiling is white and the floors are white. There's not a stitch of furniture in here. Just a blanket in the corner with a small, flat pillow. These two additions look like add-ons—a last-minute thought placed in here to make it look "roomy."

I'm in the corner of the room, my back against the wall,

as far back as I can get from the door. I know I'm alone in here, but I can feel eyes on me, tracking my every move.

No one's come in here to check on me. Are they going to leave me in here to rot? I want to say no, but I'm starting to doubt myself.

Very faintly, I can hear a baby crying. My heartbeat sky-rockets. In my mind, I can vividly see Evelyn lying in her bassinet. She's scared and I'm not there to comfort her.

The very thought makes me want to vomit. If she was here right now I would reach out and count the beats of her heart. And then I would know I'm alive. I would know that I have a chance of surviving this.

"Bad mom . . . bad mom . . . bad mom . . ."

I don't know what my brain's doing—bringing up dark moments from the past. No matter how hard I try to ignore the words, I can't, because the actions from the present back it up. I am a bad mom. I let go of her. I didn't fight the nurses and doctors hard enough.

There's so much I didn't do.

I start to shake so violently, my teeth chatter.

I think that nothing can compare to the insanity and fear suffocating my soul, but a deep dark voice in my head tells me that I'm wrong.

"Why can't you just listen?"

I scream and stare into the eyes of Wes. He's to my right, kneeling so his knees brush against my arm. I want to jerk away but I'm trapped.

He brushes the hair from my face and tucks it behind my ear. "I told you to leave this alone, didn't I? All this time I've been trying to protect you from this."

I draw my legs up to my chest and rest my forehead on my knees. He's not here . . . he's not here . . . he's not here.

This is all just in my mind. That's what happens when fear takes over.

But he's here. Nothing about him is made up.

"They took her away," I groan. "They took my daughter away."

"This is all your fault." Wes's voice goes from being sweet and gentle to menacing and cruel. "I had a beautiful life planned out for us. You realize that, don't you?"

Maybe if I close my eyes, maybe if I talk over him, he'll just disappear.

"Close your eyes and count to ten. Soon it will be over before it ever began," I chant.

"Stop it," he growls.

I don't. If anything, my voice becomes louder with every word.

"Soon it will be over before it ever began. . . ."

"Stop it!"

His hands curl around my arms. He's shaking me, screaming at me to shut up.

Close your eyes and count to ten. Soon it will be over before it ever began. Close your eyes and count to ten. Soon it will be over before it ever began. Close your eyes and count to ten. Soon it will be over before it ever began. Close your eyes. . . .

39

The door slowly creaks open.

I don't bother lifting my head. My hand slaps erratically at the wall over and over and over. The noise my palm makes against the padding is the only reminder that I'm still alive and present.

"Victoria, I'm so sorry." Dr. Calloway bends down until she's kneeling next to me. She wears an expression of concern. I stare at her blankly. "I didn't know you were in here all night. I would never approve of this."

She places her hand on my shoulder and I jerk away from her touch. Someone can only take so much before they break. "I'm so sorry," she repeats.

Dr. Calloway holds her hand out, but I stand up on my

own. She didn't shut the door behind her, and now I can hear the very faint voices of nurses and patients.

"How long have I been in here?" My voice cracks.

"Just one night. No more than nine hours."

Impossible. It feels like years have gone by.

Right then the image of Evelyn slams into my mind. "Where's my daughter?"

Dr. Calloway holds her hands out in front of her. "She's fine. She's just fine."

"Where is she?" My voice is frantic now. Until I see her with my own eyes I won't be satisfied. The scariest part of this room is the separation. Countless times I heard her cries. But after a while, I don't know when, they stopped.

And then I begin to fear the worst.

I know it sounds impossible, but when I searched for my own pulse, telling myself that if I could find my own, then my daughter was still alive, well, I didn't find it.

"Where is she?" I yell.

"Victoria, she's fine. But I need to talk to you about something I found in your file. I—" Dr. Calloway's lips are moving, but I can't hear a word over the beating of my heart. I try to listen. I really do.

But my mind is screaming at me to find my daughter and I can't avoid it. Ducking beneath her arm, I run out into the hall.

"Victoria!" Dr. Calloway calls out behind me.

"I need to know she's okay!" I shout and run down the hall. It doesn't take me long to reach my room. The door is wide open; one look inside and I know Evelyn's not there.

I quickly move toward the dayroom. The hallway is empty.

A therapy room next to the locked doors is open. A nurse is ushering a group of ladies into the room. She makes the mistake of leaving one of the doors open. I run through it and into the dayroom.

All eyes are locked on me. I probably look like a maniac. At this point it's hard to care. My appearance is the last thing on my mind.

Where is she? Where is she? Where is she? I turn in a circle, and then I see Alice. She's standing next to the nurses' station. My daughter is in her arms.

My daughter.

Alice sees me. The cocky demeanor that she had while she encouraged the doctor to inject me is gone. She looks terrified. Of me.

"Give me my baby." The minute the words slip from my tongue I have a sense of déjà vu. This trips me up for the barest of seconds. I grab my daughter, ready to kill for her if I have to.

I hold her tightly in my arms. She's crying. I try to soothe her but she won't calm down.

"Look what you did. . . ."

Wes's voice is whispering in my ear. I whip my body around. He's not there. The television is on just as usual, but no one's watching it. Board games are paused. Books are on the table and multiple sets of eyes are on me.

And that's when I see him.

He's outside, walking along the length of the building. Plain as day.

I take a step forward but stop when he disappears out of my line of vision.

"No, no, no . . ." I whisper. This isn't happening again. Not again. He's not getting away so easily while I'm trapped in this prison. I walk toward the dining room. In this hall the blinds are always open, letting in bright white light, and in this case they give me a clear view of Wes.

His hands are in his pockets, and his eyes remain looking forward. He has a dark smirk on his lips.

My pace matches his, step for step. In front of me the hall cuts to the left and right. In front of me is the back door where the nurses take their smoking breaks.

I slam my shoulder against the door; it opens but a siren goes off instantly.

"Hey!" a nurse shouts behind me. "Come back here!"

Once I'm outside I take off. Wes already has a lead on me. He's running toward the woods, cutting a trail between the long grass.

Barefoot and with my daughter in my arms I run after him. I can hear multiple voices behind me, but I don't stop. I can feel it in my bones that this is the coup de grâce and everything has been leading up to this. All I can think about is that I have to catch up with Wes. The dry grass snaps beneath my feet. My heart is pounding so fast I think it is going to burst from my chest.

The alarm seems to be getting louder. And then I hear Sinclair's voice. He's yelling at me to stop.

But doesn't he get it? For weeks I've been trying to untangle my past, undoing the knots, and I knew I was so close to having my life back. It was right there. I could practically touch it.

"Wes!" I shout. "Stop!"

He continues running. My muscles burn so badly I want to collapse in one big heap and greedily suck in all the air I can.

Yet we draw closer and closer to the trees until the next thing I know, I'm swallowed by them. The grass gives way to damp ground covered in leaves, pine needles, and broken branches. They puncture my feet. I barely register the pain. My heavy breathing mingles with the drone of the alarms. I lose my footing on uneven ground. I stumble a bit but remain upright.

Evelyn is screaming. This time I feel her heartbeat. It's as frantic as my own.

But Wes remains unfazed. He jumps over fallen tree trunks. Dodges along slopes.

Sinclair's still behind me. He continues to call out my name. I feel the weight of his stare on my back.

Clouds move in front of the sun, surrounding me in further darkness. The wind picks up, rolling through the trees. Strands of my hair whip into my face, blurring my vision before I impatiently pull them back.

We keep running. I don't know where we're going or what will happen. Wes is ahead of me, weaving in and out of the trees, stepping over thick branches as if he's done this many times before. Finally the trees thin out and in the middle of nowhere stands a small cabin. Wes runs inside it, leaving the door open.

I hesitate.

And then I step into the cabin. I'm panting, ready to drop from exhaustion. But I stop dead in my tracks when I see what's around me. On the wall, my face smiles back at me.

There is not a square inch that isn't covered in pictures. Some of them are of me alone. The others are of Wes and me through our entire relationship.

The small cabin has been transformed into a replica of our master bedroom in our old house. The same four-poster bed. Same bedspread. Same rug. The dresser against the wall has a wedding picture of us in a silver frame.

I feel like I'm in a funhouse. I won't be surprised if the floor shifts beneath me and reveals a secret room with more surprises waiting for me.

Wes claps loudly. I whirl around. "Congrats on making it here." He tucks his hands into his pockets and rocks back on his heels. "For a minute there, I didn't think you had the courage to get up and leave. Pushing those women out of the way?" He whistles. "Ballsy."

I stand perfectly still, gasping for air.

"I bet you want to know why we're here. Don't you?"

All I can do is nod.

"I wanted to show you where I lived all this time," he explains. For greater emphasis, he lifts his arms and gestures to the small space. "Do you like how I decorated?"

He advances and without thinking I take a step back. It is my first instinct around him. He just laughs at my fear. "Why do you look scared? I won't hurt you. I'm on your side, Victoria. I want to help you remember."

Sinclair's voice becomes louder. I take comfort that soon I won't be alone.

"You didn't want to help me!" I yell. "You made it look like I was making up your visits."

"Not true. I walked in and out of Fairfax every single

time. It's not my fault that their security is complete shit. By the way, I came to see you because I care about you."

My breaths even out but the beating of my heart doesn't. "You're lying."

"Again, that's not true. I care a lot about you. I *love* you."

I point a shaky finger at him. This isn't a time for him to twist things around and make me look like the crazy person. "You're fucking crazy."

"Now, come on. That's a cheap shot, Victoria. Everyone is a little crazy. You have to be to survive in this world."

"Why are you doing this?"

The floor creaks underneath him as he comes closer. "You're my wife. I love you."

The look in his eyes, the possession in his words shows that this cycle will never end. I'll never be free of this man. If I ever am I'll also be six feet under.

"No," I groan. "No, no, no."

Sinclair bursts through the door. His chest heaves as he looks me over. I'm too scared, too much in shock to walk toward him. He takes a few steps my way but stops when he sees Wes. His face goes pale.

Wes is nonplussed by this arrival. "Guest number three's here. Good, good. We're just waiting for one more person."

"Wes?" Sinclair asks in disbelief.

"What's wrong, Montgomery? You look like you've seen a ghost."

"What are you doing?"

"Why does everyone keep asking that? Have you not been paying attention to Victoria these last few weeks? The love of our lives wants the truth. So I'm going to give it to her."

He continues to speak, but my past is waiting for me. Lurking above me like a hive of bees, it buzzes, the noise louder with each passing second.

It hasn't touched me but I can already feel the sting of its truth.

Funny how just a mere hour ago I was anxious to escape. Anxious to seek the truth, boldly reach out and grab on to it. But now I'm terrified. Suddenly I can't breathe. My heart starts to palpitate. My head starts to spin.

My vision is starting to blur and all those whispers from the past are growing louder in my head. I try to focus on Wes.

"At first, I thought we should all reunite at the house. I mean, that's where we all met. That's where the betrayal started. So that's where it should all end, right? But I had it all wrong. That's not where it started. Not by a long shot."

Time starts to crawl. The air becomes thick. Stale. And it's almost as if I'm breathing in the past.

"It's clear you're angry," Sinclair says to Wes, talking to him as you would a child throwing a tantrum. "But let's think clearly."

"I am. In fact, I'm beginning to think I'm the only person in this fucking room thinking clearly." He looks at me, his eyes beguiling. "Victoria is the catalyst. Everything begins and ends with her."

That's all it takes. Six simple words.

Six seconds to say.

Six seconds to destroy.

One second Wes is clear across the room. The next he's

lunging for me. His arms are extended, fingers spread. He tackles me full-on.

I land flat on my back. The air whooshes out of my lungs. There is no time to be dazed and out of sorts. I have to react. Push him off me. Protect Evelyn.

Yet it's too late.

Hands wrap around my neck, squeezing tighter and tighter. With more pressure the smile widens across Wes's face.

I close my eyes and I see flashes of pain. Screams of agony. Blood. I see my hands curling into mud. I see myself close my eyes.

I count my breaths.

Six of them and then I slip away. . . .

40

May 2015

I believe that everything always comes full circle.

Lives end.

New ones begin.

Sometimes the circle connects when you take your last breath. Sometimes it happens way before but, oh, I promise you the pieces will touch and when they do, nothing will be the same.

The chapter of Wes and Victoria finally came to a close. He came over earlier tonight and signed the divorce papers. A deep sense of relief settled over me. Everything officially felt final.

The last week I'd done nothing but pack. My routine consisted of going through everything and taping up boxes. And tomorrow I would be moving out. The cable and Internet were shut off. The silence was so unnerving that I had my laptop open and put in a movie just to hear some noise.

It was bizarre to see the house so bare. The last time I saw it like this, I was filled with optimism and hope for the future, and while I was now leaving with those same two emotions, I was also not doing so blind. I knew the road Sinclair and I were going down together wasn't going to be smooth. There would be bumps.

But I loved him. More important, I trusted him.

We were going to be okay.

I stared out the kitchen window, taking a small break from cleaning the counters, with the smallest smile on my face. Just a few days earlier, Wes left for a business trip. The day he left he sent me another email. He finally agreed to sign the divorce papers. He said he'd do it when he got back from his trip.

At first I was skeptical. I wanted to hang on to his words and believe him, but if my history with Wes had taught me anything, it was that Wes loves playing mind games.

But this time he was telling the truth. He came over tonight, his keys turning in the lock, so reminiscent of happier times we'd had. When he came into the kitchen, I was shocked by his appearance.

The normally put-together Wes was a wreck. His hair was sticking straight up, as if he had spent hours tugging at it. He had a day's worth of stubble and his eyes were bloodshot.

He looked around the house. Years of stored-up memories were just behind his eyes.

"Where are the papers?" he asked.

"Right there." I pointed to the kitchen island and leaned against the sink. I twisted the dishrag so tightly around my hand, it threatened to cut off my circulation. Wes pulled out a pen. He'd probably read through the paperwork a million times by now, but he still scanned through it all. At the final page he lifted his head and finally met my gaze. I didn't look away.

His eyes were tormented. His mouth opened and closed, as if the weight of the words were too much for him. His eyes closed for a brief second and then he signed the documents.

"Thank you," I finally said.

Wes crossed his arms and shook his head at me in disbelief.

"What?" I asked defensively.

He shrugged. "Nothing. I just . . . I just didn't think it would ever come to this. I know love can fade and marriages fail, but never once did I believe that would ever happen to us."

"Me either."

Wes held my gaze a second longer and then pulled out his car keys. "I need to get going."

He left minutes later and then it was just me and the wind howling against the house, and the rain hitting the window in hard, angry pelts. The weather had been terrible all day and it showed no signs of letting up. Just an hour ago Falls Church and all surrounding cities had been issued a severe thunderstorm warning.

A bright strike of lightning lit up the sky. Thunder sounded loudly, making me jump.

But even in the dark I could place each flower in my back-yard. I could sketch out the roses and calla lilies. That was the only thing I was going to miss about this place. I had poured so much love and care into that backyard. I tried to tell myself that wherever I went, I could plant and grow a brand-new garden and would have Evelyn next to me. I would teach her everything I'd learned about flowers.

I patted my belly, my hand forming soothing circles. She kicked and I smiled. I was giving her a better life.

Quickly I packed up another box and taped the top of it. This one was filled with pots and pans and was too heavy for me to pick up. I slid it on the floor over to the corner and took a deep breath. I looked around the almost bare kitchen. In probably an hour, the entire room would be packed and I would officially be done. It was bittersweet to see the house empty, but also exciting; I was starting a new life with Sinclair and our baby. I looked down at my swollen stomach and lovingly rubbed it again.

And it was then that the front door opened. My head shot up just as Wes walked through. He brought in the smell of rain and a cold gush of air. Goosebumps formed on my skin.

"What are you doing here?"

He slammed the door behind him and walked into the room, a dead look in his eyes.

I leaned against the doorjamb, watching him carefully.

"I've done some thinking. . . ."

"About?" Fear trickled up and down my spine.

He snorted loudly and began flipping through the documents. I reached for the folder but he jerked it away. "Wes," I said a little too urgently. "Give it to me."

When he got to the last page, my vision blurred. It was all downhill from here.

Wes looked up at me, his face composed. But his eyes . . . they were two dark pools of hate.

Suddenly my tongue felt too big for my mouth. I needed to calm him down before things got out of control.

So I said the truth: "Wes, you just signed the papers. There's no going back."

He laughed as if I'd told him a joke. "We're done?" Wes gestured to my stomach. "I'd hardly say we're done."

"I'm leaving," I said more to myself, an affirmation that this was the right plan, the right path.

Wes picked up the papers and stepped toward me. I didn't move, although I was dying to get as far away from him as possible. When he was standing right in front of me he raised those sheets of paper and tore them in half, then let them flutter to the floor.

Wes smirked and stared down at me. He was too calm and composed. Right now he was fractured ice. All too soon he was going to break apart. I couldn't stop shaking.

"You've been planning this for a while. That shocks me. But nothing should really shock me about you anymore, should it?"

"Wes—"

"You're so ready to start your new life and leave me behind, aren't you?"

Panic made my blood freeze, because his eyes were dead. Cold. Void of any emotions. He could hurt, or worse, kill me, and not feel a thing. I had to get out of there. Out of the corner of my eye I glanced at the door just a few steps away.

"Why are you looking at me like that?" He advanced slowly. "Why are you looking at me like I'm the bad guy in this? I'm just stating the truth."

"You're not making sense," I whisper.

"I'm making perfect sense, Victoria."

With small steps, I inched closer toward the mudroom. My purse was on the counter right next to the doorway. I could grab for it as I ran out the door.

Wes mirrored my movements, slowly stalking me like I was his prey. "Why do you look so upset, Victoria? Why does everyone get so torn up over the truth? Huh? Why does everyone think it will hurt them? I say, give me the truth. Let me have it all!"

He extended his arms and I was afraid that when he lowered them back down, they'd make contact with my body.

"Wes." I held out my hand in front of me. "You're angry. And I get that . . ." I smiled and tried to take a deep breath. "But let's be practical about this and not yell."

"I'm yelling and it's your fault! You've brought me to this point, because everything begins and ends with you, doesn't it?"

There was no way for me to answer his question correctly. I'd get it wrong no matter what. The air was sucked out of the room. Gone was my patience. I turned on my heels and ran toward the kitchen.

"Answer me!" he yelled. I could feel his words reaching out, sinking their hideous claws into my flesh.

It was then that I made a move for my purse. Wes got there quicker and snatched it away, then threw it against the wall. I jumped and watched the contents spill out.

"Tell me what you were thinking tonight." He paced back and forth, his cold eyes never leaving mine. "Did you really think a piece of paper would magically allow you to disappear from my life? Hmm?"

I didn't answer.

One second the kitchen island was blocking us and then before I could react there was nothing keeping us separated. Wes tackled me to the floor. I landed so painfully on my right side I gasped. Pain rocked through my body. Behind my lids I saw bright white spots.

Call it motherly instinct but my hands flew to my stomach. The baby kicked and that single, small kick was a reboot for me, giving me enough strength to crawl backward, toward the door.

Tears started to pool in my eyes. The light above me blurred slightly. I couldn't lie there and do nothing. I had to fight. If not for me, then for my baby.

Some unseen force overtook me. I'll never know what it was or if it was simply that maternal instinct to protect what I loved. But I wiggled enough room to lift my knee and hit him between his legs as hard as I could.

Wes dropped back, landing with a loud thud.

I tried to stand up but the pain was unbearable. So I crawled.

My keys lay on the floor, just a few steps away, where they had fallen from my purse. All I needed to do was grab them and leave as quickly as I could. But my legs wouldn't cooperate and my body wanted to react. It wanted to curl up in a ball and wait for this pain to go away. It took me twice as long to move.

Behind me Wes moaned, muttering curses beneath his breath. He sat up and grabbed the lip of the kitchen island for support and when he did, a knife fell to the floor, clattering loudly.

Wes stared between the sharp blade and me.

Go, go, go! my mind screamed. I turned around and hurried for the keys.

Wes was shouting but I couldn't make out his words. He grabbed one of my arms, twisting it painfully. I screamed and my arm was abruptly pinned on my back.

I didn't have a chance to protect myself. The knife went down and I felt this searing pain, like flesh burning, melting apart, so slowly.

It felt like it was never going to end.

Wes dropped the knife and stared down at me, smiling. He was panting and I was barely breathing. I pressed my palm flat against my belly, thinking that if I pressed down hard enough the blood would go back inside my body and the wound would heal itself.

It seeped through the cracks of my fingers. I stared up at Wes with pain and accusation.

Wes jumped away and would have kept moving if he didn't slam into the refrigerator. "Look what you made me do!" he yelled. Fear and panic were in his eyes. He stared at the blood with hunger and fascination.

I squeezed my eyes shut. I pressed down on the wound and winced. The pain intensified.

He started to pace the floor, telling me that I made him do this. That this was entirely my fault. I was his wife and I was supposed to stay.

I was starting to feel less pain. My body was starting to feel weightless.

And then he glanced at me over his shoulder. His eyes widened and it's as if I had come back in focus. He grabbed my cellphone and dialed 911.

As he talked to the operator, he raked a hand through his hair, gripping the strands so tightly it looked like he was going to rip chunks out.

In a terrified voice, he told the operator that I had hurt myself. Knife wound. Lots of bleeding.

The operator continued to speak but Wes was staring at me with that bone-chilling smile of his. With the phone in his hands, he walked over with slow steps. He knelt next to me. The knife was only a reach away but it didn't matter; the damage had been done.

I thought it was the end. For my life as well as my baby's.

Wes slid down the cabinet and sat next to me and stared up at the ceiling. The only sounds were my pants and the operator: "Sir? Are you there? I need you to talk to me."

We said nothing. I couldn't even if I tried. I was starting to see bright lights, thousands of shades of yellow. So beautiful.

"Are you there? Sir?"

Nothing.

"Sir, I need to know everything is okay."

Wes brushed the hair away from his forehead as he hung up and dropped the phone. I wanted to flinch but my head wouldn't obey.

"Look what you made me do," he repeated.

Over and over he repeated that phrase. And then he

glanced at me, his eyes wide. An idea was taking shape in his mind. I couldn't move.

"Please, don't," I whispered.

He picked the knife up. "You hate me now, don't you?"

Wes put the knife in my hand, but my fingers couldn't get a firm grip. "Do it," he urged me. "Do it. I know you want to."

I shook my head. My clothes were becoming soaked with my own blood. I was shaking. Wes's eyes were wide, frantic. "Do it!" he screamed.

The knife dropped to the floor. Wes loomed over me and brushed a hand across my cheek. "Everything I do, Victoria, I do for you. Can't you see how much I love you?"

His voice was fading away as I drifted in and out of consciousness and soon he stopped talking.

I don't know long I stayed in that position. I closed my eyes. I felt so much pain, physically and emotionally, that I was almost numb. It was a terrifying thing, not to feel. I hummed to block out everything. I hummed because it reminded me I was still alive.

I was still breathing.

I still had a life that depended on me.

I refused to think that this was the way everything would end.

Outside, the rain picked up.

Slowly, I rolled over and got on my hands and knees. A slice of blinding pain streaked through me, making me gasp. I moved toward the keys and ignored the sound of my blood dripping onto the floor.

Before I crawled outside, I glanced over my shoulder, for one last look at my old life.

Wes was now standing, staring down at the blood smeared across the floor with a dazed expression.

I told myself to breathe. That I couldn't think about him. I lifted my arm. I turned the doorknob weakly. The door cracked open and I slipped out onto the back porch. It took me minutes to make it down the steps. The rain hit my skin, powerful enough to wash the blood off my hands. Twigs snapped underneath my palms and cut open my skin. I barely registered the sting. I kept crawling. I counted my steps.

Twelve, thirteen, fourteen . . .

My hair fell around my face like a black curtain. I started to tell myself that if I kept moving, my life would be so good. So, so good.

I told myself that the warm substance making my pajama top stick to my skin was just the rain.

There was no blood on me.

No pain.

Nothing.

I was fine.

I hummed louder.

Fifteen, sixteen, seventeen . . .

It was getting harder and harder to move. The ground was getting closer and closer. The tips of my hair were dragging in the grass. I started to hum louder and louder until I was full-out singing.

Eighteen, nineteen, twenty . . .

The car was in sight. I pressed down on the unlock button but I didn't have enough strength for it to work.

Twenty-one, twenty-two, twenty-three . . .

I had to keep moving, but I was starting to feel dizzy.

And at twenty-four steps my knees gave way and I dropped to the ground in a big heap. The water soaked through my bottoms, chilling me to the bone.

It felt as though my body was fighting so hard to stay alive. But something inside me was giving up. It was dying.

There was nothing but blackness and the cool, wet ground beneath my cheek. My eyes closed. I pressed a protective hand over my stomach. I hummed a beautiful hymn.

My eyes started to close. I drew in one final breath before my world went dark.

41

May 2015

I distantly heard the sounds of a baby crying.

My head lolled to the side. Slowly, my eyes opened into slits. My vision was blurry, as if a white veil were over my eyes. I opened my eyelids wider and my vision cleared. The crying let up too.

Beep, beep, beep . . .

Wires were connected to my body. A blood pressure cuff was wrapped tightly around my arm. I couldn't find the source of the noise.

I saw a woman in scrubs looming above me. I jolted and she laid a cold hand on my arm. "You're up," she whispered. Her lips curved into a wide smile. "You've been asleep for a really long time."

Furtively, I glanced around the room. The smell of bleach invaded my nostrils. Hospital smell. I tried to remain calm and continued to look around. The blinds were open, letting in bright light. On the ledge of the window were flowers and balloons with phrases that said "Get well soon." Or "Praying for you." Or "Thinking of You."

I swallowed. This wasn't good. Not at all.

I glanced at the nurse with nothing but fear in my eyes. "What happened? Why am I here?" I went to sit up and felt a slashing pain that shot straight to my stomach. I sucked in a sharp breath and grabbed the railings next to me. The nurse guided me back down to a lying position.

"Lie down." Her voice was so quiet and sweet. "You have all the time in the world to heal."

Her voice calmed me, but her words alarmed me. "What happened?" I whispered. Her hand stilled on my arm and her soft smile dimmed. "Let me go get your doctor."

"Wait—"

She walked toward the door but before she left she smiled at me. It looked forced. "Your mom is here. She'll be so happy to know you've woken up."

Beep, beep, beep . . .

I stared around, searching for the noise. "What is that?"

"It's the heart monitor, honey." I stared at her blankly. "I'll get your mom," she said one last time and then she was gone.

The door shut behind her. All was silent except for the sound of the machine, the consistent beeping, and my frantic breathing.

Wide-eyed, I turned and stared at the heart monitor. The

noise started to increase. I squeezed my eyes shut but all I saw was crimson red. I heard screams. I felt Wes's anger and it was strong enough to smother me. I felt fear and pain.

But that was it.

"Honey!" My eyes flew open and I saw my mother hurrying to my side. Tears streamed down her cheeks and for the first time in her life she was not completely put together. Dark circles were under her eyes. No lipstick. Her hair was pulled back. She looked like a completely different person, but the look in her eyes, the concern and strength . . . that's the mother I knew and loved. To know that something hadn't changed made me grip her hand tightly. "I've been so worried about you."

"Mom," I croaked. "You need to tell me what happ—"

"Shhh . . ." She brushed my hair behind my ear. "We can talk about everything later."

"But I don't re—"

And right then a commotion sounded outside my door. It was a man's voice. I lifted my head from the pillow. I knew I'd heard it before. I just couldn't place it.

My door opened and I saw a flash of a tan arm and dark hair, before he was pulled back.

"Sir, you can't go in there!"

"Let me see her," he growled before the door slammed.

My mother stood up and hurried to the door. She cracked it open an inch.

"You can't keep me from her!" the man screamed.

I wanted to get up, and once again, I tried. I really did. But I couldn't move. The pain was just too strong. It shot straight down my body to my stomach, making me suck in another sharp breath. My mother quickly shut the door, but not before I heard her say, "Go right now. Leave her alone."

"Who was that?" I asked.

My mom stopped walking and peered at me carefully. Her mouth opened and closed repeatedly as she stared at the door and me.

"Who was that?" I repeated.

She waved her hand in the air, as if she were shooing a fly. "No one. It was absolutely no one."

"Mom—"

"Honey. I promise. It was no one."

Much like the crying baby, the voice started to fade. I heard nothing but the soft squeaking of shoes and murmurs of voices and it was almost as though a voice was in my head.

So I believed her; my mind was blank. It held nothing and here she was offering me up comfort. So I greedily took it like a hungry child.

My hand trailed across the hospital sheets and gripped her hand tightly.

I knew there was pain. I could feel it deep within my chest.

My mother brushed the hair away from my forehead, a thing she used to do when I was little girl. "The doctor is going to be in to speak to you."

"About what?"

She hesitated. "About your condition."

"Mom . . ." I took a deep breath. "What happened?"

Her eyes widened. Her mouth opened and I thought for a quick second that she was going to tell me the truth, then someone knocked on the door loudly.

She pulled away and faced the door like a mother hen on the attack.

An old man with a white coat entered the room and her shoulders dropped.

He looked in my direction and his expression brightened. He was an older, balding man with a belly that protruded over his pants, and rosy cheeks. He almost reminded me of Santa Claus.

He looked too happy, too friendly to be a doctor.

"Well, it looks like my patient is finally up," he said as he walked toward me. He held out his hand. "Dr. Wendell."

I shook it. "Hi," I said quietly.

He gave me one last smile before he opened up his chart and got down to business. He sat in the chair right next to me. My mother sat on the opposite side, gripping my hand as though it were a lifeline.

"Now, I wanted to speak to you about what has happened. . . ." His mouth continued to move. My mom stared at me, a grave look on her face. But I couldn't hear a single word.

In my mind I saw flashes of crimson blood. So much of it. No matter where I looked it was all around me.

My hands and body were drenched with it.

I felt pain. Searing pain in my stomach that made me gasp.

Ignoring the doctor, I pulled down my blankets to my hips and pulled up my hospital gown and saw a hideous scar on my abdomen.

And then I realized the truth.

My baby. The one good thing in my life was gone.

My baby.

My baby.

My baby.

My baby was gone.

"I'm so sorry. . . ." The doctor patted my arm. I felt numb. "I really am."

My mother wiped away my tears.

I shook my head.

The beeping became faster. The doctor glanced at the machine.

I kept waiting for one of them to say this was all some kind of sick joke. I kept waiting for the nurse to walk into the room with a tightly wrapped bundle in her arms.

It never happened.

The doctor stood. The beeping increased. "Victoria," he said quietly, "I need you to calm down."

I couldn't, and how could he expect me to? My baby was dead.

Everything was gone.

He spoke to my mom. But, again, their voices were muffled.

He called the nurse. She came running in and moments later the doctor administered more drugs into my IV.

"No," I moaned. My lips started to quiver. "My baby . . ."

But my words faded and I slipped into darkness.

Give me my baby, give me my baby, give me my baby. . . .

I was released from the hospital three days later. I had to walk around my room, proving to my doctor that my C-section scar was healing correctly. Anytime he tried to speak to me about my loss, I turned him away.

I didn't want to hear it. I was barely making it hour by hour.

The day I packed up, I felt numb. I had a destroyed marriage. A husband who the doctor said had died.

I lost my child.

And I had . . . I had something else. There was a huge chunk of my memories cut out and stolen from me. But I didn't care. If they were gone I probably couldn't handle it. There was a reason they were gone.

As I prepared to leave I told my mom that she could keep the flowers or donate them. I couldn't look at them. I turned away every visitor that wasn't my mom or Renee. My mother wanted to drive me home, but I told her Renee was going to pick me up. I couldn't bear one more pitiful look from my mother.

I left dressed in pajamas and a broken heart. I breathed through the pain and tried to tell myself that it was nothing. I refused to look at the stitches.

It was nothing.

It was nothing.

It was nothing.

The entire drive back to my house I felt numb. I watched the people and buildings pass by but I didn't really see. Everything was in black and white.

My entire world was destroyed. It felt unfair that everyone else would be so . . . happy. Why couldn't they suffer with me? Why couldn't they feel this pain? And when would it end?

It was nothing.

It was nothing.

It was nothing.

The longer I chanted that in my head, the better I felt. I closed my eyes and imagined my pregnant belly. It was a good thought and for a second I could breathe.

Renee and my mother agreed on one thing: They didn't want me to stay at the house. But I did; everything else in the world was stolen from me, but this was not. Renee tried her hardest to change my mind but I wouldn't be deterred.

We pulled up into my driveway. I opened my eyes and stared at the house. I saw home and nothing else.

When I unlocked the front door and stepped into the foyer it was deathly quiet, but the smell of bleach slammed into me. You could hear a pin drop. It was the unnatural quiet that moves in after something awful.

The house was bare and boxes were everywhere. My mother told me I was getting ready to put the house on the market and move. I couldn't picture myself doing that. Wes and I had built this place to start a beautiful family. Why would I move?

Renee grabbed hold of my elbow. "You okay?"

I gently shook her off and gave her a weak smile. "Good. But we need to turn on the radio or TV; it's too quiet in here."

"Everything's packed away but we can watch some videos on the laptop."

I walked up the stairs hating how empty the place was. In my mind, I could picture a male's voice and laughter. It echoed in the foyer and gave me chills. "We need to unpack some boxes."

When Renee didn't reply, I stopped and glanced over my shoulder at her.

"Let's just take everything day by day."

I didn't reply. We walked into the master bedroom. It was completely empty. The blinds were open. Sunlight poured in and ran across the floors. Dust motes danced in the air. "Where's my stuff?"

"I have no idea. A lot of things were packed and ready to go. We'll have to ask your mom."

That should have been enough to put me over the edge, but I was determined to stay. I dropped my bag in the middle of the room. Uncomfortable silence circled around Renee and me.

She leaned against the doorway, staring at me. "You don't have to stay here. You can come home with me. Or stay with—"

"It's my house. I have to stay here."

Renee ended up staying till midnight. I finally talked her into helping me unpack a few things. Towels. A few plates and silverware. One down comforter. She offered to stay the night with me if I wanted her to.

I insisted that I wanted to be alone.

"All right," she sighed. "I guess I'll be going. I was thinking that I could come over every morning for a bit. I have to go into the flower shop for a few hours but I can return around five or six. I've spoken with your mom and she's agreed to stay with you during the afternoon."

"You don't have to do that. I'm fine."

Renee sighed and grabbed her purse. "No, you're not. I'm coming over here whether you like it or not."

"How will you coming every day help?"

"I—"

"It won't," I interjected. "I just need to be alone."

"I know . . . but I don't want to leave you alone. I worry about you."

"I need to be alone. For a few days, okay?"

She stared at me for a long second before she agreed. "But I'm coming over at the end of the week. No matter what."

And then she left.

It made no sense. This was the time that I should be leaning on a shoulder. But I was wrapped in grief and pain and just wanted a moment to myself.

A moment to try to think everything through.

That night, the silence was too much. I slept in the middle of the room, staring blankly at a movie playing on my laptop. My ears started to ache, and then ring, and soon I heard the distant sounds of shouting.

Finally, I gave up. I moved down the hall and stepped into the baby's room. Instantly I felt a calming peace drifting over me. The curtains were open, letting in light from the moon. Boxes were stacked against the wall. A crib was slightly put together, but the crib mattress was out, leaning against the wall.

This felt all wrong to me. I wanted to see everything put together. I wanted to walk in here and see a beautiful room, just waiting for a beautiful baby.

I turned on a light, closed the curtains, and got to work. No box went untouched. Clothes were hung. I put the mattress back where it belonged. The rocking chair was placed in the corner. I draped a yellow crochet blanket on the back of the chair. Diapers and lotions were placed on the changing table. I couldn't hang anything on the wall yet since I didn't have a clue which box the nails and hammer were packed in. Tomorrow I would search for them and hang the pictures.

I didn't know what time it was, but I wasn't stopping until everything was back where it belonged.

When I was down to the last two boxes, I finally sat with my back pressed against the crib and dragged one box in between my legs. It wasn't taped shut. The flaps were tucked in on each other. On the side, in black permanent marker were the words VICTORIA'S STUFF.

The second I opened it I was hit with a musty smell. I scrunched my nose and covered it with my T-shirt. There was nothing but a bunch of homemade arts and crafts. Baby dresses that I assumed I wore as a baby. A small scrapbook filled with pictures of me. At the very bottom was a beautiful baby doll.

I gasped and reached for her. I remembered this doll. As a little girl I carried her everywhere. Her name was Evelyn. She had the most beautiful blue eyes. Her cheeks were rosy. She was wearing a white crinoline dress. The skirt was wrinkled, but the dress itself was in pristine condition. On her feet were small red Mary Janes.

Looking at her brought the biggest smile to my face. This doll used to give me so much happiness. Not a single bad memory was attached to her.

I put the rest of my childhood belongings back in the box, but Evelyn stayed outside. She belonged in here. I stood up and placed her on the rocking chair. "You belong right here, don't you?"

She just smiled.

Exhaustion started to take over. Yet I didn't want to leave this room. So I grabbed my comforter from the bare master bedroom and padded back to the baby's room. This time, when I lay in the middle of the room with the comforter tucked beneath my chin, I fell asleep.

I woke up a few hours later.

At first I forgot. I had forgotten everything that had happened, but all too quickly it hit me and I couldn't breathe.

I didn't cry.

I didn't sob.

I didn't breathe.

I just curled up into a ball and stared at the other side of the room. I felt so much pain. It wouldn't stop at me. If I let it go it would attack everyone else. So I held it deep inside me.

Another day passed.

And then another. I ate very little and slept even less. Renee and my mother called. I told them I was fine. The doorbell was constantly ringing. I never answered it. Sometimes there was pounding that never ended.

My eyes kept fluttering open and shut. I would get only two to three hours of sleep and then it was dark again.

This routine lasted for days.

"What am I going to do?" I asked Evelyn.

Lately I had been talking to her a lot. She never replied, but this time she cried.

I sat upright and crawled across the floor until my face was level with Evelyn's. Then she blinked at me, looking me straight in the face.

Her arms moved, reaching out toward me. Fingers spread.

She wanted me to hold her. And a slow smile spread across my face. When I picked her up she rested her head against my chest. For the first time in days I felt happy. Complete.

The longer I held her, the more solid my heartbeat became. I could hear it beating in tune with this beautiful baby.

Evelyn. My beautiful baby Evelyn.

Tears spilled down my cheeks. This was my baby. I never lost her to begin with.

"Hi, sweetheart," I whispered gently.

She stared up at me with her beautiful blue eyes. I cradled her for the rest of the night. A few times I dozed off but it was never for long. I couldn't stop staring at her.

My daughter.

Early in the morning, before the sun was up, Evelyn started to fuss. I went downstairs and made her a bottle. In the quiet of the house I fed her, feeling better than ever.

This routine spanned the next few days. I was on cloud nine. Everything was clicking into place. The sharp, aching pain in my chest started to fade. I could breathe without gasping.

I felt important.

Needed.

Loved.

And that's the best feeling in the world.

Then one day, the doorbell rang. I didn't know what day it was. Time was starting to blend together and I didn't care.

I opened the door. "Renee!" I greeted her with a smile.

She stared at me with visible shock. "Hi." When she saw Evelyn in my arms, her smile faded. Fast.

"Come in." I opened the door wider. "Come in. Meet Evelyn."

She stepped inside but kept her distance. "Who is this?"

"My daughter," I said proudly.

"Your daughter," she repeated.

I glanced over at her. "Yes," I said again slowly.

Renee dropped her purse and stared at me with wide eyes. She looked nervous and terrified.

"What's wrong?" I held Evelyn tighter. "You're scaring me."

She didn't reply, just grabbed my shoulders, her grip impossibly tight. "We need to get you out of this house."

"I'm fine. I have Evelyn."

"Right you have Evelyn. But don't you want Evelyn to see the outdoors?"

I hesitated and stared down at Evelyn. "I don't know. . . ."

"Well, I do." Renee looped her arm through mine and tried to drag me out the door. I stubbornly stayed put.

"I can't leave," I said. "Evelyn needs her car seat."

Renee sighed. "Okay. Let's get her in her car seat."

"I need to pack her diaper bag."

Renee smiled wanly. "Sure. You do all that stuff."

I hurried around the house, gathering everything I would need. In the front closet was the car seat. I pulled it out and very gently buckled in Evelyn. She momentarily cried at not being held. I smiled and kissed her cheek.

"All right," Renee said, her voice surprisingly high. "Are you ready to go?"

I stood up and lifted Evelyn's car seat. "Yep."

When I stepped outside, I immediately wanted to go back

inside. I could feel someone's eyes on me, watching every step I took. I looked around in paranoia and hurried to the car, strapping Evelyn in and double-checking to make sure she was okay.

I slammed the car door and hurriedly got in the front seat. Before I buckled up, I twisted around to check on Evelyn again.

"Where are we going?" I asked.

Renee backed out of the driveway. "I want to show you this place that I found. I think you'll really like it."

"What's it called?"

When the car was in drive she answered me, looking at me very solemnly. "Fairfax. I think you'll like it."

42

Last memory. Last moment.

Last everything.

This is my finish line. But there's no celebration.

The truth that I've spent days and months suppressing slams into me as hard as it can. I fall to my knees as a guttural cry escapes my mouth. "Oh God, oh God," I moan. "My baby."

In my arms is Evelyn. Finally, I see her for what she is. Just a plastic baby doll with lifeless eyes and a perpetual smile on her face.

Abruptly, I drop the baby to the floor and watch her fall.

This doll is not my daughter. The one that belonged to me was killed. I lift my head. All because of this man.

Everything inside me aches. It's impossible to breathe without clutching my chest. Hunched over, I close my eyes. I want to scream the pain out of my body, but it's futile; if anything the agony just multiplies.

"Stop screaming." Wes is pacing, staring at me with a blank look.

It's all too much. Sinclair is beside me. I'm in such a state of shock, I can't move.

I think I'm paralyzed.

"Stop screaming, stop screaming, stop fucking screaming!" Wes rushes toward me and I shrink backward until my back slams into the wall.

Sinclair holds out a hand. "Wes, let's talk calmly."

"I'm calm," he says and smiles as though we're all having a small get-together. "I'm perfectly calm. But she"—he points an accusing finger at me—"isn't. And now I can't think straight."

I thought that things couldn't possibly get worse. The loss of my child was enough to send me spiraling downward. Even now I fight the urge not to retreat from the memories and ignore them altogether.

"Why did you do it?" I ask, my voice choking on the words.

Sinclair steps forward. "Victoria, listen to me—"

Wes stops pacing and turns his attention to Sinclair, the tip of the knifepoint right at his chest. My blood turns cold.

"Why is the sky blue? Why do we need oxygen to live? You could drive yourself crazy trying to find out all the answers but just know this: It had to happen. Yet you can't seem to realize that. All you choose to see is that I'm the villain. Everyone needs to have a villain in their life, don't they? A person they can dump all their problems on. And you . . ." He shakes his head, as if he's disappointed in me. "You look like the victim. You relish playing the victim role because as long as you have someone to blame then you never have to look at yourself and what you've done." There's anticipation in his eyes, as if he's saved the best for last. "Let me tell you the truth."

43

~~WESLEY~~

May 2015

You can treat the world one of two ways: as your friend or opponent.

Go down the path of the first and you're doomed. You'll say things like, "That's the way life is." Or my favorite: "Chin up, pal. Next time will be better."

But there's no next time and by the time you realize that, you're already gone.

I've taken the path less chosen. The one people are afraid to take. But life is one giant game of chess and the world is my opponent. Every move and choice has a motive behind it. My guard is never down.

You learn so much going down this road. And soon, life

will start to admire you. It'll give you hints here and there and it's your job to pick each one and collect them like rocks.

I've learned so much from life: when to smile. How to engage and what to say at just the right time. It's also showed me that you never strike back when you are hurt.

You wait.

Through that wait a seed of patience grows, takes root. It calms you down, tells you to watch and wait, when all you want to do is react. The urge to grab hold of your opponent's pain and throw out their strength. But patience tells you to wait; you don't want your opponent to become suspicious.

You let them live life completely unaware that the whole time you're tracking everything they're doing. You'll learn all there is to know about them.

Soon . . . soon it's time to strike.

And your anger? Oh, it's there. But you don't use it yet. So you mold it, twisting it this way and that, knowing that the longer you hold it back the more furious it gets.

Don't worry, it will all work out in the end.

When all is said and done, when you let your pain free, it will hit your opponent so forcefully that their life will drain away, like blood from a wound.

And Victoria's life was all around me.

It covered my hands, streaked the floor, and dirtied the countertops. On one white cabinet was a streak of her fingertips, dragging down, down, down. But this wasn't how I wanted it to play out. Plan A—my best-laid plan. The one that I'd spent years crafting was down the fucking drain and now I needed to go with Plan B.

Very slowly I stood up and reminded myself that Victoria and I would have a great life together. I knew the second I saw her, walking down the street, so sweet and distracted, that there was nothing in the world that would keep me from her. Including a moment like this.

I loved her. She was this beautiful doll who was so open and composed, but held so much back.

It was fascinating.

My beautiful doll was much more cunning than I ever thought. It's as though she had risen to the occasion and showed me just how perfect she was for me.

I picked up the knife. Without a second thought I swiftly swiped it across my forearm, watching with a satisfied smile as dark red freely flowed down my arm and trickled onto the floor.

I cut my other forearm. The pool of blood started to pick up and on my knees I moved, making sure that her blood was mixed with mine.

Just as I predicted, the cops were close. I could hear the faint but growing sound of sirens.

I stood up and let the knife fall to the floor. Blood was splattered across the kitchen cabinets, oven door. A few drops had managed to make it onto the counter. Not a drop was on the divorce papers.

It was an impressive scene. I could have stared at it all day long.

Reluctantly, I hurried toward the doorway and dragged my fingertips down the wall. I slammed my palm against the other wall, watching as crimson stained the white walls. Then I ran into the mudroom, toward the back door. I made sure to keep it open. Not all the way, just slightly cracked. Before I grabbed Victoria's shoes and took off my own.

Her blood trailed across the deck and down the steps. With the rain pouring down, it was slowly disappearing, turning into a soft red and trickling off the side of the deck.

I hoped she lived; we were just getting started.

I ran across the lawn and jumped the fence, surrounded by trees and overgrown grass. The sirens grew closer and I kept running. They wouldn't search for me, at least not right now, and when they did, I would be hiding right underneath their noses.

Adrenaline coursed through me so strong I felt unstoppable. I barely felt the ground beneath my feet, or the branches and wet grass.

The cold rain beat down on my face. I smiled and picked up the pace. Not too far ahead I saw the outline of the abandoned factory. My legs started to ache but I pushed forward. The closer I got the more I could see the graffiti on the red brick. A handful of windows were boarded up but most were broken, with shards of glass hanging on to the windowpanes. The factory was fenced in with a lock on the gates.

I made a sharp right, running along the length of the huge building until I finally saw a gray Ford Taurus that had seen better days, carefully hidden from plain sight. I grabbed the key tucked above the tire and popped the trunk. My duffel bag sat where I'd stored it hours ago.

As I quickly changed, I thought of what was going on at the house. I could picture it vividly: Two or three cops were probably there by now. Probably an ambulance, its lights creating a kaleidoscope of colors. The property would be roped with yellow police tape. They'd call for more backup. Victoria had probably arrived at the hospital, if she hadn't died on the side of the road, that is. A cop would be there shortly to talk to her.

Police would start searching the area. Neighbors would begin to filter out of their houses, curious to see what was going on. Word would slowly spread and by tomorrow afternoon, reporters, journalists, camera crews, and photographers would be camped outside the house. The beautiful Bellamy Road home would have the attention it deserves.

I smiled to myself as I tossed my bloodied clothes in the duffel bag and put it back into the trunk.

The car door slammed behind me. The engine came to life and I pulled out onto the road. This, out of everything, was the crucial moment. I had to blend in—look like I was an innocent resident just minding his own business.

Reflexively, my hands tightened on the wheel. My eyes kept flicking between the road and the rearview mirror for anything suspicious. But there was nothing. The drive went smoothly and soon I was driving past Fairfax. Very few lights were on inside. The parking lot was practically empty, save for the nurses working the night shift, their cars all parked next to one another.

A mile later I slowed down and made a right onto a gravel road.

Water was starting to fill the potholes that peppered the uneven road. Trees flanked me on both sides and all too quickly the gravel gave way to plain dirt, with only a strip of dirty tire tracks shining in front of me. I'd been on this path so many times I turned the lights off. It was a jarring drive;

the potholes were getting deeper by the second and the trees became farther apart before they gave way to reveal a small cabin. It was buried in the middle of the forest and no one knew about it.

I loved it that way. It was my oasis.

My home.

A bolt of lightning flashed, momentarily revealing the porch in front of me. Alice stood there, her arms crossed over her chest, back hunched as if she were ready to fold in on herself.

The second I got out of the car she ran down the steps. "Where have you been?"

"Where do you think I was?" I said over my shoulder and grabbed the duffel bag from the trunk.

Next to the cabin was a dinky shed that looked one wind gust away from collapsing. I walked toward it. Alice followed behind me. Her nervous energy lingered all around her. If she was going to be like this all night she could just leave right now. She'd only mess things up for me.

"It shouldn't have taken this long," she fretted.

"Plan A is out of the picture."

"What happened?"

"What happened is even better than I could've hoped for," I said over my shoulder.

"I really think that—"

Quickly I turned around. "We don't have enough time to sit and chat. Go wait inside. Give me ten minutes and I'll be ready."

"Ready for what?"

"Just go."

Finally, Alice turned on her heels and walked back toward the cabin. I pulled out a set of keys from my back pocket and quickly located the smallest one. Not even the strong smell of the rain could compete with what poured out of the shed. Anyone else would've made a face, covered their nose with their hands. Some might vomit.

I did none of the above. I walked forward and stared down at the two bodies. They looked so peaceful, almost as if they were sleeping. Funny how just hours ago they were both walking around, still assuming that they had all the time in the world. But everyone is placed on this earth for a short amount of time. Surely they knew that.

I dropped my bag onto the ground and stared at the girl thoughtfully. She told me her name. I don't remember it. And does it really even matter?

She was my second doll—a prop if there ever was one.

But my prop was useless now.

I turned my attention to the male body. I crossed my arms and grinned. This body was extremely important. I savored every moment stealing his life away.

Behind me the door creaked open. I turned just as Alice stepped into the doorway. Sure, I could hide the body. I could block her from the sight and tell her to get the fuck out. Or I could get this over with and show her my plan. Her eyes adjusted to the dark. She walked forward and looked beyond me. It was only a matter of seconds until she reacted. She screamed so loudly my ears started to ring.

"Can you not be so dramatic?" I asked. Already she was getting on my nerves.

She took a step forward and pointed a shaky hand toward the bodies. "What did you do?"

"Will you relax?" I turned back around and brushed back strands of the woman's hair. It was so dark, so shiny. Just like Victoria's. "She's still alive. I haven't decided what I'm going to do with her."

"I don't care about the woman!" Alice yelled. She pointed to the man. "I care about him!"

"You can care about him until you're blue in the face, but it won't change a thing. He's dead," I said bluntly.

Alice was shaking. Tears streamed down her face. She looked at me with fear. But for what reason? I was her son. And I was making everything right.

"He was your brother," she whispered brokenly. "Your *twin*."

I stood up and wiped the dirt off on my jeans. "We weren't raised together."

If she stopped crying long enough, she might actually hear what I was saying. What's more annoying than emotions? Tears. They're just annoying and pointless.

She hurried forward and loomed over Wes's dead body. She reached out to touch him but at the last second pulled away.

"I had to do it. You understand that, right?"

Alice went pale and moved away from the table and dug the heels of her palms into her eyes as if she could erase the image in front of her. If I could have, I'd have climbed into her head just so I could see why she was reacting so dramatically.

"Fairfax is no place for a baby . . . Fairfax is no place for a baby . . . Fairfax is no place for a baby . . ." She started to mumble over and over.

This was why I had no empathy for Wes. We might have been twins but the similarities stopped there. Alice gave him up. She kept me. Wes had a life in the world. My life circled around Fairfax, where Alice worked and my father was a patient.

But in a bizarre twist, he was the golden boy in Alice's eyes.

Never once did I feel a stirring of guilt as I watched him and Victoria, waiting for the perfect moment to strike. I just wanted to take something away from him. And take I did.

If there was anyone to blame in this entire situation it was Wes. He turned his back on his wife and I slipped into his life so easily. Like it was meant to be.

I'd love her better.

I'd be the perfect husband for her.

In the end, she would thank me.

Patience ran out and I walked over to Alice, gripping her tightly by the shoulders. "Stop crying."

She lifted her head long enough to look at me.

"Will it make you feel better that he died quickly?"

People can be cruel in this world. Wes could have had a much worse ending than the one he got. I could have drawn out his death, made him suffer. But I didn't. I just walked up behind him and stabbed him above the heart, right through the arteries.

Quick and efficient.

When you really stop and think about it, I went easy on him.

"Oh for fuck's sake." I grabbed her by her shoulders and spun her around and pushed her out the door. She continued to sob and I shook her as hard as I could. "You have to stop crying." I gestured toward the shed. "I had to do that, okay?"

"But—"

"No buts. I had to. Victoria made me do this."

Her eyes clouded over with anger. All of it was directed at Victoria. I smiled and dropped my hands. "You shouldn't cry; you still have me."

Quickly I moved toward the car and started to pack things up. The entire time she stood there, immobile in front of the shed. I walked around her and when it was time to pick up the body, I glanced her way and pulled out a pair of Victoria's shoes and handed them to her. "Put these on."

She held them away from her body like they were a ticking time bomb. "Why?"

"Do you want a play-by-play of my plan and to waste time, or do you want to help me and I can explain later?"

Alice gnawed at her lower lip and then slowly cradled the shoes to her chest. When she looked at me, I saw that her eyes were back to being flat and I knew the unnecessary emotions were gone. I knew I had an ally in her.

This was the person who had raised me.

After that, everything worked like a well-oiled machine. I quickly unzipped my bag and pulled out a fresh pair of clothes. I quickly undressed. The cold air brushed against my skin, but I felt nothing; the adrenaline flowing through me was so heady, so powerful, that I felt unstoppable.

When I was done changing I put on a pair of latex gloves and got to work changing his pants. His shirt had to stay. But his pants couldn't. He needed equal amounts of his blood and that of Victoria.

In the end, it took me three minutes and fifteen seconds to change Wes and myself.

It was a personal best.

He was missing one last thing: his cellphone. I pulled it out of my duffel bag and placed it in his back pocket, anticipating the moment when the police would find it. Which they would. Emails would be pulled. So would phone records. Their entire marriage would be ripped apart. They would turn to Victoria for the answers. I was okay with all of that as long as I was one step ahead of them.

As Alice patiently waited in the car, I rolled Wes's body into a blanket and carried him over my shoulder.

It took a little maneuvering, but I was finally able to fit his body in the trunk. I ripped off the gloves and quickly got into the car.

The rain had let up, lightly pattering against the windshield and the roof of the car.

Before I pulled out onto the road, a police car with its sirens and lights on sped by, going in the direction of what was once Victoria's house.

I took a right and drove toward the lake. I watched the police lights fade in my rearview mirror. The corners of my mouth pulled up. I pressed down on the gas.

Chin up, Victoria.

Your next time is about to begin.

44

I stare at him, this stranger, in horror.

There are no words for what I'm feeling. It's like someone snatched my heart from my chest, leaving a cavernous space in its wake. Just when I thought it couldn't get any worse it does.

Guilt gnaws at me, hissing that I not only failed my child, but also Wes.

Not once in my entire marriage had I ever questioned his parentage. It just wasn't a thought in my mind. He blended in with his parents. Perfectly groomed. Charming smile. For so long I thought he was the villain. A psychopath. The cause for my pain.

But I was wrong this whole time. The realization causes buckets of pain to fill my heart.

How could I have not believed him? How could I think that he was capable of such evil?

My mind refuses to believe it all, though. It brings up memories, trying to poke holes in the story. "It isn't possible."

"Isn't it though? Wes was always working, always distracted. The house tour, the dinners, seeing you with Sinclair were all moments that Wes didn't want. So I took them. The fact that he worked in my favor was just a happy accident."

No, no, no. Don't believe him, my mind pleads.

But deep down, I know he's right.

"So what do you think?" Nathan asks conversationally. "Did I do a good job telling my story? Are you happy now that you have all the answers?"

I don't reply.

Sinclair grabs my arm and tries to pull me behind him, but Nathan reaches out and holds me back. With the tip of his knife he brushes my hair behind my shoulder. Sinclair freezes and so do I.

The blade is so close to me. One false move and he could end it for good. I should fight him. Try to move, but what's the point?

Nathan gives me a tender smile. "Shhh . . . don't cry for me. Everything's better now. I was born from crazy. I grew up at Fairfax and I survived. So have you."

Alice looks unfazed, staring down at the table with a blank look in her eyes.

"We belong together," he says to me.

His hand reaches out and I can't help but flinch.

I dodge behind Sinclair, trying to put as much distance between Nathan and me as quickly as possible. My shoulders hit the wall.

He looks past Sinclair, almost as if he's not there. "Why are you looking at me like that, Victoria? I did this for us!" he screams.

My body starts to shake to the point I'm almost convulsing.

"Stop looking at me like that," he groans.

Finally, he takes a step back, tugging at his hair. The grip on the knife never lets up. I feel broken, the edges of my life all around me, but all the screaming . . . all the memories that were trying so hard to link back together have clicked into place.

"You have only yourself to blame," Alice says. She stands next to Nathan, staring at me with so much hate. "You made him do this."

"How?" I ask in disbelief.

"You've been so ungrateful, so spiteful to Nathan. You've never appreciated Nathan like you should!" She gazes at Nathan with love. "You were never good enough for Wes and you certainly weren't good enough for Nathan. So I helped him."

"Do what?" My mind is on the brink of falling apart into tiny pieces.

"I helped him get in and out of Fairfax to see you," she explains slowly, as if she's talking to a child. "I let you believe he was Wes. You had to be punished for cheating on Wes and for making Nathan hide from the world!"

I can tell that Alice truly believes every single word that comes from her mouth. But to me it's just a jumbled mass, swirling in my head, making me more confused.

"You are an ungrateful little bitch!" she screams.

Nathan turns and narrows his eyes at her. "Stop yelling. Can't you see that you're scaring her?"

And just like that, Alice pipes down, as if Nathan is her master.

With the knife dangling from his hand, Nathan walks over to me. I move even closer to Sinclair. Nathan doesn't seem to notice; he has this glazed look in his eyes that makes a bolt of fear run through me.

"Say you love me, Victoria."

My lips remain closed.

"Say it!" Nathan screams. "Say you love me!"

The longer I remain silent, the wilder he becomes. Sirens start to grow louder. In a few minutes the police will arrive. His eyes drift to the door. His hands are starting to shake. Perspiration forms on his forehead. There's a look of recognition in his eyes. Almost as though he realizes that there's no running. It's all over.

And then Alice steps forward. "Just drop the knife," she says, her voice a pleading whisper. "She's not worth it, okay? We can leave now and start over somewhere else. But this all has to stop. She'll never understand you."

He whips his body around and stares at Alice. He lowers both hands to his sides. "It can't stop. Don't you get it?"

Sirens are closer. Help is only seconds away but it feels like time has stopped altogether.

Panic and fear start to build inside me. I feel like I'm going to be sick. But Alice is right. This has to end.

Before I can think twice I lunge forward, beating Sinclair by seconds, and jerk the knife out of Nathan's hands. He turns around and his eyes widen. I see the fear in his eyes as I raise the knife.

Now or never.

With both hands curled around the handle I drive it as hard as I can into his chest.

He grunts. It's a sound that comes from within his chest. He falls to the ground.

I jump on top of him, pull out the knife, and plunge it even deeper. Blood coats the blade and handle, making my hands slip. Yet that doesn't stop me. I keep stabbing.

Anger is a hurricane of an emotion. It can sweep into your life and tear everything upside down. It steals all rationality until you have no choice but to expunge the emotion out of your soul before it eats you alive.

At this point, that's all I want. For this to end. For my soul not to be haunted any longer.

My vision starts to go blurry, but I keep stabbing him. I can't seem to stop and at this point, I don't know if I want to.

"Victoria!" someone shouts. But the voice sounds far away. "Victoria, stop!"

I raise the knife one more time, only to have someone stop me. I turn and look into the eyes of Sinclair.

Very slowly my surroundings start to come into focus. Alice is screaming, her body half-draped over Nathan. His eyes are open, staring lifelessly at the ceiling.

I look down at my hands and find them coated with blood. A sob tears from my throat.

"Let go of the knife. He's dead." My labored breaths punctuate each second that passes by. I don't want to let go. I'm almost afraid to. But my arms slowly extend and with shaking hands, I drop the knife into Sinclair's waiting hands.

This can't be happening, I tell myself. *This can't be happening.*

But deep down I know that it is.

Alice cradles Nathan's head in her lap. Copious amounts of blood seep out of his wound. Alice doesn't seem to care. She lets the blood coat her skin and rests her forehead against his head. "Fairfax is no place for a baby. . . . Fairfax is no place for a baby. . . ."

Alice continues to scream out in pain. I can't be in this room anymore. I stagger out of the cabin with Sinclair right behind me. Greedily, I suck in all the fresh air that I can. Just then two cop cars pull up, their flashing lights making me wince. They run up to us, take in our appearance. They're speaking. I watch their mouths move but I can't make out a single word.

Sinclair points to the shed. One stays with us, the other goes inside.

My shoulders are stiff but I can't stop looking around. The pain around my heart starts to spread, seeping into my veins until soon it's all I can feel. I breathe it in. Exhale it out.

I gasp for air.

I feel hands touch my back and jerk away.

"It's okay, it's okay," Sinclair says.

Nothing is okay, and I don't know if anything will be okay. "He killed them both," I croaked.

Saying the words out loud just makes the pain intensify. "Our baby's gone." My hands wrap around my knees. I want to curl up in ball, compact this agony, and make this pain go away.

Sinclair's hands gently hold my face. I try to push out of his hold but his grip is unshakable. "Stop, Victoria. Please." My tears trail down my cheeks and onto his hands as I stop fighting him. "He didn't kill our child," he whispers.

At first I don't think I've heard him right. My body stiffens.

My hand stills and I think my heart does too.

He looks me straight in the eye and says very slowly: "Our child is alive."

The center of my life, my existence gives way over his words. Out of everything I've experienced today, I know that this is the one thing that will break me.

I shake my head, wanting to believe his words but terrified to hold on to them.

"The doctor was trying to tell you that he survived. He was trying to tell you that during the surgery you lost too much blood. Your uterus was taken out . . . *you* almost died."

My lips start to quiver. Sinclair reaches out and covers my hand with his. "I promise you, our child is alive and well."

My emotions have been jerked left and right and instinctively I want to believe what he's telling me, but right now, there's no room for hope, or even happiness. My mind is processing so much information. It's almost too much.

Powerful, racking sobs overtake me and a deep keening makes my body shake. Sinclair holds me and says against my ear over and over and over: "Our baby's alive. . . ."

What comes after this is unsure. But deep in my marrow, I know that right now I'm at the bottom and the only thing to look toward is the top.

Epilogue

There is no straight and narrow path to the truth.

It takes you on back roads and shortcuts that are bumpy and unsafe. Sometimes you end up at a dead end and have to turn around and start over. Sometimes you become so lost, you begin to feel helpless. The idea of finding the truth seems like a long-lost dream.

But you will.

You always will.

"Are you ready?"

I glance at Dr. Calloway. "I am," I reply confidently.

We're walking down the hallway, toward the library. Sunlight filters in. It's impossible to contain my excitement. It feels like I've been waiting years for this moment.

After the truth came out, I came back to Fairfax; I was so far from being mentally stable. It was chaos at first. Uncovering Nathan's deception led to another trail of evil. Alice was arrested and charged for being an accessory to murder.

And Melanie, the girl from the photos? She was discovered moments after the police arrived that fateful night. She was one of the lucky ones and made it out alive.

There are many labels that the press will use for Nathan and he fits every single one. But to me he will always be the devil reincarnate. Logically, I know that he'll never hurt another soul again, but I still deal with paranoia daily, that he's watching me and will attack when I least expect it.

Very slowly, I picked through the pain, trying to rebuild my life. What's the most unbearable pain is the time I lost with my child, and the fact that I never believed Wes when he was innocent the entire time. Sometimes my guilt chokes me. Sometimes it doesn't.

I simply have to take everything day by day.

When we stop at the library doors, I exhale a shaky breath.

"Everything will be okay," she replies softly.

"I know."

"You should go in," Dr. Calloway urges. "Everyone will be here soon."

I nod and open the door and step inside. The library is deathly quiet. The door shuts softly behind me. I drum my fingers against my thighs as I pace the room. What if this goes badly? What if I'm really not ready? I've made a lot of progress, but is it enough?

Or will I just crumble?

I continue to pace when someone knocks softly on the door. I stop short and jerk my head toward the door, my hands laced in front of me. Sinclair peeks his head into the room. His eyes instantly find mine. "Knock, knock."

I swallow loudly. "Hi."

"You ready?"

It's the second time that question has been directed my way, but this time it's I who smile widely. "Absolutely."

Seconds later, the door opens. Sinclair steps through with our child in his arms.

Peter Montgomery.

He's beautiful. So beautiful. During a few of my sessions, Sinclair has been present, showing me pictures. But those pictures don't do our little boy justice. They don't capture his bright green eyes. Sinclair's eyes.

The tears are impossible to push down. With the back of my hand I wipe them away but after a few minutes I give up. The tears won't stop. But it's good. These are happy tears.

His hair is a light shade of brown. Closer to my hair color. The tips of his wispy strands curl at the edges. I feel a small seed of pride sprout up in me; almost pride that he has something of me.

I'm so happy, I can't even think of the time that's been lost. All I can think is that I am lucky. So incredibly lucky to see him.

Sinclair stands directly in front of me, trying to tilt Peter forward so I can get a better look at him.

"This is your mom," he says softly.

With his big doe eyes, Peter stares at me blankly.

"Hello," I whisper. My hand is shaking as I reach out and

brush my fingers against his cheeks. Very slowly, a smile graces his face. A small dimple appears in his left cheek. I'm looking at a mini-version of Sinclair.

Nothing and no one can prepare me for this moment. Not so long ago, I was convinced that my heart and mind were broken. Thousands of shards. I thought I was unfixable.

But this boy is the staple that puts me back together. Links me with Sinclair.

"He's beautiful," I say.

"He is," Sinclair agrees, an impossibly wide smile on his face.

Hesitantly, I hold my hands out, desperately hoping that he'll come into my arms but knowing there's a good chance he won't. I was forewarned before this meeting that there was a possibility that Peter wouldn't let me hold him. And I'm okay with that. I know he needs time.

At first he curls close to Sinclair. Some of my hope deflates. But then he whirls back around, as if he's double-checking to see if I'm still there.

My hands reach out farther and Sinclair hands him over. I smile and blink rapidly, trying to keep the tears away.

I wrap my arms around Peter and bury my face into his neck. I'm so happy my heart feels like it's going to burst from my chest. Holding my son, feeling his steady heart beating like mine, is more than I ever imagined.

I've missed out on seven months of his life. I've missed a lot of memories, but I remind myself that I have thousands of good memories just waiting for our family.

I look over the top of Peter's head and meet Sinclair's gaze, tears brimming in my eyes.

I love him for standing by me for all this time. I love him for taking care of our son when I couldn't.

I love him for so unapologetically loving every part of me. Flaws and all.

I'm allowed to stay in the library for a few hours. Sinclair and I talk the whole time. Wide, brilliant smiles on our faces. I get to feed Peter. And when he needs his diaper changed, Sinclair happily lets me take that job. I tickle his stomach and cradle him close to my chest, the whole time a smile on my face.

I'm not perfect.

Or even considered "recovered." But I know I'm close.

I know I'm better.

There will always be flaws in my life, but they will be beautiful.

Sinclair reaches out and holds my hand.

"Heartbeat?" he asks.

With my son in my arms, I say, "Heartbeat."

Acknowledgments

A huge thanks to my beta readers: Melissa Brown, Christine Estevez, Claire Contreras, Trisha, Rai, Megan Simpson, Tosha Khoury, and Lori Sabin. You are all amazing!

Thank you to Darla—whether I'm just venting or sending you a random chapter in the middle of the night, you're always there and I'm so grateful for everything.

A big shout-out to the ladies in the Unravel Support Group. All of your passion for the characters at Fairfax is amazing and so encouraging!

Thank you so much to my editor, Linda Marrow. Your enthusiasm and faith in this book has meant so much. *"Fairfax is no place for a baby."*

My heartfelt thanks to my agent, Amy Tannenbaum.

Thank you for your never-ending patience, reading through the multiple drafts of Victoria's story, and your amazing suggestions!

As always, thank you to my husband, Joshua, for always taking care of the kids and letting me escape into the world of my characters!

College seemed like too much stress for me. Traveling across the world, getting married, and having four kids seemed much more relaxing.

Yeah, I'm still waiting for the relaxing part to kick in. . . .

I change addresses every other year. It's not by choice but it is my reality.

While the craziness of life kept me busy, the stories in my head decided to bubble to the surface. They were dying to be told and I was dying to tell them.

I hope you'll enjoy escaping to the crazy world of these characters with me!

Caliareadsandwrites.blogspot.com
Facebook.com/CaliaRead
@Caliaco22